A FALLING FOR FABLES NOVEL

BREWED IN MAGIC

A FALLING FOR FABLES NOVEL

BREWED IN MAGIC

JENNA WOLFHART

For anyone who has ever wanted the fantasy version of a wintry Hallmark romance movie

AUTHOR'S NOTE

Dear reader,

Welcome to the Isles of Fable! Whether you're new or a returning visitor, I hope you'll feel right at home. Here's a mug of your favorite beverage, a roaring hearth, and a pet dragon to keep you company.

Brewed in Magic is the second stand-alone book in this series, however, you can read these romances in any order.

This is a light-hearted palate cleanser for those days when you need something fun. Get ready for lots of banter, cozy moments, and a bit of spice, while our characters try to save a winter festival and fall in love.

xoxo

Jenna

O C E A N

THE ISLES OF
FABLE

CASTLE
RUINS

SUNLIT
RIDGE

RIVERWOLD

MILFORD

WHISPERING
WOODS

ASHBORN
FOREST

MOUNT
FORGE

WYNDALE

HEARTHAVEN

I

LILIA

I hauled the wooden keg into the back of my wagon, whistling an old, familiar bard's tune that was as upbeat as birdsong. My brother, Rivelin, grabbed a barrel and slid it beside the others. The wagon groaned beneath the weight of all that ale. I'd spent the past few weeks elbow's deep in malted grains, and this was my biggest brew in years.

My brother stepped back, frowning, but his golden eyes were soft.

"You sure you don't want to stay in Wyndale until spring?" His breath frosted the air, even though the leaves had only begun to shed their verdancy for the musky reds and browns of autumn.

Smiling, I pushed up onto my toes and ruffled the long silver hair that draped around his pointed elven ears. "I'll be fine, Riv. I always am."

"Maybe so. But Daella and I would love to have you stay, if you'd like." His voice softened. "You don't have to spend the winter months wandering the roads alone, Lilia. You always have a home here with me."

I sighed. Rivelin meant well. He worried about me when I took my Traveling Tavern on the road, even though I'd been doing it for years now. But Wyndale wasn't my home. It never had been. And if I didn't keep moving, I swore my bones would jump out of my body, and run off on their own.

To be a wanderer was in my soul.

"Maybe next year," I replied. "But Riverwold is expecting me for Yule Festival again, and you know how popular the Traveling Tavern is there. I can't let them down. Plus, I need the coin."

I motioned at my old wagon and its peeling paint. It was in desperate need of a fresh coat of silver. Had been, for a couple years now. But I only had a bit of gold in my pocket, and it was reserved for food. I did have a pouch full of rare Galdur sand—Vindur, or *air magic*, specifically—which harnessed the elemental magic of our world, and was worth far more than gold. It was hidden away for emergencies only, though.

"You won't have to worry about coin if you stay here," he argued. "You could live with me and Daella until—"

I palmed his rough cheek, quieting his words. "I have to make my own way, Riv."

"Yeah." His jaw tightened, then he shook his head

and donned a strained smile. "I know you do. But you can't blame me for trying. I just—"

"Adore me?" I grinned and booped his nose. "I love you, too, big brother."

His half-orc wife, Daella, ambled around the corner. As always, she wore a cropped leather tank that revealed her muscled green abs—even when all the summer's warmth had faded from the air. She offered me a brown paper bag. The bottom of it was warm and sticky.

"From Mabel. She thought you'd want some snacks for the road," Daella said.

My stomach grumbled in anticipation. Mabel made the best mushroom pasties around. "Thanks, Daella. You're the best."

"She absolutely is," Riv murmured.

My brother turned to gaze at her, his eyes so full of love I thought he might burst. *They're so sweet.* A cord of longing tugged at my gut. I'd never had that, not with anyone. I probably never would. It meant growing roots and watching vines crawl up your body, so tight and unyielding they could suffocate you.

My skin itched at the thought.

As lonely as the road was, it was the only place for me.

I took the pasties and tucked them in the front compartment of my wagon, where I kept the supplies I might need on the road. Then I turned back to her, smiling, and took her gloved hands in mine. "You take care of my brother, all right?"

"Always. But I just have one more gift. Don't you dare turn it down, either."

Daella pulled a small sheathed dagger from her back waistband. Surprised, I looked at Rivelin. He nodded.

"A weapon?" I asked.

Hearthaven had long kept a 'no weapons' rule. We had always lived in peace here, unlike in the mainland, where ice giant invaders had nearly killed off all the orcs in a long and brutal war. That war was over now, and the orcs were slowly coming out of hiding and taking back their land. Most of the giants had returned to their icy kingdom. There was no more bloodshed, thank the gods.

"It's just for hunting," Rivelin said.

Daella snorted. "No, it's for self-defense. You've got a lot of ale and food in that wagon. Watch out for thieves on the road."

I dealt her a gentle smile. When Daella had washed up on our island's shores only a few years back, she'd come bearing a dagger and a violent past. The island—and my brother—had slowly pulled her into its gentle, peaceful embrace, but sometimes she forgot that constant danger didn't surround us. We didn't have thieves.

Well, for the most part, anyway.

"Thanks. I'm sure I'll find a use for it." I added the

dagger to the front compartment, sandwiched between the food and my bedroll.

And then it was time to leave. I didn't say good-bye. I never did. The last time I'd spoken that word, it had been far too final. A farewell I could never take back.

"See you soon, then," I said.

I grabbed the yokes and hauled the heavy wagon down the windy, dust-caked road, wheels rattling with every step. I didn't give in to the temptation to look over my shoulder. I could picture the image clearly enough. Rivelin and Daella would be standing at the base of the stairs that led into their blacksmith shop, wistful tears in their eyes. Rivelin's jaw would be tight. Daella would hook her arm around his waist and drop her head to his chest, and they'd stand there watching me until I was nothing more than a speck of dust on the horizon, driven onward by my unending wanderlust.

The wagon jolted to a stop. Frowning, I looked down. A muddy, leaf-clogged section of the road had caught one of the wheels. I released my grip on the yokes and sagged against them, wiping the sweat from my brow. Already, the sky was fading into a dusky blue and a bitter wind snapped at my cheeks. I'd only been traveling for a few hours; it was always harder during autumn. A week's travel could turn into two—sometimes three.

I grabbed Mabel's parcel from the wagon—now cold—and took stock of my surroundings. The oak trees of the Ashborn Forest loomed around me, blocking what little light was left. Darkness pulsed from the dense brush on either side of the road, and the distant snap of twigs echoed like a drumbeat.

A shiver went through me. I didn't much like this part of the journey. Once I was through the forest, it was all rolling plains and castle ruins for a few days, horizons that felt endless and full of hope. But this place felt suffocating. Shadows seemed to form faces in the woods. 'Course, I'd always had an overactive imagination, especially as a child.

And it wasn't as if I was *completely* alone.

I brought my fingers to my lips and released a high-pitched whistle. The noise rent the silence, and a shriek answered from the deepening sky. I pulled out two of Mabel's pasties and nibbled on one. The tops of the trees began to shake.

A dragon soared over the canopy, his membranous wings pumping on either side of his scaly form. He swooped low at a frightening speed, his beady eyes trained on my face. I lifted the second pasty and smiled. In answer, he opened his maw and revealed dozens of teeth as sharp as any blade. He loosed a roar that would have sent even the bravest man running.

Luckily, I was no man.

"Hello, Reykur," I purred.

He thundered onto the road. Heat stormed toward me, thawing my nose. Shaking his head, he inched toward me, his talons churning the dirt. But he stopped several feet away—he'd burn me if he came any closer.

Only orcs, like Daella, could safely touch dragons.

I tossed him Mabel's treat. He caught it mid-air and swallowed it whole, not bothering to chew the thing. Then I swore he batted his red eyes at me, as if asking for another.

I laughed. "Greedy little thing, aren't you? Well, I guess I shouldn't complain. Without you, I'd freeze when winter comes."

Only a few people knew my little secret—Rivelin, Daella, and a friend of mine in Riverwold named Nilsa. Reykur liked to follow me around when I travelled, at least during the colder months. During summer, he spent more time soaring through the skies. Often, I wouldn't see him for weeks. But during the shortest days and coldest nights, he rarely strayed far from my side.

I'd never asked for his help, of course. One day, several years back, he'd just shown up. Ever since, he'd been following me around. His internal fire meant I didn't need to worry about frost or snow swallowing up a campfire. And I could sleep in my wagon instead of outside on the ground.

The bag crinkled as I extracted another pasty.

Reykur watched me greedily, his forked tongue slashing at the ground.

But then his head swung up. He went preternaturally still, his eyes locking on the road behind me. The unmistakable rumble of wagon wheels soon followed. Frowning, I turned and peered into the gathering dark. Who else from Wyndale would be traveling on this road so late in the year, and this close to nightfall? Surely Rivelin and Daella hadn't decided to join me. I couldn't imagine my brother leaving his beloved forge for a few months.

"You best get scarce." I turned back to Reykur and tossed him the second pastry, then tucked the nearly empty bag into my wagon. "If it's not someone from Wyndale, well…I don't want to think about what they might do."

And even then, they didn't much like him there, what with him burning down someone's house a few years back. It hadn't been his fault, but some of the residents there were still wary of him.

The emerald scales along Reykur's snout burned red, his internal fire flaring to life.

I shook my head at him. "Don't be so testy. They just don't understand you mean them no harm, all right? But one day they will."

He snorted, swung his head around to show me his ridged back, then leapt from the ground. Only a moment later, his winged form vanished into the leaden clouds above. The heat seeped from the air, replaced by a chill so deep it pierced my bones. Shivering, I tugged my cloak around my body and knelt beside my wagon wheel. It had sunk even further into the mud while I'd been distracted.

Sighing, I scooped some of it away from the wheel, then tried to tug the wagon forward. It didn't budge.

The distant clattering grew louder. With a frustrated sigh, I tried to pull the wagon again, sweat gathering, muscles straining. Breath hissed through my clenched teeth. I used every ounce of strength I could find, and absolutely nothing happened. The wagon didn't even twitch.

"There a problem?" an unfamiliar voice called out from the rear of the wagon. The rattling stopped, replaced by the heavy thud of footsteps.

My heart pounded. This was really embarrassing. I should have noticed the mud sooner and steered around it. I'd spent years building up the strength and endurance to haul my wagon around for weeks on end. I didn't much like the idea of asking a random stranger on the road to help me.

He stepped around the corner. Nearly as tall as the wagon, he towered over me. His broad shoulders strained the black linen tunic he wore, the sleeves rolled up and the top buttons undone to reveal a muscular chest. Crimson hair hung down to his shoulders, curling with wild abandon. His eyes were the color of fire, widening just slightly when he caught a glimpse of me.

I probably wasn't what he'd been expecting.

And the feeling was mutual. He had sharply-tipped ears, but he smelled nothing like an elf with his odd mixture of musk, spice, and magic. Most residents of Hearthaven were folk—elves, dwarves, pixies, fire demons, and shadow demons—but he was something else, I was sure of it. I couldn't help but notice his jawline. It was like someone had taken a chisel and carved him from stone.

Yes, I'd definitely never seen him before, and he certainly wasn't from Wyndale. I would have remembered him.

It was then I realized his mouth was moving. He stopped talking, then cocked his head.

I blinked, my cheeks heating. "I'm sorry?"

The left side of his lips tilted up in a half-smile—or a smirk. "I asked if you're all right. Do you need to sit down? You look a bit flushed."

2

LILIA

"**N**o." I dusted off my trousers. "I'm quite all right, thank you."

His eyes drifted down the length of me, snagging on my hips, before moving on to the mud-drenched wheel. "Ah. Looks like a pothole got you. Should be easy enough to pull your wagon out of there, though. Move aside."

"I don't need your help." The words flew out of my mouth before I could stop them.

Truth was, if he didn't help me, I'd have to camp here for the night. That was well and good, but what about tomorrow? And the next day? Eventually, someone else might come along the road, but how long would that take? I only had a month to reach Riverwold for the festival, and it was a long journey from here. There was just something...*off* about this man. The way his eyes seemed to dance annoyed me.

Internally, he was laughing at me, I could tell. I couldn't give him the satisfaction of being right.

He folded his massive arms. "No, of course you don't need help. You were just stopping here in the middle of the road to—"

"To camp," I cut in. "It's dark now. Time to have dinner and get some sleep."

He looked pointedly at my slanted wagon. "I normally like to camp on the *side* of the road, rather than smack dab in the middle of it."

"Well, you're certainly welcome to do what you like." I shrugged off his words and moved to my supplies, hastily tugging out my bedroll. I had no plans to actually sleep on the ground, but I hoped this would give him the hint to move on. But he just remained where he was, watching me. Frowning, I tossed my bedroll onto the ground, then shoved aside the burlap flap of my front compartment to grab my canteen of water.

My wagon suddenly jerked forward.

I stumbled back. The crimson-haired man had his beefy hands on the yokes. He winked, releasing the wagon and pointing at the wheel, now free from the muddy pothole.

The blood rushed into my cheeks. "Why did you do that?"

He arched a brow. "You're welcome."

He dusted off his hands and left me where I was, returning to his own wagon that he'd parked behind mine. I eyed his broad back and the hair that curled across his neck. He climbed into the back of his wagon without saying another word.

I sighed, slumping against the wooden side of the only house I'd ever called home. What was I doing? The stranger had only been trying to help me. And how had I repaid him? Shaking my head, I wandered over to his wagon. It was smaller than mine, though the oak sides gleamed like they'd just been polished. The panels weren't faded by wind and rain like mine was. I ran my hand along the side of it. Smooth, too. *Wonder what kind of goods he sells.*

Wonder where he's traveling to sell them, too.

There were a few merchants who travelled throughout the Isles, but I'd met all of them. Or at least I'd thought I had. Most of them dealt in cloth, jewellery, shoes, and scented soaps or perfumes. None of those items seemed to fit this man. In fact, if I were to guess, I'd assume he hocked weapons, but…surely not.

I knocked on the side of the wagon. His head poked out the back a second later. Laughter still danced in his eyes, and I fought back a huff of annoyance.

"Sorry. I should have thanked you for pulling my wagon out of the mud," I said. "I'm just not used to asking for help."

"That's quite all right," he drawled, and then he vanished into his wagon again, effectively dismissing me.

I frowned. "I really am going to camp here."

"Good night, then," came the muffled reply.

"Are you going to…I don't know, move on?" I asked. Reykur wouldn't return until the man left, and my cheeks were beginning to feel numb. I wanted my warm dragon, a nice meal, and a cozy sleep in my wagon so I could get an early start in the morning. As it was, the man seemed in no hurry to get moving.

The burlap flap on the back of his wagon rustled—he didn't have a door like I did—and he leapt onto the ground with more speed and grace than most folk possessed. In the dark, his eyes seemed to burn as bright as a dragon's fury. It was difficult not to stare at them.

"Why would I move on?" he asked. "Like you said, it's dark. Time to set up camp for the night."

Of course. I should have expected. I opened my mouth, then snapped it shut. I couldn't tell him to go somewhere else, especially not after he'd helped me. That was rude, and I'd already lost my manners once. Besides, he was right. It was fully dark now. Even though Hearthaven was a safe island, traveling at night came burdened with too many challenges.

With a shrug, I nodded. "All right. Sleep well, then."

I turned to go.

"Wait," he said.

My chest tightened, and I glanced over my shoulder at him. He slung his hands into his trouser pockets and rocked back on his heels. Gone was the mocking laughter in his eyes. He motioned at the ground between us.

"Fancy sharing a fire, a few ales, and some stories? It might be dark, but it's early yet. Might be nice to have some company for once."

I swallowed, ignoring the strange patter of my heart. "You have ale?"

"A little."

"I..." Fighting the urge to search the skies for the unmistakable shadow of dragon wings, I grasped for an excuse. I couldn't remember the last time I'd shared a camp with anyone other than Reykur. When I worked festivals and village squares, I barely got a moment alone, constantly surrounded by roaring laughter, cheerful singing, and raucous chatter. The past few weeks in Wyndale had been just that, and by the end of my visit, I'd longed for my solitude. The endless hours on the road soothed my soul, whittling away the splinters that gathered along my edges anytime I spent too much time surrounded by other people.

But...he was just one person, and this was just one night. I had a lot of long days of solitude ahead of me before I reached the village of Milford and then River-wold beyond it, when the chaos of the festival would swallow me whole for weeks. But for now, it was quiet.

"One ale," I finally said. "But then I really do want to get some sleep."

I gathered some logs while he rustled around in the back of his wagon, then watched him start a fire in the middle of the road with nothing more than his bare hands. Interesting. Most folk couldn't conjure fire without Fildur sand—the elemental fire magic. He must be some kind of fire demon, then, despite his lack of horns and red skin.

After I spread my bedroll beside the flames, he ambled over with two tankards of ale. Froth bubbled down the sides and dripped onto his hands. He handed me one and settled on the bedroll beside me.

Startled, I took a sip of the ale. I hadn't expected him to sit so close to me. Did he not have his own bedroll? As the bitter liquid burned down my throat, I watched him out of the corner of my eye. He stared into the flickering fire, the color of the flames casting his hair into an even deeper crimson.

"How's the ale?" he suddenly asked.

"It's fine, thank you," I answered, wondering if I should choose politeness or bluntness. I went with the latter. "But I can tell you aren't used to serving it. The froth takes up half the tankard. Not that I mind much."

He chuckled. "And what else can you tell?"

"You brewed this yourself," I said, taking another sip. "It's a little too bitter to be something you picked up from an alehouse or a brewery. But I might only notice that because I've tasted pretty much every ale on this island. This one is different, tangier than the others. What kind of grains did you use? I think you could add something sweet to the recipe to make it better. Maybe some honey? And make sure your grains aren't stale."

He was silent for a moment, and I thought I might have offended him. Honesty was always the best policy, as far as I was concerned, but not everyone appreciated it. When the silence stretched on too long, I cleared my throat.

"Anyway, you haven't told me your name," I said.

"Ragnar," he said, arching a brow. "And you?"

"Lilia."

"Nice to meet you, Lilia." He clinked his tankard against mine. "Here's to adventure and endless horizons."

I sat up a little straighter, smiling. "I can drink to that."

I took another sip. This time, it went down a lot easier, even if the bitterness remained. Ragnar downed the rest of his drink in a single drag, then wiped the froth from his lips with the back of his arm. His sleeves were still rolled up, despite the chill, and the strength of his forearms rippled as he reached for my now-empty tankard.

"I'd offer you another, but I'm worried I'll get another lecture about my grains." A slow smile spread across his face.

I grinned and glanced away, peering into the

bottom of my tankard. My fingers curled around the wood. "I'd apologize for my unsolicited opinion, but you did ask me how it was, and I don't much like lying—especially when it comes to ale."

He laughed. "So, I suppose that means you don't want another, then?"

"Well, you supposed wrong." Quickly, I looked up at him. His fiery eyes bored into mine. "Despite the ridiculous amount of froth and the regrettable bitterness, I'd very much like another."

"Now you're just twisting the knife." Shaking his head, he pressed a hand to his heart.

"You can take it."

"No, I'm far too wounded. I'm going to expire within seconds." He held out a hand and winked. "Double the froth this time, then?"

A giggle popped from my throat. "Why hold back? Let's just go for an entire tankard full of it."

I passed him my tankard, and our fingers brushed. The warmth of his hand bled into me, like a shock of heat. I blinked and snapped back my hand, far too quickly to be normal. But he didn't seem to notice. He wandered back over to his wagon in a relaxed yet confident gait.

I took the opportunity to press my hands to my cheeks. They were blazing hot. What had gotten into me?

He returned a moment later with the refilled tankards. This time, he'd done them with a proper pour, and only a small amount of foam perched on top. When he settled down beside me again, he lay all the way back and pointed up at the carpet of sky visible through the trees.

"I love clear nights," he said, his voice rumbling deep in his chest. "Look, you can see the constellation of Freya."

I set my tankard beside the bedroll and reclined on the ground, my hair spreading around my head like a puddle of silver. "You don't strike me as someone who memorizes the constellation of the gods."

I wasn't looking at him, but I could still *feel* his head shifting, and then his gaze pinning the side of my face. "What *do* I strike you as? Besides a terrible brewmaster, of course."

Rolling over onto my side, I pushed up onto my elbow, and cushioned my head with my hand. I swept my gaze across him. He was pure power and strength, and that hint of magic I'd smelled earlier mingled with the fire he'd built. "You must have fire demons in your ancestry, which means you probably don't need this fire to stay warm tonight. You also helped me with my wagon, even after I was rude to you. So you like helping other people, and you don't expect thanks for it. In fact, I think you'd rather not be thanked. You have this rugged look about you, one you embrace. It means people might think you're the opposite of how you truly are, and you like that. It's more fun for you when you prove someone wrong."

He turned toward me, mirroring the way I'd

propped my head against my hand. "Clever. Do you know what that tells me about you?"

"Oh, I'm certain I'm going to find out."

His eyes sparked. "You've been a merchant for a long time, and you know how to listen to people and understand their life stories. You let them unload their worries on you, which means you've learned what makes people tick. You're observant. You have refined taste, at least when it comes to ale. I bet if I looked in that wagon of yours, I'd find some kegs. That thing you're hauling around isn't some normal wagon. It's a tavern, isn't it?"

I fought back the smile but lost. A full-on grin stretched across my face. "Lilia's Traveling Tavern. It's fairly well-known around these parts, which tells me something else about you, even though I'd already guessed: you're new here."

"You caught me." His eyes travelled across my body. "So, I stumbled upon a beautiful, famous tavern owner on the road. What are the odds?"

Heat stormed my cheeks. "Well, I travel a lot, so it's not that strange. 'Course you just arrived on the Isles, I'm guessing, so I might be one of the few people here you've met. Maybe the first? And if you look at it that way, it might be fairly random, but—" I blew out a breath and stopped. This was mortifying. A man had given me a compliment and all I could do was babble nonsensically.

I sat up, grabbed the tankard, and gulped down

some ale, forcing myself to stare into the flames rather than look anywhere else.

A hand gently touched my hip. Chest burning, I dragged my gaze from the fire to meet Ragnar's. But he'd lain back down on the ground. He raised his other hand, pointing up at the sky.

"Let's watch the stars together," he said. "Before the clouds roll in."

I stared at him for a moment. There was something strange in his expression I couldn't read, like his thoughts were only halfway here, like he saw something more than just Freya's constellation in the sky. And it occurred to me that perhaps he was more like me than I'd originally thought. Anyone who called the road their home must be.

I lay back down beside him. Our shoulders brushed, and even though my heart pounded in my chest, I knew nothing would come of it. Not tonight at least. We watched the sky together in comfortable silence. And soon, the heat from Ragnar's body lulled me into a deep, dreamless sleep.

3

LILIA

Chill seeped into my bones. I sat up, blinking at the dull morning light. My bedroll slid down my front, where it had been tucked around me sometime during the night. The ashen remains of the fire scattered in the wind like a cloud of ground peppercorns. I rubbed my swollen eyes and glanced around. Only an empty space sat behind my wagon now. Ragnar was gone.

I sighed, swallowing down my unexpected disappointment. Of course he'd moved on already. He clearly had somewhere he needed to be, and helping me get out of the pothole had slowed him down. He wouldn't have stopped so early last night if it hadn't been for me. And so he'd set off before first light.

It was for the best anyway. If we'd left at the same time, it would have felt like we were journeying together. We would have shared more stories, and likely more ale, and a few more campfires along the way in a dance of strangers to friends...to strangers again. It would have been harder to leave when he eventually took one fork in the path and I took another.

For him, anyway. I never let myself forget that every hello came with a goodbye.

Still, I paused by the muddy tracks after collecting my bedroll. They were fresh enough that Ragnar couldn't have left that long ago. If I hurried, I'd catch him up. So I took my time. I inspected my wheels, whistled for Reykur, and fed him the last of Mabel's treats. As I finished preparing to leave, the dragon sat chomping away in the middle of the road, his spiked tail thumping like he was an oversized hound.

"It's just you and me," I told him. "Now and always, all right?"

Reykur tilted his head to the side and huffed.

"Don't you make that sound at me. *He* left first. And besides, I barely even know him. He's just some man I met on the road," I said. "There's nothing special about that. I meet lots of people all the time."

Reykur just continued to stare at me with eyes I swore looked sad. Ignoring him, I gathered the yokes in my hands and started down the road again. The wagon heaved, bucking against the rough ground, and this time, I was careful to steer the wheels away from muddy potholes. I didn't think I'd be so lucky if I got stuck again.

The day passed as slowly as the wagon. And my dragon never once left my side.

Musical chimes drifted on the wind. I slowed and wiped my sweat from my brow, wincing at my throbbing feet. Down the gently rolling hill, Riverwold's thatched roofs formed a patchwork quilt of homes a few miles from the hazy coastline. Smoke curled from stone chimneys, and the lush scent of apple pie made my mouth water. I'd never been more relieved to see civilization. The month-long journey weighed heavily on my aching shoulders. Even my bones felt tired.

To the north of the village, the festival grounds were already crammed full of merchant wagons and colorful tents. It had taken me longer than I'd expected this time, and preparation was in full swing. It was still two weeks until Yule, but folk from all around the Isles would begin pouring into the village any day now—if they hadn't already. Over the coming days, muted celebrations would build to a crescendo of folk music, pie-eating competitions, and packed crowds that danced and sang and drank the nights away. Yule marked the death of one year and the birth of another. It was how the folk of the Isles ushered in harmony, happiness, and bounty for the coming months. And even though I was exhausted by the end of it, I always left Riverwold with hope in my heart.

Reykur lumbered up beside me, sniffing the pie

scent on the air. I fought a smile. The greedy dragon sure did love to eat.

"You'll have to head to your favorite lair in the mountains now," I said. "I'll bring you some pies when I can."

He huffed, and the red of his flank burned hot.

"No, not this time. They're still terrified of dragons." I smiled sadly. "But I'll try to make them see some sense, all right? Maybe next year it'll be safe enough for you to join the celebrations."

Snorting, he shoved up from the ground and soared toward the mountains, his wings cast wide against the mottled sky. I shielded my eyes from the sun, watching him vanish into the clouds. My heart ached. It wasn't fair that he had to hide. He'd never hurt someone intentionally, but the people of Hearthaven struggled to forget the past. Years ago, cruel folk on the mainland had used dragons for their powerful magic—until the magic had consumed them, driving them to do terrible things.

As a response, the empire had killed almost every dragon alive, convinced they were the cause of it all. Only four eggs had survived. My brother and I had smuggled the newborns into Hearthaven, where we'd raised them. After Daella had bonded with one of them, the people of Wyndale had softened toward the dragons, but the other villages of Hearthaven had yet to shake their fear.

"I'm sorry," I whispered. He would have to spend most of Yule alone.

It wasn't right, and it wasn't fair, but maybe I could change some minds this year.

I hauled my wagon the rest of the way down the hill alone, and a light dusting of mist began to drift from the thickening clouds. When I reached the outskirts of the village, several bundled children ran past giggling and screaming, their ruddy cheeks bright from the cold.

Smiling, I trudged past them down the road that rimmed the edge of Riverwold. Even though winter was upon us, dense vines curled up the sides of the stone buildings, twisting around the branches of the thatched roofs. A few blue winter flowers sprouted from the carpet of grass that flanked every home and every stretch of road. Ravens circled overhead, cawing in delight.

At the end of the lane, I came to the sprawling meadow that backed up against a patch of woods. I slowed to a stop, the sounds of the gathered merchants washing over me. Hammers pounded stumps into the ground to hold down tent ropes. Saws scraped through wood as signs were built. Dishes clattered. Laughter boomed. And the steady buzz of conversation was an undercurrent beneath it all.

"Lilia!" a voice proclaimed from behind me.

I turned. A small dwarven woman with braided black hair bustled toward me, her green eyes as bright as her smile. She wore bells in her hair that twinkled with her every step. Her curvy hips swayed beneath her woollen trousers.

"Nilsa," I said, beaming. When she reached me, I wound my arms around her. She squeezed me back.

"You're late," she said, pulling away and tapping me on the nose. "What took you so long?"

I laughed. "Nice to see you, too. How's the inn?"

She waved dismissively. "The inn isn't important. It's the same as always. We need to talk about you. Did something happen on the road? You're usually one of the first to show up. We thought you weren't coming."

The image of Ragnar and his rugged face popped into my head, but I instantly shoved it away. She wasn't asking about a random man I'd met on my journey, a man who almost felt like a figment of my imagination now. I'd seen no sign of him on the road since he vanished that morning, and no one in Milford had mentioned him when I'd passed through. 'Course I hadn't asked about him, either, though I'd spent one long night wondering if I should.

I cleared my throat. "It was just muddier than usual. I had to take it slow so I didn't get stuck."

"Well, that's good to hear." She looked at the wagon and noted the peeling paint and the flecks of mud coating the lower half. "I'm sure Steffon can manage to find you somewhere to set up shop."

I frowned. "What do you mean? I always take the spot beside the willow tree."

Nilsa winced. "Like I said, we thought you weren't coming. So…we gave your spot to another."

"Oh."

"I'm so sorry, Lilia. If we knew, we would have saved it for you, but as it is, Steffon was worried we wouldn't have a tavern in the usual spot. And you know how everyone feels about their ale. It's not Yule without it."

"Wait." My frown deepened. "Are you saying another tavern showed up?"

She shrugged. "Looks like you're not the only one out there anymore. Though, I have to say, I tasted his ale yesterday, and it's nowhere near as good as yours. It's kind of bitter, if I'm honest. So I'm sure you'll still do well enough this year, even if you don't have your usual spot."

"The tavern owner is a *him*?" My voice rose an octave. "With bitter ale?"

My chest felt hot. It couldn't be him. Could it? This was a ridiculous coincidence, that was all. It had to be someone from Hearthaven or one of the other Isles. Not the handsome man I'd met on the road. Not the one I'd stargazed with.

Nilsa peered up at me. "I thought you'd be happy about the bitter part. Means he can't compete with the best brewer in all the Isles."

"Where is he?"

"Last time I saw him, he was at his wagon by the willow tree."

I fisted my hands. "Not for long."

29

4

RAGNAR

I unloaded another keg from the back of my wagon while chaos raged around me. Shouts peppered the air from the woodcarver next door; high-pitched voices weaved together in a whimsical song from the performer tent across the way. And there were a hundred more voices scattered through it all. Wooden rods were dotted here and there, each one decorated with a multitude of colorful ribbons that fluttered in the chilly breeze. Yule wasn't for another two weeks, but it felt like the damn festival had already begun.

Even though I'd heard stories about this place for years, nothing had prepared me for it. At least forty merchants had swarmed this little island town for the coldest, darkest, and longest night of the year. All to 'celebrate' life. They were still coming, too. About an hour ago, I'd noticed the shadow of another wagon up on the ridge, heading this way.

And if these were just the merchants, I could only imagine how many thirsty patrons would come. Hundreds, I'd bet. I could already feel the weight of the coin in my pocket.

With a smile, I swiped my half-empty tankard from the rickety table I'd set up outside my wagon, swigging my ale. The bitterness of it burned my throat, and I nearly spat it out. It really wasn't very good, was it? But there was no time to brew a fresh batch before Yule, so I just had to bank on everyone being desperate enough for a drink to ignore the taste of it. I hadn't seen any other taverns here, and the inn only seemed to serve wine and spirits.

"You," a voice snapped.

I looked over the rim of my tankard. A scowling, silver-haired elf with hips to die for glared at me, her arms folded over her chest. My heart pitched forward. It was the girl I'd met on the road weeks ago, the one I'd thought might head this way. The one I'd kept looking for over my shoulder, wondering if she might catch up to me. A part of me had hoped she would, even if it meant I'd leave here with a much-lighter coin purse. She was a much better brewer than me.

I lowered my tankard, but I was so distracted looking at Lilia that I missed the edge of the table. The cup tumbled onto the grass, spilling ale across my boots.

"Well, look who it is," I said with an easy smile. At least I hoped it looked easy. I didn't want her to know what was really going on in my mind. "Fancy seeing you here. What are the odds?"

"Pretty high considering you vanished in the middle of the night just so you could beat me to my festival."

"*Your* festival?"

She pointed at the willow tree, whose frosted branches draped over one of the few vacant spots throughout the festival grounds. The dwarf beside her —Nilsa was her name, I believed—had told me to put some tables and chairs there for patrons, not that I had any with me. Hopefully, I could borrow some from one of the Riverwold residents.

"I've been coming here for years, and everyone expects to find a tavern right here beside the willow tree. They even bring food over from the other stalls to eat at my tables, and I decorate the branches with ribbons and—"

"And they will find all that here." I motioned at my wagon. "Ragnar's Traveling Tavern is now officially in business."

Her cheeks flushed red. "You are not calling yourself that. The Traveling Tavern is *my* name. It belongs to me, not you and your...your frankly disgusting ale."

A booming laugh escaped my throat. "Well, then. At least you've finally told me what you *really* think of my brew."

"You lied to me."

"I spoke no lies."

"I'm sorry, I hate to interrupt...whatever this is," Nilsa piped up, tugging on Lilia's cloak. "But how do you know each other?"

"We met on the road," Lilia said, her eyes narrowing. "Ragnar tricked me with a random act of kindness. He wanted to beat me to Riverwold and steal my business."

"That does sound fairly misleading, Ragnar," said Nilsa.

I folded my arms. "I didn't trick anyone."

"No?" Lilia took a step toward me, her eyes flashing. "Why did you sneak away in the middle of the night, then?"

"It was barely pre-dawn, not the middle of the night."

"Close enough." She walked a few more steps closer, bringing a whiff of her perfume with her— something akin to lavender. Gods, she smelled so damn sweet. "Look into my eyes and tell me you had no idea who I was and where I was going. Tell me you didn't know you needed to get here first to have any hope of competing with the Traveling Tavern."

I met her gaze, but I didn't bother to respond. When I'd first come across her in the road, I *hadn't* known who she was. But it hadn't taken long for me to realize. Lilia was one of the reasons I was here. My brother had heard about her tavern and how popular it was—and he'd heard how well she lined her pockets with coin. He'd always dreamed of visiting the Isles with his own tavern. And now he never could.

Her eyes scanned my face as she noted my silence, and then she nodded. "Move out of my spot, Ragnar."

"Hmm, I think not."

"If you don't move your fates-damned wagon, then I'll do it for you."

I smiled, my arms still crossed over my chest. "I'd like to see you try."

A tall shadow demon with curved black horns bustled over from the path, frowning. In his multi-colored tunic and patchwork trousers, he looked as if he'd tossed on one of the performer tents. He'd introduced himself when I'd first arrived a few days before, and I'd learned he organized the entire festival *and* he'd been named the Defender of Riverwold, which apparently meant he was something of a sheriff. Thin and reedy with waist-length hair, he didn't much look like one, though.

"Is there a problem here?" he asked.

"*Yes*. Thank fate you're here, Steffon." The bright smile Lilia dealt the shadow demon was a complete contrast to the expression she'd targeted at me. "This man is trying to set up his wagon in my usual spot, and you know how important it is to have my Traveling Tavern here. All the regulars will be confused if it's not."

He wrung his hands. "Yes, about that. I'm sorry, Lilia. I did worry about giving away the willow tree, but you were just so *late*. We're already seven days into the month! I'm afraid there's nothing I can do. You know the rules. First come, first serve."

Her mouth dropped open. "But—"

"I can't bend the rules for you, Lilia. Not this time." He gently patted her arm. "Get here earlier next year, eh? The spot'll be yours so long as you make it by the first day of Ýlir."

A pixie fluttered over from the performer tent, her luminescent wings buzzing with excitement. A sheen of sweat covered her dark brown skin, and she sucked in great lungfuls of air.

"Sorry, Steffon. We need your help," she began, casting Lilia an apologetic look. "We've just been practicing our routine for Yule, and we've realized we don't have enough space where we are. Is there somewhere we can move our tent?"

"Yes, yes, of course." Steffon patted Lilia's shoulder again. "Take your wagon to St. Olaf Row. I'm afraid that's the best I can do."

"But that's in a far back corner of the grounds..." Lilia trailed off as she watched Steffon wander off with the performer. Her shoulders sagged, and the soft breath she sighed burrowed into my bones. I rubbed the back of my neck, my jagged scar rough and puckered even after all these years. It was a reminder of why I was here.

"You'll get plenty of business no matter where you park your wagon," I told her. "We both know your ale is far superior to mine."

She frowned and backed away. "Don't try to act all nice now."

"Fine. I won't."

"Good." Spinning on her heels, she strode away, the muddy bottom of her blue dress swirling around her worn leather boots. I leaned against the side of my wagon, watching her wend through the crowded meadow. She was spitting mad. Not that I could blame her. I would be, too, if a random stranger had butted into my territory, especially after we'd spent the night together—*platonically*, of course. Not that I hadn't wondered…

It was a shame things had gone this way—that we had to be rivals. She was a fetching lass, with her fiery eyes and curvy hips. But she was going to do her damndest to take every last drop of business, I could tell. And despite being hidden away in the back corner, she would likely succeed.

I couldn't let that happen.

5

"**S**orry, Lil," Nilsa said with her hands clasped before her apron-clad body. "It's not too bad, though, right?"

I situated my wagon just so and stepped back to observe it. St. Olaf Row—named after a merchant who had slain a dozen sea serpents to protect a ship and its sailors—curved along the back edge of the festival, right where the meadow bled into the woods. It was as far from the town itself as one could get. Many of the merchants back here were newcomers who'd only just arrived for their first Yule in River-wold. They'd had no idea how quickly better spots got claimed, so they were as late as me.

As it was, I'd picked a spot sandwiched between a candlemaker and a baker with plenty of room on one side for my tables and chairs. A pocket of young ever-greens rose behind it for my decorations. It was no willow tree, but it would do.

"I'll make it work," I said with a brisk nod.

Nilsa looped her arm in mine and leaned against me. "I'll be sure to tell everyone who's staying at the inn that they should head your way. You'll have no trouble getting business."

"I'll get some," I said. "But the willow tree is over near the front, where all the performers are. The stage, too. Plus, Karl is only a few stalls away with his smoked meats. Everyone likes to congregate over there. I just…I need the coin, Nilsa."

She sighed. "I know, love. But like you said, you'll find a way to make it work."

I nodded. Right now, the wagon had a dreary, dirty look about it after being on the road for so many weeks. But once I gave it a wash, hung up my banners and lanterns, and extended the brilliant silver awning out the front, my tired wagon would be transformed into the cozy tavern that it was. And I doubted the annoying man with the bitter brew had considered the importance of ambience.

Nilsa cleared her throat. "So, that Ragnar…he's handsome, eh?"

"Him?" I shifted on my feet. "Not in the least."

"Hmm." She chuckled. "Something happen between you two on the road?"

"What? No." I pulled away from her. "Why in fate's name would you think that?"

"It's just, you seem *awfully* perturbed about a stranger. If I didn't know better, I'd think he was a lover who'd betrayed you."

"That's ridiculous." Shaking my head, I moved to my wagon and rustled around in the side compartment until I found what I was looking for. I pulled out an iron candlestick holder and held it aloft. Nilsa's face lit up, but when she reached for it, I tucked it behind my back.

"I asked my brother to make this for you, but I'm only handing it over if you swear you won't try to play matchmaker again this year," I told her. "Especially with *you know who*."

She stuck out her tongue. "You're no fun."

"I have no desire for a relationship."

"What about a roll in the hay? We've got plenty of it in the stables."

I gave her a look.

She sighed. "I only do it because I love you, Lil. You spend so much time alone, wandering the roads without anyone to talk to."

"I have Reykur."

"A dragon who can't speak Nynorsk."

"Do you want the candlestick holder or not?"

"Yeah, yeah." With a defeated laugh, she held out her hands, palms up. "I won't play matchmaker with you and Ragnar. Now give it here."

Somewhat satisfied, I passed her the forged metal, smiling at the exuberant bounce of her feet. The wide base held up a curving rod that transformed into a winged dragon, its maw open for the candle at the top. She'd been asking for one of these for years— from my brother, specifically. Riverwold had a blacksmith, of course, but she'd never seen a dragon with her own eyes, and Nilsa was insistent she wanted an accurate portrayal of one to decorate her inn.

"This is perfect," she whispered, then reached for her coin purse that hung from her belt. "Here, I've been saving up some gold for—"

"Oh, don't you even try. It's a gift. From me to you, all right? Put your coin away."

"But you just said…"

"Riv made that, not me." I shrugged. "But if you really want to pay me back, make sure you send plenty of patrons my way as soon I get set up. And swing by for some ale yourself, eh?"

She dealt me a beaming smile. "I'll drag them all over here kicking and screaming if I must."

I laughed. "Maybe not kicking and screaming. It's a long two weeks until Yule. I'd prefer repeat patrons."

"Don't knock it. Might liven things up a bit." She glanced around at the quiet corner of the meadow, then nodded toward my wagon. "Guess I should leave you to start getting set up. See you at the inn later on?"

Clouds scuttled overhead, blocking the setting sun. It would be dark in an hour—tops—and most of the merchants and performers would call it a night. Even though I'd arrived late, the long evenings of celebrations wouldn't have begun just yet. And I was glad for it. With my aching feet and tired soul, I was looking forward to an early night in a warm bed instead of long hours spent out in the cold.

"I'll be there sooner rather than later," I said. "Can't wait to see where you put that candlestick holder."

Clutching the dragon to her chest, Nilsa scurried off. I sighed and leaned against my wagon, taking in the raucous energy of the grounds. The wagons and carts on St. Olaf Row were mostly silent, but lights and sounds drifted toward us from the other paths. For a few moments, I just breathed it all in, smiling. The laughter, the singing, the distant cheers. It felt good to be back here again, even if it wasn't exactly what I'd expected this year.

A dwarf wandered by, his arms laden with crates. He shot me a rueful smile and carried on to a cart that had a smoking pipe painted on the side. A pixie fluttered past on the tips of her toes as she spun in elaborate dance moves. When I clapped, she gave me a bow and then danced down the path out of sight.

Crimson flashed in the corner of my vision.

Heart suddenly pounding, I shifted toward it. Ragnar stood at the end of St. Olaf Row. He scanned the wagons as if he were searching for something—or someone.

His gaze landed on me, and I stiffened. He took in my location and the merchants on either side of me, then he turned on his heels and walked off.

An hour later, I lugged my pack through the winding paths of the festival until I reached the town proper. The tents and wagons melted away to the stone maze of Riverwold. Yellow candlelight already spilled from every window, and smoke whorled from chimneys, spit into the air by the soothing hearths I ached to sit beside. Window boxes overflowed with blue winter flowers, and vines curled in and out of the stones, like the buildings and the earth itself were one. The rich scent of pie spiced the chilly air.

I nodded to passersby. Many were familiar faces, both the residents who called this town their home and the merchants I knew from the regular festival rounds. Many of them travelled to Wyndale during the warmer months for the annual Midsummer Games, or across the sea to the mountains for the dwarven competition in the spring. But while they nodded in return, none spoke to me now. They wandered together in groups, chattering amongst themselves.

I traced my path through the streets, passing the fishmongers—closed for the evening—the apothecary, and an alley where cats prowled through piles of discarded food scraps. When I reached the end of the lane, I swung a right. The Ship's Anchor Inn sat on the other side of a large courtyard that was currently packed with dwarves, fire demons, elves, and even a few humans.

As I walked through the crowd, the warmth from the packed bodies radiated through me, chasing away the chill in my bones. I pushed inside. The sound of a hundred voices rose like thunder, drowning out the dark-haired elven bard on the small stage on the far wall.

Nilsa's inn only had three tables, but they were so long at least thirty patrons could fit on each bench. There wasn't a single seat free on any of them, and as the days progressed, it would only get harder to enjoy an evening meal here. Soon, patronage would spill into the festival itself, when the outdoor feasts became a nightly affair, ending with the biggest of them all— Yule. Riverwold could really use a second inn for the festival, but the town didn't get enough visitors during the rest of the year for it to make much sense.

A hearth blazed beside the stage, sending a soothing warmth through the cramped room. Decorations for Yule hung from the wooden beams that lined the low ceiling: antlers wreathed in dried berries, miniature wooden shields that hung from twine, and tokens carved with images of the gods. Drinking horns lined the walls, where they were stored until special feasting days like Yule.

I approached the oak counter, where my gift had taken a place of honor. A single crimson candle rose from the dragon's mouth, flickering brightly. Nilsa bustled out from the kitchen with five plates perched precariously on her arms and hands. When I breezed over and collected two of them, she shot me a grateful smile. I helped deliver the salted pork and boiled potatoes to a group of pixies before following her back over to the counter.

"Thanks," she tossed over her shoulder, wiping sweat from her brow. "It's busier tonight than I expected. Doesn't usually get this packed until closer to Yule."

"It's a cold night," I told her. "And most of the wagons aren't fully set up yet, so everyone's coming in here. You really ought to convince someone to establish a second inn."

"Two inns wouldn't survive here on the northeast side of this island," she said, waving her hand dismissively. "It's hard enough to make do as it is." Sighing, she rounded the counter and leaned heavily against it. "Anyway, you want some of my bean stew? I made it just for you, even when it seemed like you weren't coming. I thought, 'I've got to make sure I have bean stew for Lilia'."

"I'd love some," I said, reaching for my coin purse. "And a room, please, like always."

Her face fell. "Ah. I forgot to mention that earlier. We're fully occupied."

For a moment, my mouth didn't work. My heart squeezed, a little painfully. I'd been staying at the Ship's Anchor Inn during Yule for six years. In fact, Nilsa had been the one who'd insisted on it the first time I'd come to Riverwold. Soon after, we'd become fast friends. Her home was my home, or so she'd said.

But I knew I had no right to be upset. The Ship's Anchor was more than just her home, and she had to turn a profit during Yule to make up for the slower business during the rest of the year. She couldn't afford to hold a room for me indefinitely. Not for the first time, I cursed my slow crusade from Wyndale to here. I should have left at least a week earlier.

Sighing, she leaned across the counter and took my hand in hers. "I'm sorry, Lil, I really am. But you've got your dragon, right? Have him come down from the mountains and stay in the woods near your camp. No one will notice."

I tossed a furtive glance at the packed tables behind me. "I don't want to risk the wrong person catching sight of him. Besides, he could set the woods aflame if he's not careful."

"That's a good point. I'll make sure you have enough logs to build a fire yourself, then." She squeezed my hand. "Now, about that bean stew. How much would you like? There's a whole bloody lot of it, so I hope you're hungry."

I couldn't help but smile. As disappointed as I was about the inn, I was glad for the warm food. "As big of a bowl as you've got. And do you mind if I take it back to my wagon instead of eating it here? I'm so exhausted, I can hardly stand."

"You've got it." She glanced over my shoulder, and her lips twitched. "Probably for the best. The only open seat is right beside your favorite crimson-haired brewmaster. 'Course…it's nice and warm in here, and you'd have a—"

"Not happening, Nilsa." Tensing, I fought the urge to follow her gaze. I should have known Ragnar would be in here. I'd passed his wagon on the way into the village, and I'd tried not to look at it. But my eyes had betrayed me. While I hadn't spotted him, I'd assumed he'd gone inside his wagon.

With a wicked chuckle, Nilsa winked and vanished through the double doors that led to the kitchen. Rolling my eyes, I settled onto the stool beside the counter and pointedly ignored the tables. I didn't know where Ragnar was sitting, and I didn't want to find out. Seeing him relaxed in the cheerful inn, surrounded by laughter and song and hearth-flame, was the last thing I wanted.

Heavy footsteps thudded against the stone floor. I kept my gaze rooted to the kitchen entrance, *willing* Nilsa to reappear with my bowl of stew so I could get out of here. But the wooden doors were as motionless as wheels stuck in mud. The footsteps slowed the closer they got until the sound vanished entirely.

"Lilia," a now-familiar voice said.

I ground my teeth. Somehow, I'd known it was him. "Hello, Ragnar. You should probably return to your seat. It's so busy in here you'll lose it if you leave it too long."

"I'm done eating now."

Out of their own volition, my eyes drifted toward

his face. He stood over me—*towered*, really. His broad shoulders blocked out the rest of the inn, and something about his insistent presence seemed to suck away all of the sound. He ran a hand through his thick, wavy hair, his forearm flexing.

Pulse quickening, I stood. "Well, the bard is only getting started. Her name is Birta. Have you ever heard of her? She's local to Riverwold, but she does travel from time to time. She's one of the best bards in all the Isles. You really ought to stay and listen."

He shrugged his hands into his trouser pockets. "If you insist."

My shoulders relaxed. I opened my mouth to reply, but Nilsa finally returned. She bustled over and handed me a bowl covered by a round plank of wood to keep the stew warm on my return walk. I thanked her and started to go, but Ragnar shifted to the side, blocking me.

"Where are you going?" he asked.

I frowned at him. "Back to my wagon. I'm tired, and it's been a long day."

"Aren't you staying here? At the inn, I mean."

"There are no vacancies. Now please move aside."

As I darted around him, he rubbed the back of his neck, frowning.

I was glad when he made no attempt to block me again. I hadn't been lying when I'd said I was tired. The utter exhaustion was like five different anchors connected to my body, dragging me into the ground.

Bone-weary, I trudged out the door and back into the cold.

When I returned to St. Olaf Row, my wagon was just as I'd left it. I opened the creaking doors and climbed inside, settling against my barrels of ale so I could tuck into my stew. The beans were rich and spicy, and steam filled the air. I polished it off far too quickly, but the warmth lingered while I spread out my bedroll in the small gap of space between my kegs and my other merchant supplies.

I closed my eyes and pulled my blanket up to my chin. But even wrapped in layers, the wintry night soon settled over me, burrowing its biting chill into my skin. I longed to climb the mountain path, find Reykur, and curl nearby his sleeping form. But it was late and it was dark, and by the time I found him, dawn would pinken the sky.

I had to spend the night cold and bitterly alone. For the first time in a long while, my heart ached for company.

6

LILIA

An explosion of sound dragged me awake. Grumbling, I sat up and rubbed my eyes, trying to make sense of things. It was silent now, but I could have sworn… Shaking my head, I started to curl up beneath my blanket again, but a burst of thunder shuddered through the wagon, making me jump.

No, not thunder. The pounding was the unmistakable sound of a fist hitting wood.

I threw open the doors and poked my head out the back. Nilsa paused, her fist raised. She gave me a sheepish look.

"Oh. You look like you were asleep. Did I wake you?" she asked sweetly.

I patted down my mussed hair. "It's fine. What's wrong?"

"Nothing's wrong." She rocked back on her heels, the bells in her braid jingling. "Just thought you might want to come on inside where it's warm. Turns out I was confused. A room's available after all."

"Wait." I blinked at her. Was I still dreaming? "How'd you get something like that wrong?"

She shrugged. "Well, Herold does their best, but it's been so busy, they marked a room taken when it wasn't! I didn't notice until dinner service calmed down. I had a couple others asking about it, but I told them it was yours." Her eyes flicked to the interior of the wagon, where my bedroll snaked between my tightly packed supplies. "Looks cold in there. Come on in, eh?"

I pressed my lips together. "Nice try. Herold takes care of the kitchen. *You* book patrons into the rooms. You didn't kick someone out, did you? I don't want to take a room from someone else, Nilsa."

"As if I would ever do such a thing." Folding her arms, she gave me a no-nonsense look. "It's yours fair and square. Now do want it or not?"

She didn't have to ask me again. I grabbed my pack—with my clothes still tucked inside—jumped from my wagon, and followed her back into town.

The inn was still heaving, even though dinner service was done and dusted. At least there were a few open spots at the table nearest the stage now. I took a seat, despite my weariness, and nursed a goblet of sweet elderberry wine, listening to Birta the Bard's newest tune. It was one I'd never heard before, sang in a melancholy yet wistful melody.

> O'er the mountains
> The dragons soar
> Deep in their hearts
> A forgotten lore
>
> But hide they do
> From eyes below
> A dragon's might
> Is not to know

My weariness deepened as she sang. There was little cheer to her words, and they only reminded me of how difficult relations between dragons and folk still were. Reykur would spend Yule alone while hundreds would laugh and sing and cheer for days here in town. All the food, all the ale, all the songs. He would know none of it. And even though he could not speak my language, I knew he wished he could be here.

Sighing, I stood. And before I could stop myself, I glanced around the room, hunting for a familiar head of crimson hair. But there was no sign of him now. I supposed he hadn't taken my advice to stick around and listen to Birta's performance. Should have expected as much. He was here to steal business, not because he understood the importance of this festival and what it meant to all of us.

I found Nilsa beside the kitchen doors, leaning heavily against the wall. Her eyes were half-closed, and she had to use the wall to keep herself upright.

"Nilsa," I said.

She jolted away from the wall, blinking rapidly. "Sorry. I was just—"

"Resting your eyes?" I grinned.

She chuckled. "It's been a long old day."

"You're telling me." I cast another glance around the inn. A few dozen patrons were still here, but a hush had fallen across the room. Everyone watched Birta with rapt attention. Ragnar truly was missing out. Shaking my head, I dragged my attention from the crowd. "How long did Ragnar stay after I left, anyway?"

Nilsa leaned against the wall again, smirking. "Interested in where he is, are we? You know, I could put you in his room, if you'd like, though I'm afraid there's only one bed…'course you could always share it with him."

"Very funny." I held out my hand. "Which room am I in?"

She dug into her pocket, then dropped the iron key onto my palm. "Room eight at the very top. I'm afraid it's barely big enough for a bed, so it's not luxurious. Now Ragnar's room on the other hand…" Winking, she giggled.

My lips twitched. "You're impossible. You know that, right?"

"That's why you love me." She beamed. "Night, Lil."

"Good night. Try to get some sleep yourself, yeah? Or it's going to be a very long two weeks for you."

"Don't you worry about me." She gently nudged me toward the stairs. "Now, shoo. You look like you're about to topple over."

The room on the top floor was just as Nilsa had described it. One side of the bed was flush with the exterior wall, and the other side hit the wall where I stood now, just inside the door. There was no other furniture, and the ceiling's wooden beams were almost low enough to graze my head. But it was warm, and the double windowpanes blocked out the draft. Without bothering to undress, I climbed into the bed. As soon as my cheek hit the pillow, I slept.

I slipped out of the inn just before dawn. Even though I could have used a few more hours in bed, my curiosity had waged war with my quest for sleep. Before the festival grounds came alive this morning, there was something I needed to see. I might not get another chance to investigate before Yule.

The air was crisp, and a layer of frost carpeted the ground. I blew on my hands and hurried to the meadow just as the sky began to fade from black to indigo. When I reached the edge of town, only silence greeted me. It was so still and calm, quite the contrast to the day before. Not a single wagon or tent stirred.

I crept past them, willing my boots to remain silent. If anyone caught me...well, I could only imagine what they'd think. Theft was rare in the Isles, and the Yule Festival practically relied on trust. We frequently left our wagons unguarded. Our wares were ripe for the taking. Not once in the six years I'd been coming here had anything gone missing.

To break that trust would mean shattering the cocoon of safety and hope that we celebrated each year.

'Course, I wasn't going to steal anything. I just wanted to have a look.

Luckily, no one spotted me before I reached Ragnar's wagon. Now that I had a chance to examine it closer, I really took it in, eyeing the smooth wood and the polished shine that had not yet been faded by time. It was a much smaller wagon than mine— maybe half the size—but it was brand new. If I were to guess, this was his first event. The quality of his ale was telling, too. Whatever he'd done before this, he hadn't been a brewmaster.

"Who *are* you really?" I murmured to myself. And where had he come from? What was his purpose here? I found it hard to believe it was as simple as selling that terrible ale. Perhaps I'd find the answers inside.

I paused by the rear wheels and waited a breath, listening for footsteps on the path. The last thing I wanted was for him to catch me in the act. When silence was my only answer, I swept the burlap aside and hopped into the wagon. Light on my feet, I landed in a crouch. It took a moment for my vision to focus.

The crimson hair was the first thing I saw. Then it was his bare torso, marked by a long jagged scar. A blanket curled across his hips, barely covering the bottom half of him. His substantial muscles gleamed from the dawn light cutting through the gap in the burlap.

I sucked in a sharp breath, so loud it could wake the dead—*and* the living.

Ragnar's eyes cracked open, and the fire in them speared me.

I froze. What in fate's name was I supposed to do now? Tumble out the back of the wagon and hope he hadn't seen me? Maybe he was still asleep.

He sat up suddenly, and the blanket slid down his front. I swallowed around the lump in my throat.

Definitely not asleep.

Maybe if I didn't move, he'd forget I was here.

Or he'd go back to sleep. I could be a dream and nothing more.

But Ragnar did not lie down and go back to sleep. He smirked at me.

"If you keep staring, I might think you like what you see," he drawled. "Is that…is that drool on your face?"

Hastily, I rubbed my chin. It was dry. Damn him.

"I should have known you were an arrogant bastard in addition to everything else. You wish I was drooling over you."

"*You're* the one gaping at *me*, darling." His eyes swept across me, then narrowed. "You're still wearing the same dress you were yesterday. Long night?"

"That's none of your concern." At long last, I dragged my gaze away from him. And much to my chagrin, he did have several wooden kegs stacked beside him. On the other side of the wagon sat a shelf lined with tankards, and the rich scent of ale perfumed the wagon. He hadn't been lying about his wares, at least. Not that it really changed anything. All this could be a cover for something else.

Or those kegs were hiding something. And I was determined to find out exactly what that was.

"Why aren't you staying at the inn?" I suddenly asked.

"You mean, the inn with no vacancies?"

I frowned. Damn Nilsa. She'd been teasing me, pretending like Ragnar was staying at the inn just to get a reaction out of me. And it had worked. Cheeks hot, I cleared my throat and grasped for an explanation as to why I was here, poking around in his wagon at an ungodly hour. While he was shirtless. And potentially not even wearing trousers.

Gods, was he completely naked?

I needed to get out of here.

"Ah, so. I think I'll be going now." I turned to leap outside and into what I hoped would be a hole in the ground—that would be better than ever having to face Ragnar again—but his deep chuckle gave me pause.

"Well, isn't this interesting?" he asked, his voice dropping an octave. "You thought I was staying at the inn, which meant you expected to find this wagon empty. Let me guess…you realized you couldn't compete with me fair and square, so you thought you'd steal my ale instead. That way, I'd have nothing to sell at my tavern, and you'd get your spot back."

"Actually, I realized you *can't* compete with me. You can shove me in a corner, but that won't make your ale any better than mine. And you know that. So there must be some other reason you're here, right?" I arched a brow. "You're not really a brewer or any other kind of merchant. This wagon is brand new, and I've never seen you before. I think you're hiding something, and I don't plan to let you ruin Yule by doing…whatever it is you think you're going to get away with here."

His eyes flashed. "Interesting theory. You must have spent all night thinking about me to come up with it."

The warmth in my cheeks deepened. "You're deflecting."

"Am I wrong, darling?"

"Am I?" I countered.

A wicked smile curved his lips. "Feel free to come closer and search me if you think I'm hiding some-thing. Or we could go visit your old friend, Steffon, instead. He might be interested to learn you were sneaking into my wagon when you thought I wasn't here. I heard they don't take too kindly to thieves on this island."

My hands fisted. "I wasn't trying to steal from you."

"I'm not the one you'll have to convince."

I narrowed my eyes. "You wouldn't."

"Try me."

I glared at him, and his smile widened. I had the sudden urge to find an apple pie and smash it into his stupid, smug face. But there was nothing in this wagon other than kegs, tankards, and his bare, sculpted chest. Eventually, I loosed a frustrated sigh.

"Fine. Let me guess. You want something in exchange for your silence," I said.

"Smart woman." He rubbed his rugged jaw, like he was deep in thought, but I could tell by the gleam in his eye he already knew exactly what he wanted. My gut twisted. There was only one thing in the world it could be. And the bastard was going to get it, too. "I'll take a barrel of your ale."

7

LILIA

I stormed over to St. Olaf Row while Ragnar got dressed, my fisted hands shaking by my sides. The bastard had backed me into a corner, and I couldn't see a way to knock down the walls in which he'd trapped me. If I didn't relinquish a keg, he would get me evicted from the festival this winter *and* every year to come. It wasn't enough that he'd already stolen my spot. Now he was taking my brew.

"Everything all right, Lilia?" Emil, a human baker with short-cropped brown hair and a jaw as wide as his forehead, called out as I stalked past his wagon. He sat on a wooden crate, puffing on one of Viktor's pipes, the sweet scent of tobacco trailing through the crisp morning air.

"Not really." I sighed, slowing to a stop before him. "I'm just…dealing with a pesky creature."

He shot me a knowing smile. My stomach dropped. Did he somehow know I'd crept into

Ragnar's wagon? If he did, it wouldn't take long for the news to spread like wildfire. No one could keep secrets during Yule. Gossip was as common a currency as gold coins.

"That adolescent dragon, eh? I saw him lurking the woods near your wagon," said Emil.

"Oh." I had a brief moment of relief before his words sank in. Then I straightened, alarmed. "*Oh.* Listen, Emil, I know—"

"Ah, lass. Don't worry. I've got no quarrel with a dragon so long as he keeps his fire away from me and mine." He sucked on the end of the pipe, then curled his lips into an O. Half a dozen smoky circles spilled from his mouth, then he smiled. "How'd you like that? I've been practicing."

"Very impressive," I told him. "And thanks. For not alarming the whole festival about the dragon. I promise he's harmless."

"Harmless?" Emil chuckled. "Dragons are never harmless. Oh, looks like the other creature you were worried about is heading right this way."

I whirled on my feet, my dress swishing around my boots. Ragnar walked toward me, his steps long and purposeful, his hands swinging confidently by his sides. My eyes raked across his broad shoulders, his rugged face, and his wild hair. My pulse fluttered in my neck; my legs itched to move. Suddenly, I felt as if I was in the eye of a storm, and I would drown if I didn't escape.

But Ragnar sidled past me without even tossing a

brief glance in my direction. When he reached my wagon, he went right to the back, yanked the doors open, and looked inside. I followed him and propped my hands on my hips, readying myself for battle. If he tried to take more than one barrel, I'd tell him exactly where he could shove my kegs.

Up your fates-damned arse.

He let out a low whistle. "You have a lot more than I thought. This could serve…well over a thousand."

A flicker of pride went through me. "Twelve full barrels. I spent weeks brewing beforehand, paying careful attention to the quality of the malted grains and how much yeast I added. I weighed it all just so. And I added a bit of Vatnor sand so it wouldn't spoil on the road. Not that you would know anything about proper brewing techniques."

"You're right. I don't really." Leaning back, he winked. "Smells like mighty fine ale, and the Vatnor sand was a smart call. I wouldn't have thought of using elemental water magic to keep it preserved and tasting sweet. So I thank you for your donation to Ragnar's Traveling Tavern."

I bristled. "I told you before. You cannot copy the name of my business."

"No?" He arched a brow. "Should I fetch Steffon, then?"

"Ugh! You're impossible." I paced back and forth, the rising fury burning my cheeks. "Honestly, Ragnar Whatever-Your-Surname-Is, you're the most infuriating man I've met in a very long time, and that's saying something. I've met some real arseholes."

He sketched a bow. "I aim to please."

Without another word, he hefted a keg from the back of my wagon and perched it on one of his shoulders, like it held nothing more than feathers. And then he strode back down the path, taking my precious ale with him.

"Reykur!" I called out in a hoarse whisper, trudging through the dense woods. The oaks had shed their leaves weeks ago, and a carpet of orange and red crunched with my every step. An owl hooted from somewhere nearby. I'd been searching for the past hour—at the very least. I was starting to think Emil had been imagining things. Reykur would be in the mountains, like he always was, or soaring through the distant skies. He'd never, not once in six years, come this close to Riverwold. And all these dried leaves were like kindling.

'Course, I'd noticed him spreading his wings a bit more these past couple of years. Ever since Daella had bonded with one of his sisters, he'd spent a lot of time flying the skies above Wyndale, and he'd seemed to crave my company more than usual. Had he thrown all caution to the wind, abandoning his lair, hoping he might be welcomed here at last? Was he that desperate for friendship? I heaved a sigh. Perhaps it had been selfish to ask him to journey with me this winter.

Perhaps he needed more than I could give him.

Just as I was about to give up the search and return to camp, a burnt patch of leaves caught my eye. The unmistakable scent of sulphur and smoke drifted on the wind. Heat throbbed toward me. I pulled out a loaf of Emil's bread and waved it in the air.

"Who wants a treat?" I called out.

A storm of wings scattered leaves and twigs into my face. I held up my arm to block the onslaught, bracing myself against his unrelenting heat. Reykur shoved through the brush and landed so close I had to stumble back. His long, scaly snout inched toward me.

"Careful," I warned him, wincing when pain flared in my cheek. "You'll burn me if you come any closer."

Suddenly, the flaming heat disappeared. Reykur huffed through his snout, then leaned closer, lowering his head so that it was only an inch away. Awed, I gazed into his face, struck by the beauty of his shimmering scales and the bright gleam of his eyes. I'd never seen him so close. His scales flared from emerald to red to orange and back again, as if he were lit from within.

I reached out a hand, then paused, waiting for the pain. And still, our close proximity didn't burn. Sucking in a breath, I erased the distance between us and gently lowered my fingers to his snout. His scales were warm and slick beneath my palm.

"How?" I whispered, too awed to speak any louder than that. "Dragons burn anyone who isn't an orc. I…"

The dead leaves beneath his powerful talons crunched. They weren't catching fire, either. But I didn't understand. This went against everything I'd always been taught about dragons—everything I'd seen with my own two eyes.

And yet, here I was, touching Reykur for the first time in my life. Tears of happiness filled my eyes.

He nuzzled my hand, leaning his impressive weight against it. Laughing in delight, I slid my other hand up the side of his snout and hugged him to my chest. I didn't know how it was possible, but that hardly mattered. His touch didn't burn, and the woods weren't aflame. If there was any way to convince the people of the Isles to accept him, it was this. They had no reason to fear him now.

"We're going to be all right, you and I." Smiling, I pulled back and tossed him the bread. He caught it in his sword-like teeth and chewed. Crumbs peppered his snout. "I'll be back soon with more food. Then we'll try to introduce you to a couple merchants. Once they realize you won't burn them, word will spread. And maybe, if we're lucky, you can attend your first Yule. Wouldn't that be grand?"

I swore my dragon smiled.

Winding through the festival grounds with a bounce in my step, I whistled a tune. I purposefully avoided Ragnar's brewhouse—I refused to call it a Traveling Tavern—even though it meant going the long way around. The last few merchants had arrived and were pouring into the meadow now, filling up the back rows. I passed a woman with a wagon packed to the brim with second-hand books, and another who already had a sign hanging on the front advertising her palm-reading abilities. A lie, of course, but a harmless one. Our elemental Galdur magic couldn't predict the future, least of all by reading the lines on someone's palm.

No matter. She'd still get plenty of business. People liked to hear what the future might bring, even if deep down they knew it was nothing more than a dream. Dreams tasted of hope.

By the time I made it back to the Ship's Anchor, the sun had crept higher into the sky, chasing away the frost. My stomach cramped as I pushed inside. I'd only had a small bite of Emil's bread all day, and the savory scent of beans and potatoes swirling through the inn dragged me forward by the nose.

By the time I reached the counter where Nilsa was busy filling tankards with water, I was practically drooling. But then she took one look at me, and her eyebrows darted up. "Where in fate's name have you been? What is that on your cheek?"

She hopped up on her stool, leaned over the counter, and picked a leaf off my face. Then she snatched a twig from my tangled hair.

"Lilia," she said as a wide smile spread across her face. "Where did you spend the night? And why are you just now returning to the inn? It's near midday."

I gave her a look. "It's a long story. And no, it's not what you think."

"How unfortunate." She reached for the jug, filling another tankard. "Wait here. I want to hear all about it when I get back."

"Do you have any more of that bean strew?" I called out as she bustled over to the tables.

"Yeah, in the kitchen. Go on in and help yourself," she tossed over her shoulder.

I nearly moaned in relief. Abandoning the counter, I pushed through the kitchen doors, where I found a pot of the stew bubbling on the stove. I spooned some of it into a bowl, then pushed through the door with my hip to find a spot to eat.

Ragnar stood on the other side, blocking my path. His arms were crossed, and his lips were curled into a scowl. I stopped short. Some of the broth splashed onto my hands, scalding me.

"Ouch!" I darted to the counter and set down the bowl. He barely shifted out of the way, watching me with narrowed eyes.

"Serves you right," said Ragnar.

"*Excuse* me?" I patted my reddened skin with the hem of my dress. A painful throb answered each dab.

"You heard me. Perhaps if you weren't a blatant thief, fate would cast a kinder eye on you."

I whirled toward him, frowning. "What are you on about? I thought I made it clear I had no intention of stealing from you, and then you said you were going to…" I lowered my voice, "…keep quiet about the *you know what* since I gave you a bloody keg!"

"The *you know what*," he said flatly, not bothering to keep his voice down. "Interesting way to describe you sneaking into my wagon when you thought I wasn't there."

"This wasn't part of the deal," I said hotly. "I'm taking back my ale."

I tried to move around him, but he stepped sideways with me. Glaring at him, I tried again, but he blocked me as easily as a fallen log in the road. My fury made my skin throb. All my earlier euphoria about my dragon's new ability melted beneath Ragnar's blatant disregard for honor. I'd had enough. And if it meant I got banned from the festival, then so be it.

"Move out of my way, Ragnar," I said in a low voice.

"Tell me where you hid my ale, and I will."

I started. That was the last thing I'd expected him to say.

"Is this some kind of demented game to you or

something? Well, go find someone else to play it with and get out of my way," I said with a scowl.

"Absolutely." He leaned in, lowering his head so that our eyes were level. The heat of him stormed toward me like a wildfire. "Just as soon as you tell me where you hid my ale."

8

RAGNAR

Lilia glared up at me, and I scowled right back. After our morning encounter, I'd deposited her keg in my wagon, right beside my own collection, and then I'd taken a stroll through the grounds to check out the half-erected merchant stalls. When I'd returned with a steaming bowl of porridge, her barrel *and* all of mine had been gone. Only a layer of dust had remained.

It was clear what had happened. Lilia had been spitting mad when I'd blackmailed her into giving me some of her ale. At the time, I'd wondered if I'd taken it too far. A part of me had wanted to give it back. She had to earn a living, too.

But then the sneaky little thing had stolen it back. If she hadn't taken mine, too, I might have let it go.

I should have seen it coming. Lilia didn't strike me the kind of lass who ever backed down.

"I don't know what you're playing at here," she

said, narrowing her flashing silver eyes. "I don't want anything to do with you *or* your ale."

"You expect me to believe it's just a coincidence that it vanished no more than an hour after I caught you trying to steal it?"

She let out a little roar that was far closer to adorable than intimidating. "I've *told* you. Five times now, *at least*. I wasn't trying to take anything from you! All I wanted was to poke around and find out what you're hiding. And if I could reverse time, I'd never go near your bloody wagon in the first place. It's given me a headache."

"Then explain how all my ale is gone." I leaned against the counter, where an impressive dragon candlestick held a flickering flame that cast a glow onto Lilia's face.

She merely shook her head and threw up her hands. And for a moment, I wondered if I might have gotten it wrong. Her annoyance didn't seem like an act... Of course, I'd met plenty of liars and thieves in my life, and I hadn't always been able to see through their falsehoods. And if she hadn't taken my kegs, then who had?

I couldn't imagine why anyone else would want them.

I'd gotten lucky when Lilia had sneaked into my wagon. She'd dropped leverage right into my lap, which I'd gladly exploited. Now I had some good ale to draw in patrons—or I had, until she'd snatched it all away.

Nilsa bustled over from a nearby table, her wide eyes darting between me and Lilia. "Did I hear you say you're missing some ale?"

"Yeah. And I think your friend here knows where it is," I said.

She snapped her gaze to Lilia. "Is *that* why you have sticks in your hair? I knew you were mad at him, Lil, but—"

"Sticks?" I swept my gaze across her, noticing a few twigs stuck to the back of her cloak. A dash of orange decorated her hair. A leaf, I realized. And beneath her cloak, she still wore that white blouse and the woollen blue dress. Her boots were coated in a layer of dust that looked a lot like crunched leaves. "You hid my kegs in the woods."

"I did no such thing." She cast her friend a helpless look. "Come on, Nilsa. You know I'm not a thief."

"Well, I wouldn't call it *thievery*, exactly. It's just…I could see you moving his belongings around just to annoy him." Nilsa winced.

I nodded. Exactly what I thought. "I think I'll go check out these woods, then."

I started toward the door.

"No!" called Lilia.

My boots scuffed the stone floor as I slowed, fighting back a smile. She had no way out now. If she tried to stop me from exploring the woods, she might as well admit her guilt.

I turned toward the counter. She shovelled a few spoonfuls of stew into her mouth, then strode toward me. Her expression oscillated between panic and determination. Clearly, her mind was spinning through ideas on how to stop me from stepping foot in those woods. I folded my arms. This ought to be good.

But instead of offering up a flimsy explanation, she hooked her arm through mine and dragged me outside.

A bitter wind whistled through the courtyard beyond the inn, but my internal furnace burned hot enough to chase it away. The pungent scent of brine drifted toward us from the fishmonger hurrying past, his cart rattling behind him. A few seagulls caught the scent and swooped toward him, but he waved his cane at them before they could snap up his fish.

"Listen," Lilia said as she quickly extracted her arm from mine. Her face reddened, as if she'd just now noticed we'd touched. "I think we need to start over, you and I. We've gotten off to a rocky start, but there's no reason for us to be against each other. You can run your tavern, and I can run mine. There'll be plenty of patrons for the both of us."

I searched her eyes for the truth behind her words. They were like pools of silver out here beneath the sun, reflecting my face right back at me. Damn, the lass seemed sincere.

"I'd agree with you," I said slowly. "Except I have no ale to run my tavern now."

She cocked her head. "You're really not making this up, are you?"

"Why would I make it up?"

"I don't know. To annoy me?"

A smile tugged my lips. "Seems I'm fairly good at that without resorting to a lie."

She laughed. "Good point." Then she held out her hand. "Truce?"

I slid my hand into hers, swallowing her soft palm with mine. Her cold fingers quickly warmed as my heat flooded into her skin and steam hissed between us. She shivered, gazing up at me. Her eyes were wide, like an open book. Earnest, kind, warm. This was how she'd looked at me the night we'd met on the road.

I wished I could trust it.

"Sure," I said, still holding her hand. "I'll agree to a truce. After I search those woods."

Her hand tightened around mine, like a reflex. I'd been right. She was only saying all this to stop me from investigating. It disappointed me more than I wanted to admit.

"There's nothing in the woods," said Lilia, but her voice was tight.

"You won't mind if I go for a walk there, then." I released her hand. "Or is there something you don't want me to find?"

She opened her mouth, then snapped it shut. With a satisfied nod, I strode away.

9

LILIA

Panic anchored my feet to the road. I couldn't risk Ragnar stumbling upon my dragon. Even if he wasn't fearful of him, he could use him against me by threatening to tell everyone I'd brought a dragon to Yule. And I couldn't hand the bastard something else to hold over my head. He already had enough.

But if I tried to stop him, he'd think I stole his ale.

I frowned and jogged after him. Ragnar's story made little sense. Who would have taken his kegs? Was he even telling the truth? And if he wasn't, what was his goal here?

Whatever it was, it felt like it was aimed right at me.

It didn't take long for me to catch up to him. His strides were long yet unhurried, almost like he'd expected me to follow.

"Fancy seeing you here again," he murmured, casually tucking his hands into his trouser pockets.

"You keep saying that."

"You keep showing up in surprising places."

"I don't think you've been surprised even once."

He chuckled, a deep, rumbling sound, like the bass of a melodious song. It was a nicer sound than I wanted to admit. Shame nothing else about him matched it.

"So what's the excuse?" he asked.

"Excuse for what?"

"Well, you clearly haven't eaten much today. Nor have you changed into fresh clothes. One might think you'd rather fill your belly with Nilsa's stew rather than follow a man around you hate."

"I don't hate you," I said quietly.

A muscle in his jaw ticked as he continued to stride purposely down the road. "I'd understand if you do. Hel, I'd probably hate me if I were you."

"Hatred is a very strong emotion. I'm not certain I hate anyone." I pursed my lips. "Well, that's not entirely true. I hated that ice giant conquerer, Isveig. But most people aren't that cruel, and thankfully, he's off the throne." I cast him a sideways glance. "As annoying as you are, you don't strike me as the kind of man who'd try to wipe out a race."

"No, I'm not," he said quietly. "I fought against Isveig."

"What?" I stumbled a few steps, then had to hurry to catch up. "When?"

"I fought in the Elven Resistance until Isveig's ice giants beat them back and invaded their lands," he said, his voice so low I could scarcely make out his words. "But if there's one thing you need to know about me, it's that I don't quit, even when most people would. My brother and I joined a group of rebels who were hiding out in Isveig's stolen city. We sneaked into his palace once, thinking we'd catch him by surprise. But he somehow found out about us, and knew we were coming. He injured me and my brother." Ragnar rubbed the back of his neck. "Nearly killed us both."

"I'm sorry," I said softly. And as he rubbed his neck again, it was as if I was seeing him for the first time. A pale scar cut across his left shoulder. It matched the one I'd seen on his chest. His powerful arms were the cut of someone who wielded a sword —successfully. This man was a warrior. It explained a lot.

"Don't be sorry," he countered in a gruff voice. "I'm glad I fought that bastard. My only regret is that I failed. Things were never the same after that. *My brother* was never the same. For reasons I'll never understand, he then joined a group who sometimes worked directly for Isveig, and he lost himself in it, lost who he once was."

Questions threatened to spill from my lips, but I swallowed them down. This was clearly difficult for him to talk about, and if he wanted to share more, he would. The haunted look in his eye...I knew it well.

I'd worn it once myself, and I never liked it when people pried.

Silence wrapped around us, but it didn't feel awkward this time. We continued down the path toward the festival grounds, the sun beaming down from a cloudless sky. The ground was soft beneath my boots, churned up from the influx of wagon wheels. Several merchants who had claimed spots nearest to town had opened their stalls to patrons. We passed a cart full of freshly baked apple pies, then another with ribbons in every color imaginable. By Yule, most of those ribbons would be braided into hair or wound around wrists and arms.

Ragnar ignored them all, even when a pixie danced toward us on fluttering wings, hoping to catch our eye.

"Not a fan of apple pie?" I asked, finally breaking the silence.

"I'd love to have a pie. But I'd prefer to have my ale."

I sighed. "Your ale isn't in the woods, Ragnar."

"Well, it's not in my wagon, so it has to be somewhere. Unless you think kegs can go *poof*, never to be seen again."

"Let me see it, then."

He stopped and swung toward me. "See what?"

"Your empty wagon." I gestured toward said wagon, visible down the path bisecting the southern side of the meadow. It squatted luxuriously beneath the weeping willow, right where mine should be. He hadn't even bothered to unpack anything yet. What a waste of a good booth.

Ragnar narrowed his eyes suspiciously. "Stalling won't do you any good, not unless you have an accomplice moving the kegs while you distract me. But Nilsa wouldn't...or would she? You two seem to be as thick as thieves. Pun intended."

I folded my arms. "From where I'm standing, you're the one who's stalling. Something in your wagon you don't want me to see?"

"Fine." He waved me down the path. "Go ahead and look all you'd like. You'll only confirm what you already know. There's nothing in there. Because you took it all."

"We'll see about that," I replied crisply.

When we reached his wagon, I threw open the burlap flaps with gusto. The scent of rugged spice and bitter ale rushed toward me, from the dark depths of...a very empty wagon. The tankards were untouched on their shelves, and his folded bedroll was propped against the far wall, but every one of the kegs was gone. Nothing was left but the shadows of where they'd stood, along with a good helping of dust.

"Huh." I released the burlap and stepped back. "So you weren't lying."

"Your turn," said Ragnar. "To the woods we go."

Ragnar strode off, and I had no choice but to follow. Perhaps I would get the chance to warn my dragon to stay back if Ragnar strayed too far from the festival grounds. I could whistle or hoot like an owl or —who was I kidding? The second Reykur caught scent of me, he'd thunder down from above with that hopeful look in his eye. He'd think I'd brought him more food.

We curved past the willow, then took the route to St. Olaf Row before dipping into the woods behind my Traveling Tavern. I shot my wagon a mournful glance. Mud still caked her sides, and there was an eerie, cold look about her, like she'd been abandoned for decades. Ragnar and his stupid game had become a huge distraction. When we were done in the woods, I'd find a pail of water, some soap, and I'd get to scrubbing.

Lilia's Traveling Tavern would be open for business by nightfall.

The canopy overhead rustled as we dove deeper into the ancient oaks and evergreens. A twig snapped, and I jumped. Ragnar cut his gaze toward me with a rueful smile.

"You're surprisingly on edge for someone who insists she's not a thief," he said as he ducked beneath a low-hanging branch.

"There could be dangerous creatures in these woods," I tried. "Why else do you think they hold the festival in the meadow? Can't have anyone wandering around in here after dark."

"Is that what you were doing in here earlier, then? Searching for one of these dangerous creatures?" He chuckled.

I snapped my mouth shut. Little did he know just how close he'd come to the truth. And, much to my dismay, I spotted my own tracks in the dirt and leaves. We were heading straight toward where I'd found Reykur that very morning. It had only been a couple hours since I'd left him here. He likely hadn't wandered far.

My heart pounded. When Reykur had started following me around all those years ago, I'd sworn to the goddess Freya that I'd do anything to keep him safe. Safe from those who might fear him, or those who might hunt him down. Ragnar had once been a warrior. Would his instincts kick in when he laid eyes on a dragon?

"Ragnar." I stopped, catching his arm. His biceps flexed against my fingers, tensing.

Slowly, he turned toward me. There was a suspicious glint in his eye, but he didn't pull away or keep moving through the woods. He waited to hear what I had to say.

"I need to tell you something, and I'm begging you to stay calm," I started.

"Let me guess." He gently shifted out of my grasp and folded his arms. "These tracks are yours, and we're about to find something you don't want me to see."

"Well, *yes*, but it's not what you think."

"So, you're telling me we won't find my kegs at the end of these tracks." He pointed at my footprints.

"It's a dragon, Ragnar. I have a dragon," I said, forcing out the words.

He stared at me in silence, and I stared right back. But my pulse was frantic, and my mouth was dry. The intensity of his skeptical gaze felt like the weight of an anvil, and if he didn't say something soon, I might burst from the seams. A part of me was desperate to take back my words, to drag him away from these woods so that no one could discover Reykur's existence.

But I also knew Reykur didn't want to go on like this. He didn't want to be a secret any longer. And we had to start somewhere. Why not with a warrior who had fought against the very man who'd tried to extinguish his kind? If anything, Ragnar would understand just how special Reykur was. I had to hope that meant he'd never bring him harm.

Ragnar's shock slowly morphed into anger. "Do you take me for a fool?"

"What? No, I—"

"All the dragons are *dead*," he said with far more grief in his voice than I'd expected. "It was a tragedy, and yet you're trying to use them to scare me out of these woods." He shook his head, taking a step away from me. "I was starting to doubt you stole the kegs, Lilia. But all you've done now is convince me you have. And I'll find them, at the end of these tracks."

The canopy rustled again. I looked up just as the trees parted, their trunks straining against the strength of the dragon bearing down on us. Reykur's powerful wings beat the air, the scent of sulphur gusting into my face. Ragnar's jaw dropped. He stumbled back and shielded his eyes, dumbfounded.

Reykur landed before us. His talons pierced the ground, wiping away my tracks. Heart thundering, I glanced from his soft bulbous eyes to Ragnar's shocked face and back again. And then I stepped between them, pressing my back against my dragon's hot snout.

Ragnar looked at me—*really* looked. He studied my face, then looked over my shoulder at Reykur, his breath whistling between his clenched teeth.

"That's a dragon," he said in a ragged voice.

"His name is Reykur, and he means you no harm," I said with as much confidence and strength as I could conjure.

Ragnar looked surprised, and then he laughed softly. "You're protecting him. That's what this is."

"With my life," I said fiercely. "And from you, if I must."

"He's a dragon, Lilia," he said, more gently than he'd ever spoken to me before. "I think he can take care of himself, don't you?"

"Against one person? Maybe so." I gave him a pointed look, motioning for him to give us some space. "But what happens when a mob goes after him? What happens if they catch him when he's sleeping? What happens if someone tries to shoot him out of the skies with a ship's crossbow? All the things Isveig did."

Ragnar spread his arms wide, holding up his hands in surrender. "You don't have to worry about any of that with me. I swear it."

"How can I trust you?" I whispered. "After everything."

He came closer until he was only a hair's breadth away. "Look into my eyes."

Hands fisted, I met his piercing stare.

"I would *never* harm a dragon, Lilia. I'd never let anyone else harm one, either."

He wasn't lying. That look—that haunted, tortured look—I knew it far too well. Heaving a sigh, I sagged against Reykur's snout. All my pent-up fear rushed out of me like a wave, leaving me light-headed. I'd been ready to fight Ragnar if need be, I realized. I would have lost against a warrior like him, but I would have fought my bloody heart out.

And by the knowing glint in his eye, he understood I would have, too.

"This is why you didn't want me to come into the woods," said Ragnar. "You never touched my kegs."

"Yeah. Does that disappoint you?"

He gazed up at my dragon's powerful form. When he spoke, his voice was full of awe. "I've never been happier to be so incredibly wrong."

And finally, I smiled.

IO

LILIA

"What can I get you two?" Nilsa eyed us warily, one hand propped on her voluptuous right hip. In the woods, Ragnar and I had solidified our truce with another handshake before deciding to make it official by sharing a much-needed meal back at the inn. My stomach was cramping from my hunger. To punctuate its desperation, it emitted a particularly obnoxious growl.

"You know I'd love some more of your bean stew, and some bread if you've got it," I said, cocking my head at Ragnar. "And he'll have…let me guess. You'll take some salted pork, two servings of roasted potatoes, and…" I smiled. "Some apple pie, if you've got it, Nilsa."

She propped her other hand on her left hip. "Well, Ragnar? Is that what you want?"

"Pork, potatoes, and pie," he said with a wink. "A man can't say no to that."

"Hmm." Nilsa squinted at me. "You and me are going to have a chat later."

I flushed, pretending to fold the cloth napkin into some kind of elaborate design, like a dragon or a whale. When she didn't get a reply, Nilsa bustled off, but that didn't lessen the weight of Ragnar's stare.

Now that we were back inside, sitting here like two everyday folk having a meal, it felt like my skin wanted to leap off my bones. Maybe I could excuse myself and return to my room. It had been a long day, even though it was only late afternoon, and I was far too aware I was still wearing yesterday's clothes.

Ragnar cleared his throat. "So."

"So," I repeated.

"Want to tell me how you got yourself a dragon?"

I tensed, casting a glance over my shoulder. The tables were mostly empty now, but a handful of dwarves were only a few seats over. "You can't talk about it so openly. I meant what I said about mobs."

"I understand." He braced his forearms on the table and leaned closer. "So I'll phrase it this way. How'd you get yourself a monstrous, fire-breathing, death-devouring—"

"Stop it," I hissed and swatted at his arm. As soon as my fingers made contact with his warm skin, I froze. His eyes zeroed in on where we touched. Hastily, I drew back my hand.

"Relax," he said with a lazy smile. "No one's paying attention to us."

"Nilsa is most certainly paying attention."

"She doesn't know about the little bird?"

"More like a large bat," I said. "And of course she does. Nilsa and I share everything with each other."

"You tell her where you hid my ale, then?"

"Keep talking like that, and I won't tell you any more about my bat friend."

He gasped, pressing a hand to his heart. "You wound me, darling."

I grinned. Ragnar smiled back. And everything within me relaxed. It reminded me of that night we'd shared beneath the stars, the way I'd felt around him before we'd turned on each other. It all seemed silly now. All that bickering, and for what? It was just ale.

Nilsa waddled over with two trays nearly over-flowing with food and drink. Ragnar and I leapt to our feet in unison and helped her unload it all. The bowl of stew was nearly the size of my head, and my bread roll could have fed at least five. But it was nothing compared to the four plates she dealt to Ragnar. Two goblets of wine joined the table, along with a jug of water.

I tucked into my food the second my arse hit the bench again.

Ragnar and I sat in silence as we ate, too famished for words. The savory spices of the bean stew warmed me from head to toe, and the freshly-baked bread, coated with butter and herbs, quickly chased away the hunger. I sipped my wine—a smooth concoction of summer berries—before stabbing my fork at the edge of Ragnar's apple pie.

"Whoa now, little thief." He chuckled, tugging his pie plate over to his side of the table. "I'm catching you in the act this time."

"I ordered the pie. Technically, it's mine."

Grinning, he pushed it a little closer to me, but then he pulled it back to his chest when I tried to snatch a little bite of it. "I'll share. But first, you have to tell me about the bat."

"Fair enough." I took a sip of wine before I started. "I have a brother. He was a warrior like you until he saw things that...changed him. Anyway, he wanted to get away from all that, so we decided to leave the Kingdom of Edda and find the Isles. It was a long journey. One night, we were camping in a cave, and we came across four newborn dragons." I smiled at the memory. "We brought them here, where we've raised them in a mountain near Wyndale. And as far as Reykur is concerned, I'm sort of his mother. Or...a good friend, I guess you could say."

"I would have said a pet."

"More than a pet."

"And so he followed you here."

Nodding, I nibbled on the remaining chunk of bread. "He likes to join me on my travels, and he's come to Riverwold every Yule for years. But he usually stays inside a cave in the Sunlit Ridge, out of sight of the townspeople and visitors."

"Because you're worried about the mobs, as you call them."

"Can you blame me?" I asked. "You know the

stories of the folk who tried to channel dragon magic and couldn't control it. And as much as I hate to say it, those stories are all true. It killed a lot of people." I dropped the bread onto my plate, no longer hungry. "But I'm hoping I can one day convince everyone to give Reykur a chance. He seems…lonely."

"He's got *you*, Lilia," said Ragnar. "And from where I'm sitting, he's damn lucky he does."

My cheeks went hot, and I fiddled with the napkin in my lap again. I didn't know how to respond to that. If he didn't start accusing me of committing another crime soon, I might very well melt into the floor.

"An absolute masterpiece," he murmured.

My heart lurched, and I lifted my head to catch him staring at me. "What?"

"The pie." He deposited half of it onto one of his empty plates, then passed it to me. "I just tried a bite. It's some of the best I've ever tasted."

"Oh." The heat of my cheeks burned down to my chest. "Thanks for sharing."

"A deal's a deal."

"Speaking of…" I cleared my throat. "What are you going to do about all your missing ale?"

Sighing, he leaned against the wall behind him, resting his head between two old shields etched with symbols of the gods. "Good question. Any idea who might have taken it?"

"Honestly? No," I said. "I've been coming here for six years, and nothing has ever gone missing. It's just not something that happens in Riverwold— or anywhere else on Hearthaven. These Isles are special. Everyone who ends up here wants safety and peace. For the most part, anyway."

"Barrels don't grow legs and wander off," said Ragnar.

"No, they don't," I admitted. "But anyone who lives here values the festival more than a few barrels of bitter ale. No offense, of course."

"None taken." His frown deepened. "So it's got to be one of the other merchants. Do any other taverns come here?"

I gave him a frank look. "I'm the only tavern *usually*. That's why I brought so many kegs. Not to toot my own horn, but my brew is one of people's favorite things about Yule. Every year, I bring more just to be sure I'll have enough for that final night, when everyone is out celebrating until dawn."

"And my wagon is in your usual spot," he said.

"Near the stage and the performer tents and all the best cooks and bakers that attend." I shrugged, taking another sip of my wine. "It's all right, though. I'll manage. St. Olaf Row's not so bad, even if it is hidden away in the back."

"Everything is starting to make a whole lot of wicked sense." He finished off his pie and stood. "You coming?"

I frowned up at him, enjoying the heat of the hearth and warming wine on my tongue. A fuzzy, happy cocoon had surrounded me, massaging away the tension that had knotted my shoulders the past couple of days. Trudging around in cold forests and spying on naked men in wagons—this man before me, I couldn't forget—was not what Yule was about. It was this. Enjoying the hearty food and drink. Sharing stories about life with strangers and newfound friends. Settling onto the bench at the coziest inn in all the Isles and not moving until it was time to stumble up the stairs and into bed.

"I'd rather stay here to be honest," I told him. "I'm sure Nilsa has a bard lined up for the evening, and there'll be plenty more pie where that came from."

Ragnar ran a hand through his wavy hair and sighed. "I'd like nothing more than to sit here with you for the rest of the evening and learn the words to all the bard's songs, but I need to look into something first. Unfortunately, I have a feeling you're going to want to see it, too."

I lowered my goblet to the table. "I don't like the sound of that."

"I hope for both our sakes I'm wrong."

Something in the tone of his voice cut through the haze. Without another word, I rose and followed him out the door, leaving a collection of coins on the table for Nilsa. A pink hue stretched across the distant horizon where the land met the sea. Even up here on the rolling hillside, the rushing sound of waves reached my ears. The call of seagulls answered. By the time we'd reached the meadow, the sun had bid its goodnight.

The festival grounds had come alive in our

absence. On the northern side of the meadow, new arrivals—attendees rather than merchants—had erected their tents, where they'd camp until the day after Yule. The beginnings of bonfires flickered in the growing dark, and elves and dwarves bustled past carrying flat stones to situate around them. A line had already formed to Karl's smoked meat cart, where plates puffed steam into the chilly air.

Ragnar went right past all of it, then kept on going when we reached his wagon. A few pixies drifted around it, looking disappointed. I recognized one of their faces. She was a regular who came nearly every year.

When she spotted me, her face brightened. "Lilia! Where's the Traveling Tavern?"

"Where's your ale?" her friend added.

"I'll be back in a moment to explain," I called back, hurrying to match Ragnar's hasty stride. But the pixies did not wait beside his cold, dark wagon. They took to the path, trailing a few steps behind us. As we carried on, others spotted our small crowd and fell into line, whispering excitedly that something fun must be going on.

"Are you following Lilia to her tavern?" came a man's whispered voice.

"Who's that with her? Is he going to put on some kind of performance for her grand opening?" someone else asked.

"He's not a performer," a third voice said. My footsteps slowed. I knew that voice. I cast a glance over my shoulder. Steffon, the organizer of the whole shebang and the Defender of Riverwold, had joined the procession.

I caught the edge of Ragnar's shirt, nearly breaking out into a jog to keep up with him. In a harsh whisper, I said, "We have an audience."

"So I've noticed," he replied dryly, not bothering to keep his voice down. "And if I'm right about this, there'll be no way to hide it. Word will get around soon enough."

"What is it, Ragnar? What are we checking on?"

But I knew. We were heading in the direction of St. Olaf Row.

Ragnar's wagon was perched in *my* usual spot. And with how he'd reacted earlier in the inn, he clearly suspected they'd been trying to take my kegs instead of his.

How long had it taken the thief to realize they'd stolen from the wrong brewer?

I'd been away from my wagon all day long. Visitors had begun to arrive, but St. Olaf Row still boasted very little traffic. It would not have been difficult for someone to steal my kegs today, if they had the mind to do it.

And someone certainly did.

II

LILIA

Crowds often gathered around the Traveling Tavern. At times, I wondered if I should hire an assistant to barkeep for me during the busier events, but then I'd remind myself I didn't much want a traveling companion, other than Reykur. But what normally drew people in was the sweet scent of my ale wending through the festival. This time, however, it was the scent of calamity.

Ragnar and I stood at the rear of my wagon. At least twenty spectators gathered round with Steffon right in front, wringing his hands in pure dismay. He must have already learned of Ragnar's missing kegs and now suspected the same as we did. The culprit had struck twice, and the blow would echo through the entire festival. And as I lifted a shaking hand to the back door, everyone held a collective breath and leaned in like trees bent in the wind.

"This isn't how I expected to open my wagon for the season," I muttered beneath my breath.

"Want me to look?" Ragnar asked.

"No. It should be me."

I unlatched the door. It swung wide, creaking on the well-used hinges. Thick shadows obscured the contents, so I hopped up on the step and ducked inside. Everything was exactly how it should be. Tankards and banners were tucked in the correct corner. Wooden stakes were propped against the square pieces I used to construct tables. Even my brewing kit had been left untouched.

There was only one thing missing. A very important thing. Well, eleven things, really.

"It's gone," I whispered into the quiet dark. "The ale is actually gone."

For a moment, a deafening silence seemed to suffocate the wagon. It was as if a powerful storm had sucked out all the air, leaving nothing behind. Heart pounding, I stared at the empty space where my kegs used to be. All those long days spent brewing, all the care and attention I'd given to the grains. It was all gone.

A dozen angry voices shattered the silence. The wagon rocked as the crowd swarmed. I fell to my knees, and my bones sparked with pain. The shouts grew louder. A few people clamored into the wagon and took a look around.

"Everyone, stop. Calm yourselves. Now!" Ragnar's booming voice rent the chaos. The shouting ceased, and the wagon stilled. The intruders who'd leapt into the wagon slowly edged back outside. Sighing, I closed my eyes, then climbed out myself.

Steffon was shooing people away, but it was Ragnar's scowls that put the fear of Freya in them. The crowd gave the wagon some space, but they lingered still. They wanted to know what was happening, and I didn't much blame them. I wished I knew, too.

"I was hoping I wasn't right," said Ragnar, his eyes glued on the crowd. "Any idea who might have done it?"

"Earlier today I would have said you."

He tore his gaze from the crowd to look at me, his lip curling. "And now?"

"Doesn't really make much sense," I said. When his brow rose, I quickly continued. "It's not that I trust you, of course. Or even like you. But if you were going to steal my kegs, you would have been a lot quieter about it. I mean, if it weren't for you, I would have gone to bed tonight none the wiser."

"Maybe I'm a mastermind, and this was my way of convincing you it wasn't me."

"That would be very convoluted, and I don't think that's your style."

"Enough," Steffon cut in, shuffling closer, his shadows whorling around his reedy frame. "We have a problem, and you two don't seem to understand the severity of it. There's no ale for the festival. Yule is ruined!"

A murmur went through the crowd. Swallowing, I cast around a desperate glance for any sign of the thief. There were several footprints surrounding the wagon, but they could be mine or Ragnar's or any of the people who had swarmed me during the missing ale discovery. There was no help to be found in the size or shape of those markings.

"We'll figure something out," I told Steffon. "It's a little less than two weeks until Yule. Worst case scenario, I can brew some more. For now, Nilsa has plenty of wine. That'll do while we work out a plan, right?"

"And you can brew some that fast?" he asked hopefully.

"Potentially," I said slowly. There were a lot of factors to take into consideration. Most importantly, I had to buy some grains. But I didn't want to see his eyeballs pop out of his head from the stress, so I decided not to go into detail. "I'll need to look into a few things when it's daylight, but I promise I'll do my best."

He lurched forward and latched onto my hand. "Thank you, Lilia. Fates bless you."

The smile I gave him was weak. Fate had not been kind so far.

R agnar walked me back to the inn, though he didn't say much along the way. I couldn't find the words, either. The future of the festival wasn't the only thing weighing on my mind. I didn't know how I could afford to brew another batch of ale, not with my coin purse so light. I'd been depending on Yule to get me through the winter and into spring. As it was, I barely had enough to pay for my room during my stay. I might have to start digging into my pouch of Vindur sand.

When we drew near the inn's courtyard, Ragnar finally cleared away the silence. "Can you really brew some ale by Yule?"

"Only if I get lucky." I sighed. "The thief didn't touch my brewing supplies, but I'll need to buy some things."

"Or the festival will have to go on without ale," he said, shrugging. "I know it's not ideal, but it could be worse."

I couldn't help but laugh. "If I hadn't already known you're new here, that would confirm it. A Yule without ale is like a Yule without music or food. Or a Yule in a rainstorm, flooding everything. The festival can still go on, but it will feel as damp and dreary as a pair of wet socks you've been wearing for weeks. You'll see soon enough, if you decide to stay."

I patted his arm and charted a path through the courtyard. When I reached the inn's door, I felt a warm hand on my waist. Tensing, I looked up.

Ragnar stood just behind me, so close I could feel his breath on my cheek.

I swallowed. His hand dropped to his side, and the chill of the wind brushed away any trace of his palm.

"Are you staying at the inn tonight?" I asked, my voice a pitch higher.

"There're no vacancies, remember?" He rubbed his neck again. "I just thought we might want to help each other out."

My pulse quickened. What in fate's name did that mean? Did he...did he expect me to offer him to stay in my bed? And if that was me helping him, how did he intend to help *me*? Surely he wasn't suggesting what I thought he was suggesting.

"I..." My cheeks flamed. "The room's too small."

His brow furrowed. "What—?"

The door suddenly swung inward, and the hearth's fiery heat rolled across me. Nilsa stood just inside, hand on hip, eyebrow waggling suggestively. "Can you two please stop blocking the door? I have patrons waiting behind you."

A throat cleared from behind Ragnar. Two shadow demons, their black horns melting into the dying light of the evening, stood behind us. I hadn't even noticed. Chagrined, I scuffled on inside with Ragnar on my heels. The buzz of conversation hushed as every head swivelled our way, but Birta the Bard continued to pluck her strings, quickly drawing attention back to her song.

Nilsa dug her fingers into my arm and dragged me over to the counter, where a candle flickered brightly in the dragon display I'd brought her. She dropped her voice to a sharp hiss. "What's going on? Everyone's talking 'bout you *and that one*. And your ale has gone missing? Some have said the entire festival is cancelled."

I wet my lips. "The festival isn't cancelled."

"And the ale?"

"The ale is in my barrels. And those barrels have relocated themselves to somewhere that is not my wagon."

"Someone stole them." Nilsa wagged her finger at Ragnar. "And I'd say that someone is you, but yours have gone missing, too, I'm hearing?"

Ragnar leaned against the counter, one ankle crossed over the other. "All six I brought with me, plus the one I had of Lilia's."

"Now wait a minute. You had one of Lilia's kegs? How did that happen?" Nilsa asked in a snap.

"Just ignore him," I said quickly. "That part isn't important."

Ragnar chuckled.

Nilsa's brow shot higher.

"Do you have any empty barrels in the back?" I asked, hoping to change the subject.

She narrowed her gaze, like she was considering whether or not she wanted to insist on hearing about the previous subject. "Afraid not," she eventually said. "Why?"

"Steffon wants me to brew." I leaned onto the counter, elbows digging into the wood. "Any idea where I can get some barrels? Some grains, too, ideally."

"See, if someone else came asking me this question, I'd tell 'em to ask Lilia," she said. "The only thing I brew is wine. That said…" She tapped a finger against the counter. "You could ask our carpenter, Tomas. He might make you some barrels."

"Thanks, I'll do that."

"I have a better idea," said Ragnar.

I looked up. He was back to rubbing his neck again.

"I tried to say this to you earlier," he said. "You've already brewed plenty. No need to brew more when all we have to do is find the missing kegs."

"And how do you propose we do that?" I asked, folding my arms.

"Simple." He dealt me a wolfish smile. "We track down the thief and take it all back."

"Whoever took it is probably halfway to the coast by now, where they'll grab a ship and sail out of the Isles. We'll never catch up to them."

"Nope." His smile widened. "I did some investigating when mine went missing. No wagons or carts were seen leaving today, which means the kegs can't have gone far. They'll be somewhere here in Riverwold, on the festival grounds."

"Ooh, I like this." Nilsa bounced on her toes, her bells jingling. "If you catch them quickly enough, they won't have enough time to drink it all themselves. You could save Yule!"

"Shh," I whispered. "If we're going to do this, we can't let the gossip mill catch wind of it. We have to make sure the thief never sees us coming."

Nilsa nodded enthusiastically. "You're right. I'll keep calm, as best I can, and make very vague inquiries of my guests. To suss them all out, right?"

"Sounds good, Nilsa. Thanks." Ragnar touched my elbow. Swallowing, I met his gaze. "I'll meet you here in the morning. We'll get a start on it then."

I nodded, my words abandoning me.

"Sleep well." Giving the hearth and the bard a regretful glance, he vanished out the door.

Nilsa leaned in close as soon as he was out of sight, her forehead dipping to mine. "Are you *really* going to make him sleep in his wagon again?"

"Oh, stop it," I whispered.

She waggled her brow at me.

I rolled my eyes. "You're far too obsessed with romance. Aren't there more important things to worry about right now?"

"What, ale?" She laughed. "If you believe a few barrels of beer are more important than the deep, life-altering connection between two lonely souls, then I'm afraid you're more hopeless than a hound without a bone."

"The only thing that connection does is tie you down." I pulled back, my heart hammering. "Besides, if I were ever to fall in love, it wouldn't be with a man like that."

She gave me a no-nonsense look. "Oh yes. Definitely not him. I mean, he's only ruggedly handsome, strong enough to toss you around, swooningly confident, and kinder than you think." She ticked off her list with each finger. "Oh, and he has good taste in food."

"Sounds like he's perfect for you, then," I quipped.

"And leave dear Herold? Never." She squeezed my hand and tugged me around the counter, bustling the both of us into the back kitchen. To speak of the devil, there they were. Herold hovered around the stove, stirring pots of bean and vegetable stew and frying buttered sliced potatoes. The scent was mouthwatering.

Herold was a dwarf, half an inch taller than their wife. They had a big ginger beard that bounced as they moved, and the bells woven in jingled a merry tune. A leather apron strained against their stocky frame, barely covering the white, stew-stained tunic beneath. Their boots creaked as they shifted my way. When they spotted me hovering in the doorway with their wife, their face broke out into a broad grin.

"Lilia!" they exclaimed, still stirring the stew without missing a beat. "Nilsa said you were here. Glad you could make it again. Save me enough of your ale for a few tankards, eh?"

I winced. "Ah, there's been an incident with the ale. It's gone missing."

Herold dropped the spoon. It collided with the side of the pan, launching a spray of beans onto the wall behind them. It ceremoniously clattered onto the floor. "The ale's gone missing?!"

"Don't worry, my love. Lilia is going to sort this out with her *friend*," Nilsa said, patting her partner's arm. She turned to me. "Now, I wasn't going to tell you this because he asked me not to, but I think it's time to spill the beans..." Nilsa giggled to herself, pointing at the bean splatter on the wall.

I folded my arms. "Nilsa, I love you, but that was groan-worthy."

"I'll tell you what's groan-worthy. That man you're so insistent on keeping at arm's length *did* have a room here. You know what he did when you arrived looking like something the cat dragged in? Well, he said to me, 'Nilsa, I'd like Lilia to have my room. I run hot, like my ancestors, and so I'm just fine sleeping out in the cold.' Bet you didn't know he gave up his room for you, now did ya?"

I blinked.

She dealt me a smug smile. "That's what I thought."

12

LILIA

It took a few moments for her words to sink in. She left me to stew in my thoughts while she bustled around her partner, wiping up the spill. When I'd first arrived in Riverwold, Ragnar had seemed just as agitated with me as I was with him. He'd come across as selfish and stubborn, unwilling to admit he'd tried to outrun me so he could claim the tavern location as his. So why would he have given up his room for me?

As I mulled it over, Nilsa tugged a pie from the packed shelves, draped a cloth over it, and carried it across the kitchen. She held it out to me. "I noticed that Ragnar is awfully fond of apple pie. 'Course I know you are, too. So do with this what you please, whether that means keeping it for yourself or delivering some good 'ole home-cooked food to the man who's staying out in the cold so you don't have to."

I took it, my heart thumping in a wild, guilty rhythm. "I didn't know he'd done that."

"Because he hasn't gone around boasting about it." She folded her arms, the steam from the stove surrounding her like a halo.

"He clearly would have done it for anyone, Nilsa. Like he said, he has some fire demon ancestry, and he doesn't feel the cold like we do."

"Then go on and eat the damn pie yourself," she said, sticking her tongue out at me.

"Hmm. And here I thought you were going to stick to your promises and not play matchmaker," I said, teasing her if only so I could get some of the focus off me.

"All I did was tell you the truth," she said with a crisp nod.

"Of course. There was definitely *nothing* more to it." I winked, backing toward the door. "I suppose I'll just keep this delicious pie all to myself. Thanks, Nilsa!"

Grinning, I spun around and headed back into the taproom while her exuberant shouts peppered my back. But when I passed the stairs that would take me up to my room, I kept going. And when I neared an empty seat, I didn't take it. I continued onward to the door, where the night would lead me back to the meadow.

It wasn't that I felt any sort of way about Ragnar, despite Nilsa's suggestive winks. There was nothing romantic happening here, nor would there ever be. It was just that he'd done something nice for me, and so I'd do something nice right back. Delivering this pie to his cold, lonely wagon made us even. That was all.

With those thoughts repeating in my mind, I quickly reached the grounds, spurred on by the chilly wind at my back. I couldn't wait to see the look of surprise on his face. He'd never expect me to deliver him an entire apple pie, especially when he likely thought I'd already gone to bed.

A peal of thunder crashed through the skies. Another gust of wind shuddered against my back, and the scent of brine thickened the air, rushing in from the distant shore. I picked up my pace. The crowd began to scatter, diving into their wagons and tents to hide from the impending storm, and yet I carried on, my head bent into the wind.

Up ahead, a burst of fire flared in the dark. I slowed and clutched the pie against me, fingers barely keeping the cloth from darting into the sky to join the bulbous clouds. Ragnar stood at the rear of his wagon with flames dancing along his knuckles. A brunette woman was with him—one of the lithe, long-limbed elves who performed on the stage. She was leaning close to him, her head titled back, musical laughter spilling from her lips. Ragnar grinned back, then motioned toward his wagon. She nimbly leapt inside.

He followed her.

My breath stilled, and an unexpected pain tore through my gut. Swallowing, I took a few steps back.

This had been a terrible idea. Of course Ragnar would want someone to help keep his bed warm. That was probably why he'd wanted to stay at the festival grounds rather than the inn. Turned out, it truly did have nothing to do with me.

And here I was, standing out in the cold wind like a fool, holding a pie I'd brought to him while my teeth chattered up a storm.

I shouldn't have come here.

Eyes burning for no good reason, I hurried back the way I came. There were a few shadow demons and dwarves still perched on some old wooden crates outside one of the tents. I handed the pie to them on the way past; I didn't have the stomach for it anymore.

When I returned to the inn, I went straight upstairs. I didn't want to face Nilsa's questions.

Mist curled into the cold room, a pale blue light splashing onto the narrow walls. Heavy rain drummed the roof and blurred the view of the town beyond the window. I shivered and tugged the heavy quilt tighter around me, contemplating staying in bed for the rest of this miserable day. This storm would keep everyone inside, and there was little I could do to set up my tavern in heavy rain.

And all my ale was gone. I truly had nothing else to do but mope about my current quagmire of a life.

Groaning, I rolled over and hid beneath the quilt. I was supposed to meet Ragnar downstairs soon, but the idea of seeing his face this morning made me feel a bit sick. Would he even show up or would he be too busy entertaining his new friend in the back of his wagon? Why trek all the way to the inn during a downpour when he could stay tucked up with her for hours?

And if he did show…what would I even say to him?

We couldn't do much to track down the thief while it stormed, which meant losing another day. Meanwhile, I could get started on a brew easily enough, and I didn't want to waste what little time we had left.

And it meant I wouldn't have to wait around for a man who'd never appear.

I peered out the rear door of the inn with the heat of the kitchen at my back. Mist-shrouded rain plinked against the stones, and the frequent thunder was like a dragon's roar. The dark haze smudged the courtyard at the end of the narrow alley. A few huddled forms scurried through it, likely visitors who'd had enough of the campground.

"Shut that door, will ya?" Herold called out from

behind their mound of pots and pans and baking trays. The taproom was a cacophony of chaotic activity, and Herold was up to their ears in food orders.

"Sorry," I told them. "I'm just trying to work up the nerve to go out."

"You lost your damn mind? We've got a roaring hearth and piles of food here. Go find somewhere to sit. And if the tables are packed, find a corner to prop your arse against. It might not be much, but it's dry."

"When I get back, I'll do just that." Sighing, I tugged my cloak's hood over my head and stepped out into the storm. The door thundered shut behind me.

Puddles splashed around my boots as I hurried through the village. According to Nilsa, Tomas kept a carpentry shop on the southern side of town, where most of the fishmongers lived. I hurried down the street. The bottom of my cloak swept across the mud, splattering droplets onto my trousers. Lightning forked through the gray skies in wicked tongues of white.

A heavy chill settled into my bones as the moments bled past. When I finally spotted a wooden sign swinging in the wind, etched with a painting of a hammer, I loosed an audible sigh. Even if Tomas couldn't help me, I'd find a brief respite from the rain inside. I dashed up a set of rickety stairs, faded from wind and time. Warm light spilled through the cracked curtains.

I knocked and waited, bouncing on my toes.

When the door swung inward, the sight of a towering shadow demon greeted me. Shadows pulsed around him, curling like wisps of smoke. His eyes gleamed bright, like stars, and his black hair was twisted in a high bun that sat squarely between his sleek, curving horns. Folding his bulky arms across his aproned chest, he arched a brow.

"We're closed today due to the storm." He pointed at a small sign in the window that said just that, but I'd been so focused on the light I hadn't noticed it.

"Looks like you're still working." I indicated his apron.

"I'm always working." He took in the sight of me, drenched to the bones. Shaking his head, he opened the door wider. "Come on in, then. I don't have it in me to turn away a drowned rat."

"A drowned *elf*," I corrected him with a thankful smile.

Inside, his shop was a mess. Planks of wood in all shapes and sizes formed a cascading mountain across one side of the room. The opposite wall held all manner of tools, but there seemed to be no rhyme or reason to where they hung. Hammers were haphazardly clinging to spools of thread, and saws were situated with the sharp side out. I gave that wall a wide berth, then realized the planks could drown me in an avalanche if I jostled them too much.

"Right." He palmed his worktable in the center of the room, hidden beneath drawings and tools. Rain beat the tin roof above. "What can I get for you?"

"My name is Lilia. I run the Traveling Tavern for the festival." I stuck out my hand.

With a grin, he captured my palm in his grip and eagerly shook it. "I've heard of you. Best ale in all the Isles, right? Maybe this year I should finally make some time to attend the festival and give it a try. I'm fond of a good brew."

This was a good sign.

"That's actually why I'm here," I told him. "My kegs have gone missing, which means there'll be no ale this year unless I can brew some more. I was hoping you had some barrels. And if not, perhaps you could build some for me."

"Gone missing?" He scratched his chin. "Well, I don't understand. How do kegs go missing?"

"That's a good question. Unfortunately, there's not a lot of time to figure that out."

"So you need some barrels. Hmm." He cast a glance at his wood pile. "I don't have any ready-built, I'm afraid, but I could certainly build you some. When do you need them?"

"In a few days."

"*Days*?" The shadow demon paced the floor, and a few strands of shadows shot out to whip the wall. I gave him a wide berth as best I could, but there was nowhere for me to go. Mumbling to himself, he shook his head, then said, "I have too many other jobs in the queue, I'm afraid. Unless you can pay double, I just don't have the time."

I hated to ask. "What's double?"

"How many barrels?" he countered.

"Five at the very least."

"Ten golds each," he said without missing a beat. "Fifty in total."

"*Fifty?*" I gaped at him. That was extortionate. Earlier this year, I'd purchased barrels from the docks near Milford for two golds each, and the carpenter in Wyndale had built some for only one. Spending ten each meant I'd barely break even. Add in all the lost barrels, and I'd leave the festival worse off than when I'd arrived.

"It's my going rate for a rush job," he said, his expression softening. "I am sorry, but it wouldn't be fair to all my other customers."

"No, I understand." I nibbled on the inside of my cheek, shoulders slumping. The problem was, I didn't have fifty gold coins. "It was a long-shot, anyway. Even with all the barrels in the world, I can't brew ale without some grains, and most of the food stock here in Riverwold is reserved for Yule."

"I've got plenty of grains."

I straightened. "You do?"

"Got them when the last ship came through." He wandered to the back of the room, where a cupboard was nearly bursting from the seams. When he unlatched the lock, the door collided into him. Piles of sandpaper, wood chips, and tiny carved figurines tumbled onto the floor.

And there, piled innocently on the top shelf, were big old sacks of grains.

"That's quite the stock," I said, trailing over to him.

"Ship came through at the docks just a couple days ago. Or was it yesterday?" He rubbed his chin, frowning. "Days all blur together, you know."

I cut my eyes his way. "What are you going to do with them?"

"I thought it might be fun to make my own beer. Nilsa likes her wine and spirits, but..." He shrugged. "Thing is, I don't really know much about brewing."

I looked down at the pouch of Vindur sand on my hip, half-hidden beneath my cloak. As long as Tomas would accept it for payment, it would more than cover the cost of all the barrels and the grains, even with the rush fee. I'd been holding on to this sand for years now, saving it for a rainy day. My hand found the pouch, and my fingers pressed into the leather. I was reluctant to part with it, but it was hard to imagine there'd ever come a time when it would be needed more than it was now.

Loosing a breath, I extracted the pouch and dropped it onto the worktable. The sound of shifting sand whispered through the shop.

He gasped and moved toward it. "Is that...is that what I think it is?"

"Eight ounces of Galdur sand," I answered proudly. "Vindur, specifically."

He wet his lips and rubbed his hands together. "Please tell me you're offering this as payment."

"It's yours if you can agree to have my order ready by…what's today?"

"Mandag," he said.

"I need them by Torsday, then—six barrels, not five. And you have to throw in the grains. I'll collect them when I come get the barrels."

"That's a lot of demands," he said with a wry grin.

I reached for the sand pouch. "Can you do it or not?"

He motioned at the grains. "They're all yours."

13

RAGNAR

"Where's Lilia?"

Nilsa deposited a plate piled high with sausages, eggs, and mash onto the table before me. I'd tucked myself in the back corner, where I could see the staircase to the upper floors as well as the front door. An hour had bled by without any sign of Lilia and her unmistakable silver hair and curvy hips.

My boots were still sopping wet from the trek over. The rainfall had transformed the festival grounds into a swamp. I'd planned on moving my wagon today so Lilia could return her Traveling Tavern to its rightful place, but the wheels wouldn't budge in all that mud.

I'd spent all night considering it, tossing and turning in the cramped wagon. If we were somehow going to turn all this around, we needed to run the tavern from Lilia's wagon. I'd caught a glimpse of her supplies when we'd discovered her missing kegs. She had tables and chairs, silver banners, and an awning to hang outside. We could find the missing ale and then sell it together, so long as she agreed to the deal.

'Course, the lass had to show up first.

Nilsa patted my arm as if reading my mind. "My partner saw her sneak off into the alley earlier this morning. I'm afraid she's not back yet."

I frowned. "We agreed to meet here for breakfast, then go out hunting for the ale."

"I'm sure she'll be back soon. You eat up while you wait. Bet you're not that hungry after eating all that apple pie last night, though." She winked. "How'd you like it?"

"The apple pie? It was delicious, but I only had half a slice for lunch yesterday. You have any more? Wouldn't mind having some after my sausage and eggs."

She squinted at me. "Oh. I could have sworn... never you mind. I'll see if we've got any ready."

I watched her sashay back to the kitchen, the bells in her hair jingling with every step. I wondered what she'd meant. Why would she think I'd had a whole damn pie last night? Must have gotten me confused with someone else.

After another survey of the stairwell and the door, I tucked into my breakfast. The warm, salty food was sorely needed after sleeping out in the soggy night. The wind had pushed the rain through the burlap, nearly flooding the floor.

The sound of the busy inn rose around me as I finished off my meal. Forks scraped plates, conversation hummed, and the crackle of the hearth formed a rhythm with the hammering rain outside. Satisfied, I pushed aside my plate and leaned back against the wall, watching a pixie flutter in the door and squeal when she spotted her friends. She rushed over to their bench and flung her arms around their necks. And I wondered what that felt like, to have someone—or a lot of someones—that happy to see you.

Gusts of wind battered the inn, and the door rattled from the force of it. The glass in the window groaned, shuddering ominously in its frame. The pixies I'd spotted earlier yelped, hauled their food and drinks into their arms, and darted to an empty spot at the table furthest from the outer wall.

Frowning, I rose and approached the counter, where Nilsa busied herself polishing some cutlery. She looked up when I neared, but she continued to shine away what appeared to be invisible smudges, her fingers moving with a frantic energy that betrayed far more than her blank expression.

"This is quite the storm," I said.

"Yes, it's the Elding. And I can't say I like it very much. We normally don't get it this bad here, especially not this time of year."

"The Elding? I've heard of that, of course, but I didn't think it was real."

According to legend, the Elding was an ever-present brutal storm that darted along the coast of the Isles. Ships routinely got lost in it when they tried to sail here. The winds and rains were harsher than anywhere else, churned up by the elemental magic of this world. Some tales said the Old God of Thunder created it himself.

She gave me a look of pure consternation. "What else in fate's name would it be?"

I shrugged. "Just a fable or a bit of lore."

"Well, it's very much real. It swings round here at times, but it usually sticks to the sea." She heaved a tumultuous sigh. "Otherwise, we'd never hold Yule Festival in Riverwold. All those visitors camping out in this. I hope they're staying dry."

"Looks like most of them have come in here." And it wasn't the merchants and the visitors I was concerned about. It was a bright-eyed elf who should have been back here by now. As if to punctuate my thought, wind gusted against the building, howling like a pack of wolves.

Nilsa dropped her cutlery, paling.

"Is it dangerous?" I asked.

"The Elding?" Her lips thinned. "It can be."

"All right." I shoved away from the counter. "What were Lilia's plans this morning? Where did she go?"

"She didn't tell me, but if I were to guess, she went

to have a chat with our local carpenter. His shop is on the other end of town. Southern side, down a road called Cherry Lane."

As I turned to go, Nilsa clutched my arm. "You find her and bring her back safe."

"Leave it to me."

I crossed the room and forced the door open against the vigorous wind, then strode out into the turbulent storm.

Water sloshed around my boots, and my hair plastered to my face and neck. The rain was so thick and hazy, I could barely see a foot in front of me. And yet I carried on, until I reached the lane on the southern side of town. I found the carpenter's shop only moments later and pounded my fist against his door.

The seconds ticked by, rain hammering my face and back. My clothes were soaked through, and the wet felt like it was sinking through my skin. Even my bones felt damp. Not for the first time, I was grateful for the magic in my blood that protected me from this.

When the door finally opened, a shadow demon glared out into the dark. The scowl only intensified when he spotted me.

"My shop is closed. Why in fate's name are you even out in this?" he snapped.

Wonderful customer service, I thought dryly.

"I'm looking for an elf named Lilia. Is she here?" I asked.

His brow knitted together. "She was, but she left a few minutes ago. Or was it an hour? Hard to keep track of the time, if I'm being honest."

I sidled closer, fists clenching. "I need you to do better than that. Was it a few minutes or was it an hour?" Because if Lilia had left that long ago, she should have made it back to the inn by now. And I hadn't passed her along the way.

She could be wandering the streets. She could be lost in the haze.

Lilia could be hurt.

"Oh." The shadow demon's eyes flicked down to my fisted hands. "Well, if you insist I clarify, then..." He pursed his lips and cocked his head. "It was closer to an hour. I think."

"Thanks." I jogged down the stairs and ignited the power I normally kept at a low smolder. The heat of my internal flames burned through me, dusting forth plumes of steam from the rain dousing my skin. My eyes caught the burn, illuminating the hazy street before me.

I clenched my jaw and strode through the storm, casting my brightened gaze around me, searching for any sign of a silver-haired elf. The power tore through me, hot and unyielding; it bubbled beneath my skin. I could only use this power for moments at a time before it threatened to burn me up completely.

"Lilia!" I shouted, breaking out into a run.

The wind hammered me from all sides. Rain pounded into my face, and that aching fire shuddered through me.

"Lilia!" I shouted again.

A soft voice answered. I might have missed it if I hadn't drawn upon my power.

I rounded the next corner. Another gust of wind slammed into me, and I staggered to the side.

"Ragnar?"

Peering into the dark, my fire-lit gaze fell upon a girl huddled in a doorframe, teeth chattering. She'd pressed herself up against the wall beneath an awning, though the wind still berated her. A tangle of silver hair spilled out beneath her hooded cloak. Her cheeks had turned a wicked shade of blue.

I rushed forward and gathered her into my arms. I expected her to protest and insist I put her down. But no objection came. And so I wrapped my heat around her, and I carried her back to the inn.

14

After a very cold and very wet slosh to the inn, the hot bath was a welcome distraction from Ragnar's ember eyes and his soothingly warm body. Like Wyndale, Riverwold was blessed with running water. Galdur magic ran through the very bones of Hearthaven. Every Midsummer, the island gifted its residents with what often felt like impossible things—like water that came from a spout. And so it had taken mere moments for Nilsa to fill the rickety tin tub with hot, soapy water after Ragnar had swept me to safety, like some kind of knight from a storybook tale.

At the thought of him, I ducked lower in the tub. It was embarrassing, really. I'd gotten turned around in the rain-drenched darkness, and then I'd taken shelter beneath an awning. Soon, the cold had numbed every inch of me.

A heavy knock came from the door. Frowning, I

ignored it at first. Nilsa likely had questions. Questions I very much didn't want to answer right now.

But the voice that called out was distinctly rough and much deeper than Nilsa's. "Lilia? Are you all right?"

"I'm fine," I answered Ragnar, my voice near a squeak.

A pause. "Is the water warm enough? I can boil some in the kitchen and bring it up."

"That won't be necessary."

"Can I come in?" came his reply.

"Excuse me?"

"I won't look," he said, clearing his throat. "But I want to talk to you, and shouting through this door isn't particularly enjoyable. Besides, I think everyone downstairs can hear what I'm saying."

He wasn't wrong. The inn's bathing chamber was only one floor up from the taproom, which would be crowded during a storm like this. The Elding would have driven most of the merchants and newly-arrived visitors inside. They'd be clamoring for warm food in their bellies, the heat of the ever-burning hearth, and some ale to wash it all down. Unfortunately, they wouldn't find any here.

When I didn't immediately answer, I heard a sigh, then the creak of the wooden floor just outside the bathing chamber. He had begun to move away, but a wild rush of words spilled out of me before he could get far.

"You can come in," I called out, "but you have to keep your back to me."

A pause. "I can do that."

As the door creaked open, I slid beneath the bubbly, soapy water so that only my head, from chin up, was visible. But Ragnar kept his word. He backed into the room, shut the door, and kept his gaze rooted to the wall in front of him. Unlike me, he still wore his wet clothes. Rivulets of rainwater dripped down his trousers and boots, forming an instant puddle by his feet. Damp strands of hair curled across the back of his neck. A bit of steam puffed from his skin.

"So…hello," I said, heat creeping up my cheeks. "What did you want to talk about?"

"Most of all, I wanted to make sure you're all right. You looked half-frozen when I found you. And you didn't even bicker with me once, so I know you were a bit out of it." His head slightly shifted to the side, but he still didn't look my way.

"I'm not that bad, am I?"

"You're fiery. But I like it."

I nibbled on my bottom lip, inching a bit lower in the water.

"What I don't like is being stood up," he suddenly said. "We had a plan, one I thought was important to you. But instead of following through on that, you went to the carpenter for some barrels instead."

An image of Ragnar with the beautiful singer flashed in my mind. A knot formed in my stomach.

"I realized our plan wouldn't work," I said softly.

"I figured as much."

"It's just...I can sort this out on my own. There's no need to go on an elaborate manhunt for a keg thief. Brewing ale is simple. And it's what I do best."

Ragnar folded his arms. "That's fine. I understand. I just have one more question, if you don't mind."

My heartbeat quickened. "All right. Ask your question."

He shifted on his feet, and his boots squelched, logged with rainwater. A guilty flush filled my cheeks. Ragnar had traipsed out into the worst storm Riverwold had seen in decades. According to Nilsa, he'd done it just to find me.

"What changed between last night and this morning?" he asked.

I swallowed. "If I'm being honest, I wasn't entirely sure you'd meet me here today. I...well I suppose I thought you might be otherwise engaged, especially with the weather the way it is."

"Otherwise engaged." He started to turn toward me, then stopped himself.

"You can face me if you want. Nilsa loves her bubbles, so there's plenty of them," I found myself saying.

Ragnar wheeled around. His gaze no longer held that impossible fire it had outside, but his eyes still felt like they were burning through mine. He didn't even try to look down at what might be hidden in the water. He merely met my stare with a deeply furrowed brow.

"I don't understand why you think I'd be otherwise engaged. Now that I have no ale, it's not as if I'd be busy with my shop. And the storm has driven everyone inside."

"Yes, well." How could I explain this without looking like a fool? Truth be told, it seemed an impossible feat. I cleared my throat. "Last night, Nilsa realized you'd left without eating, so she gave me an apple pie to deliver to your wagon."

That wasn't the *entire* truth, but at least it made it seem like I'd been doing Nilsa a favor rather than... well, whatever it was I thought I'd been doing. And I didn't want to think about that too much.

His lips tilted up in the corners, which blasted a strange heat through my belly. "So that's what she was talking about earlier. But since you never showed up, I'm guessing you ate it all."

"No." I looked away. "Like I said, you were otherwise engaged. I didn't want to interrupt."

"I wasn't... Oh." He chuckled, which was quite the opposite of the reaction I'd expected. It was far worse. The bastard was laughing at me. Why I expected anything different from him—

"You saw me talking to that singer," he said. "And you thought I was inviting her into my wagon for the night. Well, I wasn't."

My head swivelled toward him. "But I saw her climbing inside, and you were right behind her."

"She was asking about the ale. Said she might have an idea who took it. Then it started to rain." He shrugged. "Thought we'd have the conversation somewhere dry, not that the burlap did much to keep out the storm."

"Oh right. I see," I said in a small voice.

A pause. "That bothered you? That I might have invited a woman into my wagon for more than just a chat?"

"No, of course not," I said quickly. "It's no business of mine. But you can't blame me for thinking you might have wanted to wait out the storm with her instead of coming all the way to the Ship's Anchor."

"Hmm." He folded his arms and leaned his shoulder against the wall. "Well, I didn't want to do that. I wanted to come here and meet you like I said I would."

Suddenly, he pushed away from the wall and strode toward me. When he reached the tub, he braced both palms on either side and leaned so close I could smell the heat of his skin. He didn't dip his gaze, but his proximity still sent a shiver down my spine, coating my arms in chill bumps despite the hot bath.

He tucked his forefinger beneath my chin, and the chills were replaced by a storm of sparks. "So let's see this thing through, darling. I'll be downstairs."

I couldn't find my voice. And when he pushed away and vanished out the door, I didn't even breathe for several long moments. Eventually, I sagged, fully submerging myself, and blew out a long breath. Bubbles erupted around me.

I tried to shove the moment out of my mind and failed. My thudding heart refused to let me.

Ragnar sat in the far corner with his back pressed up against the wall. His keen eyes surveyed the door leading outside, as well as the counter where Nilsa was in deep conversation with a tipsy pixie whose wings were tossing her from side to side liked a ship caught in a storm. I slowed on the bottom step, suddenly unsure if this was a good idea.

Not that I'd ever been sure.

As if sensing my presence, Ragnar looked my way. He visibly stiffened. With a slight smile, I cut a path toward him, my long dress swishing around my booted feet. I'd chosen one of my favorite ensembles. The bodice laced up the front, dipping low over a white blouse with frilly edges along the sleeves and the collar. A necklace dangled between my bosom, the gemstone in the center glinting from the reflection of the hearth's firelight.

When I reached his table, I tossed my braided silver hair over my shoulder and settled onto the bench across from his. "You always sit in that corner, even when there are plenty of open seats."

"It has the best view of the door. Where else would you sit?"

I leaned forward onto my elbows. "Well, I'd sit anywhere. But I'm not expecting someone to barge through the door. Things like that don't happen here in the Isles."

"Someone stole all our kegs."

"Point taken." I frowned. Truth was, I didn't know how it could have even happened. The island usually protected us from these kinds of things. No one could land on our shores unless they had good intentions, and those who already lived here valued the lack of crime too much to steal.

"You want some food before we start hunting for our thief?" Ragnar asked, his deep, melodic voice cutting through my thoughts.

I pointedly looked at the window. Rain slashed at the rattling glass, and the heavy boom of thunder still echoed from time to time. The worst of the Elding had passed, but I'd had enough rain for one day. I wasn't going out there hunting anytime soon.

"I noticed several of the merchants at the table near the door," he said. "We don't have to go out in the storm to start asking questions."

I cocked my head, smiling. "I think this calls for a slice of apple pie, then."

15

LILIA

"**D**id you happen to notice anyone hauling big barrels of ale across the meadow?" I asked hopefully.

The dwarf's eyes darted to Ragnar's scowling face and back to my smile again. We'd taken a fairly obvious approach. I'd chatter nicely with everyone while he stood there looking threatening. So far, it had done nothing to scare forth any answers.

"Was I supposed to?" the dwarf asked, scratching his long, forked beard. "'Cause I didn't know I needed to be on the lookout for any barrels."

"No, it's just...well, they're my barrels, and they've gone missing." I indicated at Ragnar, who seemed to take that as a signal to deepen his scowl. "His, too. We're tavern owners, you see."

"Are you Lilia?" the dwarf asked, perking up.

"That's right," I said with an encouraging nod.

"Well, then who does that make *him*? Never heard of you having an assistant."

I smiled smugly up at Ragnar. "He just started working for me today. Isn't that right, Ragnar?"

"Hmm," was all he said.

I fought down a giggle, then turned back to the dwarf. "Anyway, about those barrels, I—"

"You should ask Snorri and Otto over there," the dwarf said, pointing to the second table over, where a shadow demon couple were locking horns. To shadow demons, locking horns was part of their pre-mating ritual. It was such an intimate embrace, I had to quickly glance away, embarrassment burning my cheeks.

"Well," the dwarf said with a chuckle, "maybe wait 'til they're done."

The rest of the evening passed in a similar pattern. We chatted with nearly everyone who'd taken refuge in The Ship's Anchor, but no one had seen a wily thief traipsing around the meadow, loaded down with kegs. I was starting to think perhaps we'd imagined the entire thing. How could someone have lugged eleven of my barrels around without it being noticed by at least *someone*?

I plopped onto the stool beside the counter, seeking a brief respite from all the *talking*. When I had my tavern up and running, I was used to constant conversation, but it was always the other way around. People liked to chat at me while they drank their ale. All I had to do was lend an ear and a kind smile, and the merry customers practically entertained themselves.

"No luck?" Nilsa asked when she stopped by for a rag to wipe up some rain leaking under the door.

I shook my head. "No one's seen anything. It's like those kegs vanished into thin air."

Nilsa cocked her head, considering my words. "What if someone had some Galdur sand? Could any of it do that?"

"Make something disappear? Wouldn't that be useful?" I reached for my pouch instinctively. It'd worn it for so long, I'd grown accustomed to the weight of it at my hip. Now that it wasn't there, it felt like I was wandering around Riverwold half-naked.

"You sure it can't do that?" she asked. "I've never had any of it myself."

"Afraid not," I replied. "Galdur sand can do a lot of useful things, like conjure water. But it's all elemental. And the elements can't make kegs of beer vanish into thin air."

A pixie fluttered over to the counter, nibbling on her bottom lip. She cast a few nervous glances behind her, like she expected someone to jump out from beneath a table. I'd seen her around before. She had big brown eyes, black hair braided in two dozen rows, and a dimpled smile that she kept dimmed for now. Patches of flour coated her leather trousers. Her soft purple tunic matched the wings poking out through the holes stitched on the back.

"I hear you're looking for a man who stole some ale," she whispered fiercely.

I exchanged a surprised glance with Nilsa. "That's right. You know of such a man?"

"I can't be sure. Maybe?" she said, dropping her voice to an even lower whisper. I had to lean in close, what with the roar of the hearth and the burble of steady conversation.

"Well, don't keep us in suspense," Nilsa swatted her with the rag. "Tell us what you think you know, and we'll find out if it's good information."

"I just don't want anyone to get the wrong idea, you see," said the pixie.

"Why would anyone get the wrong idea?" I asked.

She huffed out a breath, shook her head, then closed her eyes. "There's a pie man who lives down by the sea."

"Ivar Olsen?" Nilsa asked, straightening. "Surely not."

I frowned. "Who's Ivar Olsen?"

I'd spent a lot of time in Riverwold, and I'd never heard that name, let alone met anyone who went by it.

Nilsa clucked her tongue. "He's no one you wish to know. Bad news, that one."

"He sure does make delicious pie, though," the pixie said. "Savory ones, not sweet like Nilsa's here."

"No, that's your specialty," Nilsa replied with a smile.

"Ah, that's right. You're the local pie maker. You make a mean mushroom and leek. It's probably my favorite dish made here in Riverwold." I shot my friend a quick look. "After Nilsa's bean stew, of course."

"Of course," Nilsa said thinly. "Anyway, what's Ivar got to do with any of this? He never comes into town, and he's banned from putting up a stall for Yule."

"Banned?" That sounded promising.

Nilsa motioned me closer. I leaned in, and so did the pixie, even though she looked like she was well-aware of Ivar's sordid history. "He got into a couple fights one year before you started coming into town. Caused a broken nose and a couple swollen eyeballs. Ever since, he's not been allowed back. Still sells plenty of pies, though, just not at this time of year. Except to the sailors, maybe."

"And you saw him in the meadow? Carrying away some barrels?" I asked hopefully.

She winced. "Well…no."

My stomach dropped in disappointment. I'd begun to hope this pie man by the sea was the answer to all our problems. He'd taken the ale to get back at Steffon for banning him from Yule, and all Ragnar and I had to do was retrieve the kegs from him. And then Yule would be saved.

"I think I speak for both me and Lilia here when I

say that isn't exactly what we were hoping to hear," Nilsa said with a sigh.

"I can probably give you something almost as good as that, though," said the pixie. "A few weeks ago, I ran into Ivar at the market in Milford. He was hunting for some exotic ingredients. Frog leaves or something. But he was also looking for some good ale preserved with Galdur sand. He told me he wants to get into making ale pie. Only problem is, no one could sell him any. The Milford taverns wanted to keep all the ale for themselves. He seemed pretty agitated about it."

She was right. I did perk up at that. "So what you're saying is, you know a man who has a bone to pick with the festival, and he also happens to be in search of the very thing that's gone missing."

"That's exactly what I'm saying," she said. "If I were a betting kind of gal, I'd bet the whole damn town that you'd find every single one of your missing barrels—Ragnar's, too—if you paid our not-so-friendly pie man a little visit."

I smiled. "Luckily for all of us, that's precisely what I plan to do. Where can I find him?"

Ragnar was deep in conversation with a boisterous blue-haired elf whose eyes and stained lips looked like he'd drank his weight in wine. Although...it was less a conversation and more

Ragnar nodding along to the extended monologue spilling from the elf, like the deluge of rain from the Elding. I edged close to the table, trying not to laugh. Then, I figured I should be kind and rescue him from the situation.

I cleared my throat, and the elf slurred his words to a halt. "I'm sorry to interrupt, but I really need to borrow Ragnar for a moment. Important tavern business, you see."

"Tavern business!" the elf proclaimed, raising his goblet in a toast. "Well, I certainly can't get in the way of that. By all means, steal away, dear tavern lady!"

Ragnar's expression was that of a man who'd been saved from downing a particularly bitter jug of ale. I fought back a laugh, waiting to the side while he murmured departing words to his new friend. Then he followed me through the raucous din of the taproom.

"Thanks for that," he said when we reached the back corner. Gazing down at me, he folded his arms and leaned sideways, shoulder against the wooden panels of the inn. I wet my lips, suddenly all too aware of how close we stood. Out of the corner of my eye, I spotted Nilsa watching us.

Finding my voice, I said, "We might have found our thief."

He arched his brow and waited for me to continue.

"A pie man, who lives down by the sea. Rumor has it he was asking around about some ale a couple weeks back. And listen to this." I dropped my voice and leaned in to whisper. It took all my concentration to ignore the brush of his chest against mine. "He's been banned from the festival for starting fights."

A slow grin spread across Ragnar's face. "Well, if that doesn't sound like our culprit, then I don't know what does."

I beamed up at him. "We should pay him a visit tomorrow, so long as the storm has died down."

A steady rain still rapped against the windows, but the anger of the wind had subsided to a few half-hearted gusts now and again. By morning, the Elding should have returned to the sea, where it would whip the waves up into a frenzy. The walk would require sturdy boots and a pair of dry socks on return, but it would be worth it to find our kegs.

"Meet you here in the morning?" he asked.

"Right here in this corner," I replied.

He arched a brow. "And you promise you won't run off on your own adventure this time?"

"Oh, I will." I grinned back at him. "Just not tomorrow."

"Sounds like a deal." He stuck out his hand. Swallowing, I slid my fingers into his warm palm and slowly shook. A few seconds turned into a minute, our hands still locked. Eventually, Ragnar let go, and my palm tensed as I lowered it to my side.

"Where are you going to sleep?" I asked, suddenly feeling awkward.

"Back in my wagon."

"But—"

"Don't you worry about me. I'll be fine." His eyes dipped to my lips, then he winked. "Unless you're inviting me into your bed for the night."

My entire face flamed with the heat of a thousand bonfires. "Is that what you want? I mean—"

Laughing, he tucked his knuckle beneath my chin. "I'm only joking, darling. I've done a lot of things I'm not proud of, and I'd probably do some of them again. But one thing I'd never do is pressure a woman into going to bed with me. So good night, Lilia. I'll see you in the morning."

His touch vanished from my skin, and he started toward the door. Words were on the tip of my tongue. It didn't feel right for him to stay out in the wet cold, but I couldn't bring myself to ask him to share my bed, either. I'd never shared my bed with anyone.

But still, I called out, "Ragnar."

Pausing, he glanced over his shoulder. "Yes?"

"Thank you," I said, my voice softening. "For searching the storm for me, and for giving up your room."

He smiled. "It was my pleasure."

And then he was gone. I didn't know whether to be relieved or to kick myself for not having the courage to ask him to stay.

16

LILIA

A heavy fog blanketed the town, smudging the buildings. Through the haze, a ball of yellow climbed higher into the sky. In a few hours, it would burn the mist away. Ragnar and I traipsed along the muddy path that led to the east, where we'd follow the twisting road down to the sea. It would take us a couple of hours to reach the small cluster of buildings along the coast, but Nilsa had packed us plenty of provisions.

"You need all the energy you can get if you're going to confront old Ivar," she'd said before shooing us out the door.

Despite the chilly start to the day, Ragnar wore an indigo vest that accentuated his muscular shoulders and the bracers wrapped around his forearms. He'd tucked the back end of the vest into his trousers, where a lump sat.

When we started across the rolling field toward

the coast, I finally asked the question that had been on my tongue since the moment he'd sidled into the taproom that morning, carrying a hint of danger and fury in his eyes. "What are you hiding beneath your vest?"

"Hiding? Who, me?" A wicked smirk curved his lips. "I would never do such a thing."

"We have rules on this island. And you're breaking the most important one. No weapons."

He cut his eyes toward me, slinging his hands into his trouser pockets. "Says the girl with something hidden in her own back waistband."

As if in answer, the soft leather sheath scraped against my back as I walked. I'd unpacked it just before we'd left, revelling in the way the pale morning light glinted across the blade. I didn't know the first thing about fighting, but the weight of it made the anxious tremor of my heart slow down.

"It's just to give me a little courage," I said with a shrug. "I have no plans to use it. Because if I did, they'd ship me off to the mines over in the Glass Peaks. If you lost your temper and did something stupid, they'd send you, too."

And we wouldn't be the first people subjected to that punishment from the island. I'd seen a couple of lawbreakers sent there with my own eyes. And while the dwarven mountains were rich with beauty, I was partial to a life spent surrounded by fresh air, sunshine, and even the winds of the Elding, rather than the deep dark of the mines.

"I'll keep that in mind," said Ragnar. "You ever been there?"

"To the Glass Peaks?"

He nodded. "I've never visited dwarven mines before, but I hear they're quite spectacular."

"I've been a few times. They have a yearly event I try to attend if I can make it across the sea in time. A big competition to find the fittest under the mountain. It's incredible to watch." I smiled, the fog parting before us. "But even the mountains themselves are incredible. I love watching the sunset there. The colors are like nothing I've seen anywhere else."

"We'll have to go there one day."

My feet slowed, scuffing the path. "We?"

"I need a tour guide, don't I? Someone to show me around, so I don't get lost. Who better than the lass who spends her life on the road?"

I drew in a sharp breath, subtly casting a glance at Ragnar. The haze had finally burned away, and the sunlight streamed across his face, catching the vibrant color of his hair. He strode purposely beside me with his arms relaxed by his sides, like this was nothing more than a simple conversation. But it didn't feel so simple, not to me. It felt like the start of something bigger—like the slightest of cracks had spiderwebbed through my protective walls.

The day passed quickly. By the time we reached the coastal path, the sun hovered high in the clear sky. Churning waves crashed far below us, slamming against the rocky cliffside. In the distance, wooden docks stretched into the froth, where small boats rocked against their moorings. A few buildings were scattered amongst the cliffs, built from bleached stone. They were accessible by a stone set of stairs carved into the side of the cliff, winding down to the sea. Just beside the path sat a cluster of carts, where they'd been abandoned by whoever lived below.

Carefully, we left the safety of the grass to trail the rocky path down to the docks. Ragnar took to the lead, testing each stone with his not-insignificant weight. Despite the cold wind that battled against us, sweat coated my skin by the time we reached the bottom. We'd reached a small cove, cut off from the docks and the houses by a cluster of boulders jutting out toward the sea just a few paces to our left. Froth danced across them.

"Wait. I need a moment." Catching my breath, I leaned against a slick, moss-coated stone and breathed in the salted air. I pulled my canteen from my waist and took a long swing. The cool water was like a tonic after that climb.

Ragnar sat on the stone beside me and draped his arms across his knees. Gazing out at the sea, he got a wistful look in his eye. "This is quite the place, eh?"

There was a calmness to it, despite the rushing waves beating at the rocky shore. It was still and frantic, quiet and loud, all at once. The air was so fresh, so bright and new. Tucked in this cove, it felt like we were in a whole new world, far from everyone else.

"I've never been to this beach before," I said with

a satisfied sigh. "Years spent wandering the Isles, and I still find new places every time I put my boots to the road."

Ragnar gazed at me thoughtfully. "You love it, don't you?"

"The Isles? Yes, of course."

"No, wandering." He gestured at the rolling sea. "Seeing new places, experiencing new things. I can tell by the way you speak of it, it's in your soul."

A smile crested my lips. "I suppose it is."

"Do you never wish for a home?" he asked. "A house to call yours with a warm hearth and a familiar bed—a place to settle your bones."

I shifted on the stone, legs tucked to my chest. "My wagon is my home. But what about you? Where is *your* home, Ragnar?"

A darkness dimmed his expression. "I don't have one."

I searched his face. "None at all? What about the brother you mentioned?"

"My brother is gone." Ragnar stood, brushing the sand from his trousers. "I came here, hoping to find a way to pay off the debts he left behind. It only seemed fitting. He was always enamoured by the idea of his own tavern. Said he wanted to start one up. But something happened that took that chance away from him."

"Oh, Ragnar, I'm sorry." I reached for him before I realized what I was doing. My fingers stopped short, brushing the edge of his shirt. Either he didn't notice, or he didn't want to acknowledge what I'd done. So I let my hand drop awkwardly onto the stone before I stood.

We took off across the beach. The wet sand coated our boots within moments. Ragnar said little, his thoughts clearly elsewhere. I let him stew. Silence was sometimes the best comfort one could give.

Once we'd left the cove behind, we found a small road a few paces off the beach. Five buildings sat in a neat little row, each one smaller than the one before, as if the largest had been built to withstand the brunt of the storms and protect the others from the insistent wind.

We followed Nilsa's instructions and found the pie man's house smack dab in the middle of the buildings. It was a squat little house that couldn't hold more than a bedroom or two. The window boxes held scraggly brown plants that had seen better days, and deep muddy gorges ran through the water-logged lawn. When we came to the front door, Ragnar rapped his knuckles against the peeling wood.

"Nilsa said he ran a shop out of here?" Ragnar asked, his voice low.

"No, I think he just sells his pies to the sailors who come through now and then," I whispered back.

"Which can't be too often, right?" he asked, leaning back to glance at the distant docks. There were only a couple of small boats docked there now, likely for fishing. No ships. "Access seems terrible for trading."

I nodded. "That's why most of the island's trade goes through Milford."

We fell silent as the moments passed. Ragnar knocked again, this time louder. After another bout of inactivity from within, my heart began to sink. We'd spent the entire evening prior searching for any hint to where our ale had gone, and this had been the only lead we'd stumbled upon. To find a measure of hope, and to have come all this way for nothing…

The door shuddered inward, the bottom of it scraping across the timber floor. A frazzle-haired human woman peered out at us, blue eyes wide and wary. She wiped a gooey brown substance across her apron, then jerked her thumb in the direction of the docks.

"Has a new ship come in already? You don't much look like sailors," she said in a husky voice that smelled of pipe smoke.

"No, we, ah…" I glanced up at Ragnar, wondering how much we should divulge. "Well, we've come down from Riverwold looking for a pie man."

"A pie man," the woman repeated in a flat voice. "Don't you lot have enough pies up there, what with your bloody festival and all its bloody drunks?"

I bristled. "Now, wait a minute—"

"Shut your yapping," she snarled. "We see plenty of them wandering around down here after Yule, checking out the little shacks beside the sea, like we're some kind of circus act. Most of the time they're three sheets to the wind."

I'd never heard anything of the sort. Of course, that didn't mean it never happened. Still, if this was Ivar's wife or sister, I didn't much trust a word she said.

"We're sober, he and I." I motioned to Ragnar. "And we just want some pie."

She squinted at us. "Well then. You've come to the right place, I suppose. What kind of pie do you fancy?"

"Ale pie," said Ragnar. "If you have it. Otherwise...mushroom and leek are always nice."

"We've got plenty of ale pie here." She stepped back and motioned us through the door.

Sucking in a breath, I nodded at Ragnar and shuffled into the building. Once inside, the door slammed behind us, as if sucked closed by the wind. A single dimly lit taproom of sorts took up most of the home. A ladder propped against the wall led to what I assumed was a bedroom. There were only four square tables with two chairs each, and barrels were stacked up along the back wall, nearly hidden in the shadows. I drifted toward them until the woman's harsh voice stopped me in my tracks.

"Pick the table closest to the fire, eh? It's cold out there," she said.

Biting the insides of my cheeks, I did what she asked. Ragnar pulled out a chair and thundered down beside me, the weight of him making the chair creak.

"Good. Sit tight. I'll be right back with your pie."

17

LILIA

As soon as she'd scurried out the back door, I leapt to my feet and ran over to the corner with the kegs. Ragnar stayed right where he was, as if he didn't dare make any sudden movement for fear of conjuring the woman again.

"Those aren't the barrels, Lil," he said.

My heart pulsed. *Lil*. Not Lilia, or darling. Lil. Something about that nickname felt intimate coming from him. Which was ridiculous. *I* was being ridiculous. We were in the lair of the potential enemy, and all I could focus on was my name on Ragnar's tongue.

Ragnar's. Tongue.

Flustered, I patted the side of my tunic and tried to ignore the heat of his eyes on my back, but that was nigh impossible. There was nowhere else for him to look but at me, not in this strange taproom. Outside, we'd had the wide expanse of the world all around us, but in here, the walls were far too close.

"You just going to keep standing there?" he asked.

I blinked. What had he said? *Oh.* The barrels.

Now that I was a few steps closer, I could see what he meant. These barrels were coated in a thick layer of dust, and the boards were warped and cracking apart. If there'd been any liquid inside, it would have dribbled out a long time ago.

"How could you tell from so far away?" I asked, keeping my back turned toward him so that I had a little longer to gather control over my thoughts.

"I let my power through a notch. It helps me see better in the dark." He patted the seat beside him. "Better come back now. I have a feeling pie man's wife will be none too pleased if she catches you poking around in here."

Straightening my shoulders, I pasted on a blank face and returned to the table. I avoided meeting Ragnar's gaze. "Well, we have to start somewhere."

"That's why we're eating the pie. You with your expert palate will tell us if they used your ale to bake it."

I cracked a grin. "The taste completely changes when you cook it, especially when you put it in a pie. You really have no idea when it comes to beer, do you? If you hadn't tried to steal my business out from under me, I might think it was cute."

"I'm cute, eh? Go on."

Blushing, I cleared my throat. "I said I *would* have thought that, if you weren't running a rival tavern. But you are, so I don't."

"Except I'm not doing that anymore, now am I?"

At that, I finally met his gaze, and I swore I felt the fire in it burn through me. "I thought we came here to get our kegs back."

"*Your* kegs," he said quietly. "If we want to save Yule, we shouldn't be serving anyone mine. I know how terrible it tastes. Also, it's probably spoiled by now."

"But what about the debt your brother owed?"

He shrugged. "I'll have to find another way to make it right."

I opened my mouth, trying to conjure a response to that. But the pie man's wife chose that moment to charge back into the taproom. She carried two plates topped with a slice of ale pie, along with mash smothered in gravy. With the frizz battling her eyes, she plopped the plates before us.

"There you go. That'll be one gold coin each," she announced.

Ragnar let out a low whistle. "This pie better be good, then."

"Better than anything you'd get up top," she said crisply. "I know you lot think the festival has the finest food in all the Isles, what with all the merchants scrabbling over each other for a prime spot, but us down here…we don't need to do anything fancy to prove ourselves."

Ragnar's lips twitched. "You're right. Those pesky merchants all fighting for sales."

"Exactly," the woman said with an eager nod.

As she turned to go, I cleared my throat. "You said this is an ale pie, right? Did you brew the ale yourselves?"

The woman stiffened, her eyes narrowing. "None of your business. You pay and you eat. You don't get to ask questions. I won't have folk from Riverwold trying to copy our recipe. You hear?"

"I didn't mean..." I trailed off as she stormed out the back door, slamming it behind her so forcefully it rattled against its hinges. I blinked. "Well, then."

"And here I thought I'd be the one pissing them off instead of you." Ragnar grinned, poking the pie with his fork. "Think this is safe to eat?"

"Why wouldn't it be?"

"I don't know. There's something not right about any of this. Where are the other patrons? Why wasn't there a sign hanging out front? This building doesn't seem much like a place of business," he mused.

"I don't think it *is* much of one," I replied. "Like the woman said, they only get a few sailors in here now and again. Sounds like a ship came through recently, which means another likely won't for a while."

He shoved his plate aside and leaned toward me. "So then what are they really doing here? If they're not running a pie shop, they have to be doing something else." He gestured at the corner, where the piles of barrels were consumed by dust. Then he inclined his head toward one of the tables. Also dusty. In fact, now that I was looking, I spied a few cobwebs in the corners and mildew on the walls. This room clearly got little use.

I nodded toward the back door the woman kept disappearing through. Ragnar silently returned the nod. In unison, we pushed back our chairs and stood. Blood rushed into my ears as we stole across the floor. Ragnar reached for the doorknob, and my breath hissed between my teeth.

"You ready?" he murmured, looking far too excited about this. I, on the other hand, felt a little nauseous. It'd been a while since I'd done anything this bold.

"No."

"Just stay behind me," he said. "I won't let any harm come to you."

I pressed my lips together, hating the way my heart kicked my ribs at the thought of Ragnar throwing himself into danger in order to save me. I could take care of myself. I had for a long, long time. And yet, I kind of liked that he had my back in this. And that I had his, too.

"Just hurry up and open the damn door," I whispered. "I don't think I can bear the tension any longer."

Ragnar twisted the knob, then kicked the door open. The wood splintered, cracking like thunder. Fisting his hands, he rushed outside. I followed close on his heels. We came into a back garden that was beyond disrepair. Weeds sprouted through the stone path wending through the swampy grass. A second building perched to the side, warm light beaming through the glass panes. The window boxes there were full of blue winter flowers, and smoke curled through the chimney.

"Ah, so that's where they live," I murmured.

The door flew open. The woman charged toward us, her frizzy hair tossed into her eyes from the wind. She wagged a finger at us, and her face twisted into a furious scowl. "You're not allowed back here. This is private property."

"We're looking for Ivar. Is he inside?" Ragnar asked in a deep voice that brokered no argument.

Narrowing her eyes, the woman backed up. "You two didn't come here for ale pies, did you?"

"Where is Ivar?" I asked. "Someone told us he's the one who makes the pies, and yet you're the only one here."

Her face paled. "What do you want with him?"

"We just want to ask him a few questions." Ragnar edged a little closer, nodding toward the much more welcoming building than the one behind us. "Is he home? All we want is a few moments of his time, and then we'll be on our way."

"He's not here," she snapped, her eyes narrowing. "Now you two better leave before I call for my neighbors. They won't take too kindly to Riverwold folk bothering me and mine."

And with that, she whirled on her feet, stomped inside her home, and slammed the door in our faces.

"Well," I said.

Ragnar sighed. "Well."

"What do we do now?"

"You heard her," he said, frowning at the door. "I think it's best we leave. As adept as I am at fighting, I don't want to hurt anyone just for a few kegs of ale."

And despite the situation—despite my empty coin purse and soggy socks—my shoulders felt a little lighter. I smiled up at him. "You know what? I'm happy to hear you say that."

The trek up the mountain was hard going. As fit as I was from hauling my wagon across the islands, I had to pause a few times to catch my breath. Eventually, we crested the ridge, marching up the final steps just as the sun was marching down the horizon. I sat hard on one of the abandoned carts, grateful for a seat that wasn't coated in mud. Rubbing my tired legs, I sighed and then took the last swig of my canteen.

Ragnar remained standing, frowning at the carts.

"Aren't you tired?" I patted the empty spot beside me. Granted, he'd have to squeeze in close to me to fit. But after all the exercise and fresh air, I was feeling quite bold about it. I was a grown woman who ran her own damn business. I could sit beside a handsome man without combusting.

His frown deepened. "Weren't there five carts when we passed by here earlier?"

I looked around. There were four now, but I hadn't counted them before. "I can't say I paid them much attention on our way down."

"There were five." He slowly circled the carts, then pointed at the ground. "Muddy tracks, heading off into the distance. Someone took one of these after we started down the path."

Pulling my legs up to my chest, I failed to comprehend his agitation. It was just a missing cart. "I'm pretty sure that's what they're for, Ragnar. People use them to take things to and from the docks. And then they leave them here when they're not in use, since it's impossible to take them up and down the steps."

"Or they use them to take things from taprooms that aren't really taprooms," he murmured.

Ah. My eyes widened. I saw where he was going with this now. "You don't think Ivar took one, do you?"

"He was suspiciously absent from his house, and his wife was acting very odd. Think about it." He paced across the churned mud. "If he did steal our kegs, wouldn't he and his wife be on edge, expecting that someone might show up on their doorstep? And so when someone did—when *we* did—he went running."

"Except he couldn't have carried all the kegs up this path by himself. One or two, maybe, but no more than that," I countered.

"Unless he had help."

Sighing, I hopped off the cart, my boots sinking

into the mud. More water oozed through the leather, transforming my feet into a soggy mess again. I'd been looking forward to dropping onto a bench beside Nilsa's hearth and having at least three servings of her stew while wearing a dry, clean pair of woollen socks.

Ragnar noticed my shiver and frowned. "We can head back to Riverwold. I meant what I said earlier, it's just ale."

"I know." I hoisted my pack higher on my shoulder. "But as long as we have a thread we can follow, we should find out where it leads us."

18

RAGNAR

U p ahead, the track vanished into the gloomy woods that sprawled across the coast. Shivering, Lilia tugged her cloak around her, her body bent forward into the harsh wind. Instinctively, I stepped around to the other side of her, so that I took the brunt of it. Still, she trembled, then stumbled over a root sticking out of the ground.

I caught her arm. She tensed at my touch, swallowing as she gazed up at me. Something within me clenched. Slowly—far too slowly to seem natural—I released her. She pressed her lips together and pulled back into herself.

"You're cold," I said, stating the bloody obvious like a fool. "Is it normally this bad here in the winter?"

"Not usually, no," she said quietly. "It can get chilly at times, but it's usually nothing this harsh. The Elding must be causing issues with the weather. If only Reykur was here, he'd stave off the worst of it. 'Course, I'd worry it might rain on him, then."

Rain and dragons didn't mix. It was the only weakness of their scales.

"I can help," I said, calling upon the force of my fire. Unrelenting pain tore through my skin, the heat of that power seeping from my pores.

Almost instantly, Lilia seemed to relax. She sighed and loosened her shoulders. "Thank you. Your power feels like sitting beside a hearth, which I'll admit, is all I can think about right now."

I frowned. "If we haven't caught up to Ivar by now, I'm not sure we will."

"He won't keep going through the night," she argued. "He'll have to stop and camp."

"And so will we." I pointed at the root that had tried to take her down. "My eyesight helps me see at night, but you're getting tired, Lilia."

Her shoulders slumped forward. "You're right. I'm exhausted. Maybe we should have turned back instead of going after him."

"Unfortunately, even if we decide to return to Riverwold, we'll have to camp tonight and start back at first light. We're hours away from town."

I expected her to wrinkle her nose at me or put forth an argument, but she merely pointed into the trees. "There's a small clearing near the edge of the woods. It looks like the perfect spot for a fire."

Lilia unspooled the bedroll she'd been clever enough to pack while I imbued a cluster of sticks with my power. As soon as they caught fire, I shoved that power down, relieved for the respite from it. I would have kept it at the surface to prevent Lilia from freezing all night, but it would have nearly driven me mad.

She tugged her bedroll a bit closer to the fire and sat cross-legged on one end, leaving room for me. As soon as I settled onto the ground beside her, she dug around in her pack and pulled out a heel of bread. She tore it in half.

"Here," she said, handing me a chunk. "It's nothing compared to the 'finest' ale pie and mash, but it's what we've got."

"Thanks. I'm sorry I didn't bring any supplies myself. I didn't expect we'd be gone longer than a day."

"You brought the fire. I'd say that's help enough."

"Where do you think your dragon is, anyway? I haven't seen him around since that day in the woods."

She smiled. "Knowing him, he's out soaring over the mountains now that the storm has passed. He'll show back up when he wants some more treats, like apple pie."

I chuckled. "He really does sound more like a hound than a ferocious dragon."

Lilia sat up a little straighter, pride shining in her silver eyes. "He's a good boy."

I bit into the bread, savoring the buttery glaze. The fire crackled and smoked, and the flames danced in the light breeze. With the trees standing sentry around us, the worst of the wind was kept at bay. For a while, Lilia and I mostly sat in silence, just enjoying the fire and the food in our belly, though I would have given up every last remaining coin for that ale pie we'd abandoned.

Eventually, Lilia laughed softly.

I shifted toward her, noting the way her skin glowed from the light of the fire. "What's so amusing?"

"This." She motioned at me, then herself, and then the flames. "If you'd told me a few days ago that we'd be sharing a fire on the road again, I probably would have dumped a barrel's worth of ale on your head."

I chuckled. "Good thing I didn't, then, eh? Would have been a waste of good ale."

"Well, I could have used that bitter dross you brewed. It would have saved someone from drinking it." She pressed her lips together, shyly looking up at me with those luminous, dancing eyes.

"Hmm. Keep talking like that, and I'll make some more just for you, using those barrels you asked the carpenter to make."

"You and your brewing skills need to stay far, far away from my barrels."

"Oh yeah?" Smirking, I leaned closer. "And what are you going to do about it?"

Lilia's eyes darted to my lips. She wet her own, her tongue swiping across them. I found it difficult to breathe. Or think. Or feel anything but a tugging, insistent *want*. She was so fates-damned beautiful. In any other situation, I'd tug her into my lap and explore those curves for the rest of the night.

But I wasn't convinced she'd want that. And so I kept my damn hands to myself.

"Ragnar?" she murmured. I nearly groaned at the sound of my name on her lips, so softly spoken, it was like a beckon from the bedroom.

"Yes?" I asked, my voice coming out closer to a growl than I'd intended.

"Do you ever wonder what things might be like if we hadn't shown up in Riverwold as rival tavern owners?" She sucked in a breath, as if anticipating my answer. The weight of that expectation made me pause and consider my words. There was something she wanted me to say, and gods be damned, I wanted to make sure I did.

"Truth be told, I'm happy things turned out as they did. Because it means I'm here with you now, sharing a campfire and talking about ale and life and dragons. How could anything be better than that?"

She seemed to deflate a bit. Inwardly, I cursed

myself. I thought that answer had been pretty damn good.

The firelight splashed across her face, illuminating her reddened cheeks and her lips. "Right, of course. I'm glad it turned out this way, too."

But there was a tightness in her voice. There was something she wasn't saying. Swallowing, she touched a finger to her lips, then looked away into the dark forest. Fates be damned, I was such a fool.

"Lilia." I reached out and tucked a wayward strand of silver hair behind her ear, my fingers gently brushing her skin. She shivered and looked back at me. The flush had crept down her neck. "Come here."

Her eyes darted back and forth between mine. "I am here."

"Come closer, so I can kiss you."

Her lips parted as a shudder went through her. I slid my fingers through her silken hair, gently tugged her to me, and then captured her mouth with mine.

19

Ragnar was kissing me. My mind caught on that thought, repeating endlessly. He had looked at me with a heat I felt within my bones, and then he'd kissed me. Heart thundering, I leaned into him, clutching his tunic. His luxurious lips swept across mine, his fingers still curled into my hair.

When his thumb brushed my cheek, a part of me came undone. I sighed against him, pent-up tension easing, while another part of me found a new reason to clench. Ragnar's hands swept down the length of me and rested on my hips. His touch set me aflame.

His kiss deepened, his tongue spearing my lips. Trembling, a moan crept up my throat. Ragnar groaned in response and lifted me onto his lap. I spread my thighs around him, one leg around each side of his hips. When the hard length of him pressed against me, an ache spread through my core. I couldn't help but shudder.

"Gods, you're beautiful," he murmured against my lips. His strong hands gripped my hips, then travelled to my backside. He shifted against me, and his length brushed my inner thigh.

I clutched at his shirt, unsure how to respond. I'd never done anything like this before.

Suddenly, my belly transformed into a bundle of nerves. What was I doing? Gasping, I pulled back, my heart hammering so hard I swore it might burst right out of my chest.

"Ragnar, I..." I wet my lips, wiping my hair out of my face. "I don't know what got into me. I'm sorry."

His lips curled into a heart-melting smile. "You have nothing to apologize for. I quite like what you're doing right now. Can't you tell?"

Oh, I could tell. There was no mistaking how hard he was. He shifted beneath me again, the length of him driving against just the right spot. Delirious pleasure clutched me by the throat, so intoxicating that I had no idea what to do with myself.

I felt very, very warm, and I didn't think it had anything to do with the heat of Ragnar's power.

"I'm nervous," I finally whispered, worried he might get annoyed by my inexperience. This was the first time anyone had ever touched me like this—the first time I'd *let* anyone touch me like this—and while I wanted to give in to the pull of this heady desire, I also wanted to run.

His eyes softened. "You don't have to be nervous with me, Lil. I would never do something you didn't want."

Releasing his grip on my thighs, he leaned back on his palms and waited for me to take the lead. My heart pounded. I reached out and slid my fingers along his rough jaw. Desire tugged me toward him, impossible to ignore. I'd been so wrong about him when he'd shown up at the festival. This man was strong and powerful, but also kind. And far more gentle than he looked, at least with me. Sighing, I leaned in and kissed him.

His lips moved gently against mine, and his hands stayed right where they were, palming the dirt. Still straddling him, I shifted closer and wound my arms around his neck. And even then, he did not rush me. His kiss was softer now, gentler, and it made my heart beat even wilder than it had before.

When I pulled back, a lazy, satisfied smile lined his lips, even though we'd barely done a thing. "I could spend all night like this, but we should probably finish our meal, eh?"

I relaxed against him. He would have gone so much further, I knew, but he saw my hesitation. His understanding of my inner thoughts made me want to kiss him all over again, but truth be told, my stomach was growling and I hadn't consumed nearly enough water for all our walking.

Slowly, I extracted my tangled limbs from his lap and settled onto the bedroll beside him. I rustled around in my pack, then produced the wrapped slices of cake Nilsa had insisted I bring with me.

His brow raised. "Cake? You've been holding out on me?"

"I was tempted to eat both of them myself, but since you didn't get to finish your pie back there, I figured I could share." I held the cake aloft. As he reached for it, I pulled it back. "Ah, ah. Not so fast. You can have this, but only if you answer a question."

He eyed me skeptically. "Just one question?"

"That's right."

"The look on your face terrifies me."

I grinned. "Do you want the cake or not?"

"Go on then," he said slowly. "Ask your bloody question."

"When I met you that night on the road, did you really have no idea who I was?"

He met my gaze, unblinking. "I didn't know you were the owner of the Traveling Tavern, and therefore, my rival. Not until you told me. I'll swear it on the elements. I'll even swear it on Freya herself. I just thought you were a pretty lass, one I wanted to spend some time with, even if it was only a night."

"So, everything we shared…"

"It was real, Lilia. It's all been real."

"Hmm." I smiled. "Good answer. However, I wonder if I should just keep the cake myself…"

"Oh no you don't!" Ragnar leapt to his feet and swept me off the bedroll. He grabbed me by the waist, tickling my stomach. A fit of giggles took me as I wiggled in his arms.

The sound of our laughter echoed all night long.

R agnar's chest rose and fell beneath me. I curled against him, my head tucked between his shoulder and his chin. Birds chattered in the trees above us, and a light haze had crept into the sky, signalling the start to another day. The embers of the fire had all but burned away, but the heat from Ragnar's body had gotten me through the night. For a few moments, I didn't move. I relished the feel of him and the way my body somehow fit into his, like the curves of me were made for the hard planes of him.

Of course, that was an entirely ridiculous notion that I had no business thinking. One night with the man, and I was getting delirious.

With that thought in mind, I sat up and patted down my hair. Ragnar cracked open his eyes and shot me a smile that bordered on scandalous. All we'd done was kiss, and yet the way I felt…it seemed like so much more had passed between us.

"Good morning, beautiful," he murmured.

I loosed a breath. "Good morning. I hope you slept all right, even though I was crushing your chest."

"I haven't slept that well in months." He smiled a crooked smile, one that sent a new jolt of heat through my core. "And you can crush me anytime you like, darling."

"You charmer," I said with a little smile, tucking my hair behind my ear so that I had something to do with my hands.

"You're cute when you're blushing."

"I'm not blushing."

"If you're not blushing, I'm afraid you're suffering from severe sunburn. Need some salve to put on it? I might have some you could use." Chuckling to himself, he laced his hands beneath his head and winked.

I swatted his chest, then let my hand rest there instead of pulling it back. His corded muscles were as hard as steel. "Someone's feeling frisky this morning."

"Oh, you have no idea."

My heart pounded. I still hadn't moved my hand, and he was looking at me like he was hungry and the other half of the bread roll wasn't what he had in mind. Suddenly, I felt far too nervous to sit. I leapt to my feet and grabbed my pack, hoisting it onto my shoulder.

"If we want to catch up to the pie man, we should probably get going," I said, my words toppling over each other.

Ragnar watched me for a long moment, then he climbed to his feet and helped me pack up the bedroll. Our heads were bent close together, and every now and then, our shoulders brushed. I was so distracted that the bedroll ended up looking like a child had packed it, all scrunched and wrinkled.

Still, I shoved it into my pack and decided I'd sort it out later. Ragnar didn't comment on my flustered behavior, and for that, I was grateful. I wished I could calm myself down. Truly. But when he looked at me—when he smiled—it sometimes scrambled my thoughts so badly, my brain turned to eggs.

"After you." He gestured to the path that cut through the woods.

Mist curled through the trees, fogging the ground. I tugged my pack higher onto my shoulder and rejoined the path we'd found the night before. Dappled morning sunlight shone through the trees; birdsong soaked the air. When Ragnar fell into step beside me, there was something so strangely comforting about his steadying presence there. It wasn't often I walked the lonely road with someone else, but it didn't feel as odd as I'd thought it might.

In fact, there was a quiet inside of me, a calmness to my pace. I didn't feel like I was running away from anything. And it was then I realized I hadn't thought of my past or my late parents in days.

"A gold coin for your thoughts," Ragnar said, his deep voice penetrating the silence.

"You don't want to know. It's sad things."

"Of course I want to know, but only if you feel ready to share." He rubbed the back of his neck. "I know all about sad things, Lil."

I nodded. It seemed like he did. So I said, "I was

thinking about my family back in Edda. I lost them all, other than my brother Rivelin, when I was young. The conquering emperor—the one you fought—he sent his mercenaries into our town after the elves rose up against him. My parents, they told my brother and I to run. We're the only ones who got away. I suppose I've been running ever since."

Brushing a few tears away, I sighed. I couldn't believe I'd told Ragnar all this. It had been a long time since I'd talked about my family. I'd been avoiding it, I realized. And instead of feeling that gaping hole inside me, I almost felt...okay. My feet didn't itch to run.

Ragnar gently placed his hand on my back. "I'm so sorry, Lilia. That bastard killed my family, too."

I looked up at him. "Because of the Elven Resistance?"

"Something like that."

I nodded, and we fell into silence, but it was the good kind of quiet, where you understood the weight of the other person's thoughts. He got me, and I got him, and no words would change our past. But this companionship, this connection...it made it all feel bearable for once.

After a long while, I cleared my throat. "So, you said you'd give me a gold coin if I shared my thoughts. Do you even have any after you paid for that overpriced pie back there? The ones we didn't eat."

He chuckled. "Perhaps *that* is how I'll earn back

the debt my brother owed. Steal a bunch of your ale, bake some pies with it, and sell it for five times the normal asking price."

"You try stealing my next batch of ale, and I'll find a use for the dagger in my waistband." I wrinkled my nose at him.

"Oh ho! She's getting feisty now."

"You haven't seen anything yet. Just wait until we catch up with Thieving Pie Man."

"Thieving Pie Man," Ragnar mused, rubbing his jaw. "That has a mighty fine ring to it. Think he'd mind if I use it on my sign when I start my thieving pie business?"

I giggled. Ragnar grinned. And I was so busy looking up at him that I almost walked into a tree.

"Whoa there." Ragnar caught my arm and wheeled me to safety just in time. Somehow, we ended up facing each other. My palms found his chest. His hands brushed my hips. Swallowing, all I could hear was the *pound, pound, pound* of my racing heartbeat.

"You have a beautiful laugh," said Ragnar, his eyes on my lips. "I wish I heard it more."

"I..."

The clattering of cart wheels jolted through me. Bones practically leaping out of my skin, I jumped back with a hand on my chest. The rattling grew louder, drawing the sound of several voices along with it.

"Is that the pie man?" I whispered, ducking behind a bush.

Ragnar peered through the mist at the road ahead, then looked behind us. Frowning, he shook his head. "It's not coming from either direction."

"Then where can they be?" Cocking my head, I focused my elven hearing on the wheels. The sound roared in my head, coming not from the road but...

I looked toward the left, through the trees, just as Ragnar did. "It's coming from that direction, but how? Surely they wouldn't go through the woods with a cart."

"The road must wind back in on itself as it heads toward the mountains." A wicked smile curved his lips. "You know what that means, don't you?"

"Shortcut to pie man," I murmured.

"Exactly." A mischievous gleam lit his eyes. "We don't have a cart, so we can go through the woods and cut them off on the other side."

20

LILIA

We crept through the brush, carving a path through the trees that would put us squarely in front of Thieving Pie Man when we came out on the other side—if we timed it right. Fallen leaves crunched beneath our steps, and twigs snapped as loudly as thunder. I wanted to shush the ground. If we made too much of a racket, the men in the cart might anticipate an ambush. The patter of my heart gained ground in my ears. We were in the Isles, where peace reigned, not conquerers hell-bent on oppression. Here, we were a community, a gathering of souls who yearned for a better world. None of this should be happening.

I slowed, my hands clenching. Ragnar continued onward until he'd noticed I'd stopped. He backtracked, his brow furrowed. When he stepped in close, my pulse somehow managed to quicken and steady itself at the same time.

"What's wrong?"

"I'm just wondering...what are we about to walk into right now? I don't want to fight anyone, Ragnar. Like you said yesterday, it's just ale. Is it worth all this?"

He tucked a finger beneath my chin. "You know I would never put you in danger, don't you? If Ivar and his friends want to fight when we reach them, we can just walk away. And we won't look back. All right?"

"And what if they won't let us walk away that easily? What if they attack?" I whispered up at him. "The Isles are supposed to be safe, but they don't feel that way right now."

"You just leave that to me." His gaze implored mine. "But if you want to go now, just say the word. I won't make you do anything you don't want to do, Lil."

Lil. He spoke my name as if he'd known me for twenty years.

A tankard's worth of courage suddenly came over me. "No, it's fine. We should at least check things out. Like you said, if anything seems off, we'll just walk away."

"You certain?"

I steadied my breathing, then said, "I'm certain."

With a nod, he led us deeper into the trees. We moved more quickly now. The sound of the cart was growing louder, and we only had a few more moments to reach the path before it passed by us.

Between the growing tension and the hike, I was sweating.

At long last, we reached the tree line. A pock-marked dirt road wound past us, snaking up the side of a hill toward the distant mountains. Soft tufts of grass hissed in the light breeze, and eagles soared through the sun-swept morning sky. The jagged peaks were dashed with snow, glittering like diamonds. It was a glorious sight. But the ever-growing rattle drew my attention away from the beauty.

Ragnar edged in front of me just as the cart drew over a slope in the road. Two human men walked shoulder-to-shoulder. They were lugging the cart behind them, their faces red from the effort. A couple of others trudged along beside them—a man and a woman, both shadow demons. When they noticed us standing in the middle of the road, they all stopped and openly stared.

"Good morning," I tried to say chirpily, but my voice sounded more like a squawk than anything else.

One of the men released the yokes and eyed me warily. He had wild, curly blond hair, piercing blue eyes, and a stocky build that suggested he'd seen his fair share of hard work. The wind tussled his curls as he walked toward us, his faded leather boots barely making a sound. The others stayed right where they were.

"Morning," the man drawled. He stopped a few feet away and eyed us from head to toe, likely wondering where we'd come from. "Everything all right? You're not lost, are you?"

"We're fine," Ragnar answered. "Just being curious, what do you have in your wagon back there? Looks heavy. Need any help?"

The man's eyes narrowed. "We're managing just fine."

My companion suddenly strode forward and stuck out his hand. "Name's Ragnar. Nice to meet you."

Still squinting, the man shook Ragnar's hand. "Ivar. Is there something you two need? If not, I'll have to ask you to move off the road. We need to pass. Days are shorter, you know, and we have a lot of ground to cover."

"You have anything to drink back there?" Ragnar lifted our empty canteen and tipped it sideways. "We didn't come prepared, and my lovely friend back there is awfully thirsty. You know what would go down really well right now? Some ale."

I pressed my lips together. Subtle. Very subtle.

"No," Ivar said, taking a step back. "All we've got is pie."

"Pie?" I tried to crane my neck to see into the back of the cart, but the three others blocked my view. All I could spot was a lumpy blanket protecting the contents beneath it—or hiding them.

Ivar continued to back up. "You two must be the ones who stopped by my house. You're here about the flour, eggs, mushrooms, and venison, aren't you?"

I blinked. "The what?"

"All the food we took from the festival wagons during the storm. Aren't you here to take it back?" He folded his arms. "I'm afraid you're too late. What we didn't sell to the ship that just passed through, we used to bake these pies. Now move out of our way, or I'll have to ask my shadow demon friends back there to *make* you move."

"Wait. You didn't just take our ale, but you stole all the food, too?" I asked, my voice rising to almost a shout.

Ivar snarled.

Ragnar deftly moved in front of me; fire flickered across his extended palm. "Careful what you say and do next, Ivar."

The pie man seemed to shrink into himself. His eyes danced as he watched the flames shift from one of Ragnar's hands to the next. "I didn't steal your bloody ale. We looked for it, and there wasn't any to take."

I frowned. How was that possible? "But you just said you took all the food."

"We did." Ivar threw up his hands. "But we didn't touch the ale. All right?"

This made little sense. If Ivar hadn't taken our kegs, where had they gone? *Someone* had to have taken them. In any other circumstance, I wouldn't believe a word he said, but he'd admitted to taking the food. Why would he bother to lie about the beer?

I touched the back of Ragnar's arm. The heat of his

fire sizzled against my fingers, nearly scalding me. Hissing, I yanked my hand back. Steam whistled from his arm.

Instantly, the flames on his palms vanished. He gently took my hand in his, bringing my fingers up to his eyes. "Lil, are you all right? Did I hurt you?"

"I'm fine." I wiggled my fingers. They'd turned a bright pink, but it would ease up in no time. "See? Just a little redness. Us elves have water magic in our blood, so I suppose that helped."

But he should know that. He was partially elven himself, wasn't he?

He brushed his lips across my pink skin. "Please forgive me. I hope you know I would never intentionally harm you."

"I know."

"Are you two done yet?" Ivar called out impatiently. "I wasn't joking before. If you don't move out of the way, then I—"

Ragnar whirled on him. Any softness I'd seen a moment before vanished from his fiery eyes. "No, we are not done yet. You stole the food from the festival? Well, we're taking it back."

Ivar's mouth dropped open. "You can't. What I didn't sell, I baked into pies."

"Then we're taking the damn pies."

Furious red crested Ivar's cheeks. "You *can't*. I spent hours baking them. Those are my pies, and I'm taking them to the Milford Market, so I can actually earn some coin. That's the only reason I'm doing this, you know? You lot won't let me step foot into Riverwold. So what else am I supposed to do?"

Ivar's shadow demon friends edged closer. Their hands were behind their backs, clearly hiding weapons. Shadows spiralled around their arms.

I frowned. "Ragnar, perhaps we should leave now. They don't have the kegs."

"Hmm. I think you're right." He motioned at the wall of trees beside the road. "We'll go through—"

A rumbling echoed through the clear sky. I looked up, shielding my eyes with my hand, expecting to spot more storm clouds rolling in. But the flash of broad wings against the blue found my eyes instead. Reykur soared toward us, bellowing fire. Plumes of smoke trailed his path.

Ivar paled and fell to his knees. He pressed his fingers to his lips, then touched the ground. "Freya, bless us. Please. Forgive me for what I've done."

Reykur flew over our heads. He swept toward the ground, thundering onto the path on the other side of the cart. Such a clever boy, trapping the cart between us like that. But I didn't want to get him involved in all this.

"Reykur, come!" I called out.

But he stayed right where he was, cocking his head at the shadow demons and the cart heavily laden with pies.

Sobs convulsed Ivar's body. He peered up at me

through tear-streaked eyes, his bottom lip trembling. "Take the damn pies. Just please...please don't roast me."

This was a very extreme reaction.

"Reykur is not going to roast you," I said. "He's just a friendly little dragon. He's harmless, all right?"

"Hmm," said Ragnar.

The tone of his grunt set my bones on edge. I snapped up my gaze. Reykur was creeping toward the cart, his forked tongue slashing at the two shadow demons. Their backs were turned toward me now so they could face him. I could clearly see their hands, and unlike what I'd assumed, they hid no weapons. They'd been bluffing.

But Reykur didn't seem to know that. Wherever he'd been, he must have somehow sensed I was in danger, and he'd come to my rescue. And if he didn't realize the shadow demons were unarmed...well, I truly had no idea what he would do. Never in a million years would he hurt someone innocent. I wasn't sure what he'd do if he thought someone might hurt me. We'd never had cause to find out.

"Reykur!" I shouted. "Everything is fine!"

But the dragon inched even closer to the cart.

The heat of Ragnar's power suddenly washed over me. I stumbled sideways, gasping when I saw the flames erupting along his arms. He strode toward Reykur, his gaze so focused on the dragon that he didn't seem to notice Ivar and his friends abandon the cart and flee for the hills. They ran as fast as their feet could take them.

"Allt er gott, Reykur. Vertu aftur!" shouted Ragnar.

My lips parted. Ragnar was speaking in the ancient orcish tongue. I'd never met an elf who could understand it, much less speak it himself. And while I recognized its cadence, I couldn't understand it.

And if Reykur could, he ignored it. The dragon swung his head from side to side, snorting in irritation. He thundered right on up to the cart, then swiped a taloned claw at the blanket and tossed it aside.

His eyes gleamed as he inspected the contents. I pressed up onto my toes so I could see inside, and it was just as Ivar had said. He'd been lugging around at least a hundred pies, and the glazed crust glistened beneath the sunlight. The savory scent of fried mushrooms drifted toward me.

Reykur suddenly dug his face into the pies and started eating. Chunks of potato and dough sprayed the ground.

My jaw dropped even further. Ragnar doused his flames, and a loud guffaw erupted from his chest. My own lips twitched from the urge to smile, even as I watched all that food vanish into my hungry dragon's mouth. After he tore through at least half of the pies, he looked up and blinked at me. I could have sworn he looked a little guilty.

"Well," Ragnar said, still chuckling. "What do we do now?"

"As far as I tell, there's only one way forward from here." Shrugging, I gave him a little smile. "It's time for me to teach you how to *really* brew some ale."

21

LILIA

Riverwold had devolved into chaos. When we aimed our tired feet toward Nilsa's inn, merchants were squabbling in the packed courtyard, pointing fingers at each other, testing who could make the loudest accusations about who had stolen from whom. Steam practically erupted from their ears. Empty crates littered the ground, and discarded ribbons were drifting on the wind.

"Well, this has certainly escalated," Ragnar said. "What now?"

"We need to find out exactly what Ivar took," I said, searching the crowd for a friendly face.

A line snaked out the door of the inn. The banging of pots and pans drifted from Nilsa's kitchen. I spotted Steffon's horns peeking out from the alley and elbowed Ragnar. Together, we shouldered our way through the crowd. As soon as Steffon saw us coming, he patted his forehead with a rag and ducked out of view.

"He looks like he's been through it," Ragnar murmured.

"Everyone is probably demanding for him to fix things, but last time I checked, not even shadow demons can make ale and food appear from thin air."

We reached the outskirts of the crowd and ducked into the alley. Steffon sat slumped on a crate in the shadows beside Nilsa's back door. His horned head was tipped back against the stone wall, and his eyes were closed. He sighed as we approached, clearly hearing our boots tapping the ground.

"Hello, Lilia. You're empty-handed, so I'm going to assume you didn't find your missing kegs," he said wearily.

"I'm afraid not," I said, perching beside him on the crate.

"Figured as much." He cracked open his eyes. "Unfortunately, I have some more bad news. There was another thieving incident while you were gone."

"I know. A lot of the food has gone missing."

He sat up straight, his dark hair falling into his shadow-filled eyes. Then his gaze shifted to Ragnar, and he frowned. "How do you know about that? Did *he* do something?"

"Leave Ragnar alone. He had nothing to do with this," I said quickly. "You remember a man named Ivar, right? Apparently, you banned him from River-wold and from the festival a long time ago."

"Wait, *he* did this?" Steffon stood and began to pace the skinny alley. Every time he turned, his cloak dramatically whipped around his black boots. "I should have guessed. Ivar has been begging me to undo his ban for years." He came to a sudden stop. "I suppose he finally decided to get his revenge by stealing everything!"

I frowned up at him. "I don't think he wanted revenge as much as he thought he could use the food to make some coin. It doesn't look like he has much opportunity down by the sea. His taproom is…very quiet." That was the kindest way to put it, I supposed.

Steffon looked at me as if I'd spoken in a language he didn't understand. "Don't let him fool you, Lilia. He's stolen so much food that we won't have enough for Yule now. All of Karl's smoked meats are gone. We'll have nothing to drink. Nothing to eat. The festival is *ruined*. I'll have to call it off. Unless…" He paused, arching a hopeful brow. "If Ivar stole it all, perhaps we can get it back. I just need a few extra hands to carry everything up that monstrous mountain path, so come on. We should ask Herold if they'll join us, too."

Nodding to himself, he started toward the mouth of the alley. He paused when he noticed Ragnar and I had made no move to follow him.

He frowned back at us. "Well, come along now. We should get going so we can be back by sundown."

"No need. You won't find any food at Ivar's house," Ragnar said quietly.

Clearly perplexed, Steffon scratched his chin. "What are you talking about? You just said he took it all."

"He did. But it's not at his house anymore," I said.

Steffon propped fisted hands on his waist. "Well, then all the more reason to get moving so we can catch up to him. He's likely taking it to Milford so he can sell it at their market. They haven't banned him there. Yet."

Shifting on the crate, I exchanged a glance with Ragnar. I didn't really know how to explain that my dragon had eaten some of the food, simply because none of the Riverwold townspeople—other than Nilsa—knew about him. And I didn't think now was a wonderful time to terrify them with this information. Tensions were already so high.

But I didn't much like half-truths, either. I'd played a part in this, and I should come clean, if only so Steffon understood the full weight of what we faced. The food was gone. There was no getting it back.

I cleared my throat. "Ivar sold a lot of it to a ship that just passed through. And the rest of it, well…you know how my brother has been keeping four adolescent dragons."

Steffon paled. "Everyone in the Isles knows about that. What does that have to do with Ivar? Don't tell me he stole a dragon, too. We'll have to evacuate the town." He wrung his hands. "He'll try to—"

"The dragon is mine," I said firmly.

"What?"

"I'm the one with the dragon. Not Ivar," I repeated, standing. "And he's been with me for years, following me around the Isles while I wander from town to town with my Traveling Tavern. He's always stayed out of sight until now, but as he gets older, his courage grows with him. And well, he found Ivar's cart of stolen food, then ate it all. I suppose he was a little hungry…"

Ragnar's lips twitched; merriment danced in his eyes. A part of me saw the humor in it, too, but I knew Steffon too well to laugh about this right in front of him. His shadows were very agitated, whipping around his body like angry black wasps.

For a long moment, Steffon didn't answer. I braced myself for his rebuke. But eventually, his shoulders slumped, the shadows stilled, and he sighed. "Well, at least someone got to enjoy the food. I'm afraid it *does* mean I'll have to call off the festival, though. I suppose it's for the best with the way the weather's been. It's just not fated to happen this year."

"Wait." I took a step toward him. "You're not angry about the dragon?"

Steffon's expression softened. "Lilia, I've known about your dragon for years now. We all have. We've seen him soaring through the sky every time you've arrived for Yule. Didn't take much to put two and two together."

"I thought everyone in Riverwold was terrified of the dragons."

He shrugged. "They were, but I think they're coming around to it now. It's been a few years and nothing terrible has happened yet. Besides, we all love you and know you'd never do anything to put anyone in danger. And if you care for that dragon, well, he can't be so bad, now can he?"

"Oh." I found myself looking over my shoulder at Ragnar, searching for his gaze. He smiled encouragingly.

"Anyway." Steffon sighed. "I best get this over with."

I touched his arm. "No, wait. Don't cancel Yule just yet. We can sort this out."

"Unless your dragon can give us back that food, I don't see how we can possibly continue on."

"We still have all our performers," I tried. "Plus, there's all the merchants selling ribbons, smoking pipes, candles, clothes, and books. I even saw someone with a blacksmith stand. There are some gorgeous metal sculptures for sale."

"The feast is the most important part of Yule," he said sadly. "And while I know it's not the end of the world, it wouldn't be the same without your ale, Lilia. Everyone gets so lively and happy, clanking their tankards and dancing to the music."

I nodded. "I'm working on the ale. Don't you worry about that. As far as the food is concerned…let me call in a favor from a friend of mine. I think I can get enough food for Yule if you and Nilsa can manage to keep people fed until then."

Steffon took a few halting steps toward me, then grasped my hands. Imploringly, he searched my eyes, his shadows coming alive again. "You can do this, truly?"

"I think so, Steffon. I'll do my best." After all, it was partially my fault.

"May Freya bless you," he murmured. A beaming smile stretched across his lips. With a quick kiss on my forehead, he released my hands and started to bustle toward the mouth of the alley, calling out behind him, "I'll reassure everyone that the festival will go on. Yule may be saved after all!"

Once he'd vanished around the corner, Ragnar stepped up to my side, folding his arms. "That was quite the promise you made. Can you really get enough food for Yule?"

"I'm not sure. Maybe." I cut my eyes toward him. "I might need some help."

He arched a brow. "Some help, eh? I'm afraid you might be out of luck. Nilsa seems entirely too busy to handle anything else right now."

"You know what? You're right. It sounds like she's up to her elbows in food orders. And since I can't think of *anyone* else to ask," I said with a slight smile, "I guess that means I'll have to manage it all by myself."

"Good thing you're capable of doing anything you put your mind to, Lilia."

I elbowed him in the side. "You're really going to make me come right out and ask, aren't you?"

He caught my arm and twirled me to face him. The heat in his eyes rushed over me, lighting up every inch of my skin. It took everything in me not to melt beneath his gaze. "You don't have to ask. Tell me what to do, and I'm all yours."

My heartbeat thrummed in my neck. "For the festival."

"Right. The festival."

I swallowed as he edged closer, backing me up against the wall. He palmed the stone on either side of my head, leaned in, and pressed his lips to my ear. An uncontrollable shiver coursed through me. His breath caressed my skin.

"I need to sort out some things in my wagon," he murmured, his lips gently moving against my ear. I barely even latched on to the meaning of his words, too focused on his chest against mine, my back against the wall, and the scent of his fire roaring through me. "Come find me when you're ready for me."

22

LILIA

"Lilia! Oh, thank fate. I need your help."
Nilsa's normally smooth black hair had
sprang free of its braid, and curling, frizzy
strands stuck out in all directions. Green and purple
stains garnished her apron, and a few breadcrumbs
clung to her cheek. Just over her shoulder, the entire
kitchen was in disarray, and her partner was nearly
hidden behind a pile of teetering pans. I hovered just
inside the back door, tempted to retrace my steps into
the alley.

"Are you quite all right, Nilsa?" I carefully asked.

Nilsa latched onto my arm and hauled me inside.
"Did you see the line out the door? How many more
people are waiting? Where's Steffon? He promised to
help chop those potatoes, and then he escaped when I
wasn't watching him."

She pointed at an overturned crate in the corner,
where she'd pulled together a makeshift workstation.

Two dozen potatoes piled on top of it, peeled but not chopped.

"He's off trying to restore some order, I think," I told her. "I've got an idea on how to save Yule."

She sagged against me. "Thank fate. I don't know how much longer I can cook like this."

"*I* can cook, you mean," Herold called out over the pile of pans. "You're over there chatting up a storm while I'm melting at the stove all by myself!"

"It's going to take a few days to sort out some more food. In the meantime, we'll get you some help." I rolled up my sleeves. "Where should I start?"

Nilsa motioned at the potatoes Steffon had abandoned. After washing my hands, I got stuck in. I'd helped Nilsa out in the kitchen before, so I knew how she liked her potatoes sliced, and I knew where to find a bowl to hold them. The next hour passed quickly, my mind calming from the steady work. Every now and then, the thought of Ragnar made me forget what I was doing. His eyes and those rough, steady hands. I hadn't yet asked him about what he'd done at Ivar's cart, how he'd known the words that only dragons and orcs could understand.

As I worked, the back of my neck prickled, like someone was watching me. But when I looked up, it was just Nilsa and Herold there, focused on their cooking. Shaking my head, I got back to chopping. The long days were clearly wearing on me.

Eventually, the crowd in line for food began to thin, and Nilsa bustled over and shooed me toward the stairs. "Thanks for your help. You look dead on your feet. Go get some rest. But tomorrow morning, I want to hear everything. And I do mean *everything*."

Nilsa was right. Exhaustion hung around me like a rain-logged cloak, dragging down my eyelids. I trudged up the stairs and climbed into bed fully clothed. A part of me wondered if I should go to Ragnar's wagon and invite him inside, but my eyes slid shut before I could swing my feet back onto the floor.

I knocked on the side of Ragnar's wagon, awkwardly trying not to spill the mug of tea I'd carried out for him. My other hand was weighed down by my own, steam curling from the top. Over-head, a bright morning sun lit the festival grounds. The mud had finally begun to dry out, and merchants were beginning to unpack their carts and wagons again.

Waiting for Ragnar's response to my knock, I bounced from foot to foot, wondering if I should try again later. He'd told me to come by anytime, but that had been yesterday. What if he'd changed his mind? What if he regretted kissing me? What if he'd slept on things and realized he was better off keeping a distance from the girl whose dragon ate all the pie?

After several too-long moments passed, I turned back to town, swallowing down my disappointment.

"Where do you think you're going?" Ragnar's deep, melodic voice sounded from behind me.

My heart kicked my ribs. Trying not to look too overeager, I slowly turned back toward him and shrugged. "Thought I'd find someone more interested in this tea."

He hopped out of the wagon, the burlap fluttering behind him. He'd donned a pair of fitted brown trousers and a blue vested top that left his biceps exposed to the chill, though he didn't seem to notice it. His hair was damp and curling around his ears. He must have taken a bath somewhere. A vision of what he might look like fully naked popped into my head. It didn't take much imagination. I'd already seen enough to have a pretty good idea.

Heat flooded my cheeks.

Smiling, he strode toward me. A few nearby merchants called out to him, but he kept his eyes on me.

"Morning, Lil," he said when he reached me. I held up the mug wordlessly. When he took it from me, his knuckles slid against mine, and my stomach transformed into a thousand frantic butterflies.

"Morning," I answered. "Sorry about the cold night. I hope the tea can make up for it."

"You know I don't mind the cold. But I appreciate the thought anyway." He took a sip, then wrinkled his nose. "What in fate's name is this?"

"Nilsa's morning brew, sure to wake you up and

put a fire in your belly." I grinned. "There's a lot of cinnamon in it."

He took another sip and then pounded a fist against his chest. "It's eye-wateringly strong."

"And I bet you're not sleepy now."

"You're enjoying this far too much." He shoved the mug toward me, but I danced back a few steps. "If I have to suffer, so do you."

"I already had three sips of my own, and that was enough."

He took one more sip, grimacing. "There. I've had my three. Please tell me I won't offend Nilsa if I pour the rest of this on the ground."

"I won't tell her if you don't mention I only had a few sips of it myself."

"Deal." Chuckling, Ragnar tipped the cinnamon concoction on the ground, adding another layer to the mud.

"So, you ready?" I asked him.

"Absolutely," he said, handing me the empty mug. "Let's see how the expert brews her ale."

"Not quite," I replied. "We have an errand to run first. The missing food, remember?"

A slow smile spread across his face. "Oh, that. Are you finally going to say you need my help with it, then?"

"I don't *need* your help, Ragnar." I sidled up to him, leaving no more than a hair's breadth between our chests. "But I will admit I want it. All I ask is for you to promise you won't tell a soul what you're about to see. That includes everyone here in Riverwold and everyone back home, wherever that is."

A cloud crossed his face, and for a moment, I thought he might refuse me. He was silent for far too long.

I frowned. "Is that a problem?"

"No." He ran his fingers through his thick crimson hair. "I just don't like to think about home, that's all." A sigh. "Of course I'll keep your secrets, Lilia. My only question is…what could be a bigger secret than a dragon?"

I smiled. "Oh, you'll see."

The Golden Falls fell in a sheet of water that was the color of ice. Sunlight gleamed across the rippling surface, transforming patches of the rushing river below into a kaleidoscope of pinks, oranges, and midnight blues. It was like gazing into another world.

Ragnar and I stood on the ridge, wind whipping our hair into knots, but his wagon perched behind us and blocked the worst of it. It had taken us nearly all day to drag the thing up the path into the lower mountain ridge. My body buzzed from the effort. My heart was pumping, my lungs were full, and every sense felt wild and alive, singing even in the cold.

After several long moments, I felt the weight of Ragnar's gaze on me. I turned to find him examining my face, his lips tilted up in one corner.

I brushed the tangled hair out of my eyes, suddenly self-conscious. "What?"

"You love this so much," he said quietly. "The wilds, the walks, the wandering road. There's this look you get when we're out here. You don't have it in Riverwold. It's pure contentment."

"Don't you think it feels good to move?"

"There's nothing else like it," he said, his eyes growing distant. "But it's been a very long time since I've really spread my wings."

"That's not true. You came all the way here from the mainland, didn't you?"

A heavy sigh was his only answer. And before I could ask him to clarify, he changed the subject. "So, are you finally going to tell me what we're doing here and why we had to bring my wagon?"

"All right. But you have to swear you won't jump to conclusions. Just…stay calm when I tell you," I warned him.

His brow arched high. "If I wasn't intrigued before, then I certainly am now."

I nibbled on the inside of my cheek. Not even Nilsa or my brother knew about this. Truth be told, I could have come here on my own, but I wanted to share this with Ragnar. Deep down, I wanted to know how he'd react. I needed to know if he was the kind of man I thought—*hoped*—he was.

"A friend of mine lives in the caves behind that waterfall," I finally said, pointing at the crystal sheet of water.

"I've never known someone to live in a cave." He cocked his head. "Is this friend another dragon? Are there more here on the Isles than the four you mentioned earlier? Is that why you're being so secretive about this?"

"Ulrika is not a dragon," I answered softly. "She's a mountain troll."

I held my breath and waited, bracing myself for either fear or anger. Maybe both. Mountain trolls were considered vicious and savage. They kept to themselves and their clans, killing anyone who stepped foot on their territory. Only a few lived in the Isles, as far as I was aware, but most people didn't know that. I'd long been afraid they'd run them out if they discovered them, all in the name of protecting the Isles. But the trolls who lived here meant no one harm. They were good folk.

"You have a very eclectic group of friends," Ragnar finally said with a chuckle. "Shall we go and say hello, then?"

The tension in my shoulders unspooled. "You're not worried about her shooting an arrow into your throat for trespassing?"

He shrugged. "You said she's a friend. That's enough for me."

My hands itched to reach out for him, but I kept them firmly by my side, even as my heart swelled. "Ragnar, I..."

He turned to me then. The sunlight curled across his broad jaw, catching the fire in his eyes. His sleeveless tunic whipped around his chest, and the spicy scent of him billowed into me. I looked at him, and he looked at me, and suddenly, the world seemed to make sense for once. *This man.* I felt like I'd been looking for him my whole life, and I'd never realized it until now.

I didn't want to be alone anymore. Not when there was someone like him.

"What is it, Lilia?" he murmured, sliding his thumb along my jawbone.

I swallowed at his touch, my heart pattering like a wild thing. "I'm sorry I misjudged you that first day in Riverwold. I assumed the worst. I shouldn't have."

His eyes searched mine, and a strange expression flickered across his face. "Lilia, there's something I need to tell you. I'm—"

"Well, if it isn't Lilia bloody Asker," a voice called out, cutting Ragnar off. "Are you going to come down here anytime soon? Or are you going to make moon eyes at your fellow for another two damn years, which is how long it's been since you visited me, by the way."

Ragnar's gaze shuttered. He snapped his mouth shut and turned toward the falls, where Ulrika was watching us. Whatever he'd been about to tell me would have to wait.

23

LILIA

Ulrika pounced on me when we dipped behind the rush of water. She swept me up into her arms and spun me in a circle, the toes of my boots barely skimming the cave's floor. She smelled like earth and wet rock, and a deep, damp chill seemed to seep from her skin.

When she finally put me down, she stepped back, like she wanted to get a good look at me. It had been two years since my last visit, but not much about her had changed. At almost seven feet tall, she towered over both of us. Her pale blue skin shimmered in the glow of the sunlit water reflecting into the cave, and long ears, as sharp as swords, cut through her matching hair. Leathers covered her chest and hips but barely anything else. And as she smiled, her tusks wiggled against her teeth.

"You look good," she said with a nod. Then she

jerked her thumb at Ragnar. "Now who the fuck is this?"

"I'm Ragnar." He held out an arm.

Ulrika looked him up and down. "You smell funny."

I nearly choked. "Ulrika!"

"What? I'm just saying the truth. He looks like an elf, but he isn't one." She held up a hand when I started to speak. "Not a fire demon, either, if that's what you're going to say." Then she shrugged. "Seems all right, though."

Ulrika grabbed Ragnar's forearm, and he took hers. They shook like two warriors who had allied against a common foe. Flummoxed, all I could do was watch as they exchanged their greetings. When they released their arms, Ulrika turned and swept through the cave as if nothing unusual had happened.

"Come! I had a hunch you were coming, so I prepared some mushroom tea," she tossed over her shoulder.

Ragnar leaned in close, our shoulders brushing as we followed Ulrika into the darkness. "Mushroom tea?"

"It's quite good," I assured him. "And besides, Ulrika doesn't take no for an answer."

"That does not surprise me in the least," he murmured.

We wound through a series of tunnels, the rush of the falls vanishing behind us. Moss and lichen crept along the walls, carpeting the stone beneath our feet. An orange light glowed in the distance. When we finally reached its source, a small cavern opened up before us.

Stone steps curved down to a sandy platform jutting out over a body of milky water, lit by gemstones hanging from the ceiling above. A small fire crackled beside a single cozy chair, where a book had been left on the cushion. There were several shelves stuffed with all manner of tools: cooking utensils, scrolls, and shovels. A row boat bobbed near the edge of the platform, laden with fishing nets and spears.

Ulrika jogged down the stairs, motioning us forward. "You coming? This tea won't drink itself."

We followed her down the stairs. She sat cross-legged beside the fire, taking a pot off the flames and filling three wooden cups with the liquid within.

"Go on. Sit." She wagged her finger at me. "You came all this way. Least I can do is host you properly."

I nibbled on my bottom lip as I eased into the seat, suddenly feeling guilty. Ulrika thought I'd come here just to see her, rather than ask a favor. It had likely been months since she'd seen another face, if not longer. I couldn't bear to disappoint her. Ragnar must have read the look on my face because he dealt me a knowing nod. He would let me decide if we should ask her for help, though he was likely having a hard time seeing what she could do here in her cozy little cave with her meager belongings.

Ulrika proudly handed me a steaming mug, then passed another to Ragnar. He took a tentative sniff.

"Drink up. I imagine you're cold from your walk here." She tensed, squinting at him, clearly eager to hear his response.

"I don't get cold," he said, lifting the mug to his lips. "But I am thirsty, so thank you."

Ulrika nodded, as if he'd said exactly what she'd suspected. "You're not from around here, are you?"

"Ulrika, *no one* is from around here, not really. We all came to the Isles from somewhere else," I cut in. "Speaking of, have you heard what's been going on in Riverwold?"

Her eyes slid toward me, and a wicked, tusky grin split her lips. "Ivar passed by this morning with a bunch of his friends. Overheard them muttering about you two in fact. And your dragon." She barked a laugh. "Seems Reykur's gotten mighty bold eating a whole cart-load of pies." Her smile suddenly slid from her face. "Wish I could have seen it myself."

A heaviness settled on my shoulders. "Ulrika, you don't have to stay hidden in the mountains all by yourself. Hearthaven, all the Isles…it's a different place than anywhere else. People will accept you for who you are."

She gave me a pointed look. "And do they accept your dragon?"

I frowned. "Well, no. Not yet. But—"

"Until then, I don't see how the people of River-wold would invite a mountain troll into their town with open arms." Sighing, she closed her eyes and turned away. Wet tracks stained her blue cheeks. "The Isles are better lands than anywhere else, but that doesn't make them perfect. That doesn't make the people in them perfect, either." Sighing, she tipped the entire contents of her tea down her throat, then wiped her lips with the back of her arm.

I sat up a little straighter. I'd come here to ask for a favor, but a better idea took shape in my mind. "I think I might know how to fix that, but only if you'd like me to try."

The distant trickle of falling water was my only answer until she leaned back on her palms, arching a skeptical brow. "I'm listening."

"You heard about the pies, right? So you must know how Ivar made them?" I asked.

She huffed. "Let me guess. Not by honest means."

"He stole most of the food for Yule, baked some of it into pies, and sold the rest to a ship that's long gone," I said.

"Don't forget the ale," Ragnar added.

Ulrika blinked. "That bastard stole your ale, too?"

"He says he didn't." I shrugged. "But someone did."

"Oh, I see where you're going with this." She shoved up to her feet, towering over me. "You've got no food or drink for Yule, so you want me to come in and save the day. And you think that'll make the townspeople warm up to me? It won't work, Lilia."

"Yule means the world to them. If you save the festival, they'll not only warm up to you, but they'll also put a crown of flowers on your head and build a statue in your honor." I smiled up at her. "Come on. You know it's a good idea."

She turned away, gazing across the milky pool of water. "'Cept, it won't be me saving the damn festival. I just happened to stumble into the right cave at the right time and nothing more. And once they find that out, they'll likely seize this place for themselves."

"We won't tell them about the cave. I'll swear it on Freya," Ragnar cut in. Even though he had no idea what Ulrika meant, he held out his arm again. Ulrika looked down at his offered hand, then back up to his eyes. With a solemn nod, she grasped his arm and held on tight, as if he were a lifeline in the dark.

"Only a monster can see into the heart of a monster," she murmured so softly I couldn't be sure I'd heard her right.

Ragnar cleared his throat. "So, do either of you want to tell me what in fate's name you're talking about?"

I looked at Ulrika, who merely shrugged. If I wanted Ragnar to understand, I'd have to explain it myself.

"Well," I began, "just think of it like this. The

island is alive, and you're currently standing inside the heart of it."

Ragnar looked around, as if seeing the cave for the first time. He took in the glowing gemstones, the milky lake, and the boat that seemed to shift on the water despite the stillness. Kneeling, he placed his fingers to the platform and brushed the sand. Closing his eyes, he breathed in.

"This is Galdur sand," he said, his eyes flying back open. "There are hundreds of them, all over this platform. You even have Fildur sand here… Do you not know how rare it is to have access to this amount of fire magic?"

"We both understand. And I'm going to have to ask for you to leave them all here," Ulrika said, coming to stand right behind him so that he couldn't bolt.

He brushed all the sand from his hands and stood. "Can I ask why? There's enough here to make you rich beyond measure."

Or to pay off a steep debt.

The thought popped into my head before I could stop it. But it was there, bubbling in the back of my mind. Because I recognized the glint in Ragnar's eyes. He only got it when he was thinking about his brother and the mainland. The debt he'd vowed to pay back. The entire reason he was even here.

But I'd assumed the worst about him once, and I'd been wrong. I didn't want to make the same mistake again. So I bottled up all that doubt and shoved it deep down. Still, I couldn't shake my uneasiness. He was clearly hiding something from me.

"I do not want to be rich," Ulrika said tightly. "The island gives me what I need, and I take no more than that."

I set my now-cold mug of tea on the table beside the armchair and went over to them. "That's why we can't tell anyone about this. If the wrong person found out about this place, they could steal all this sand and drain the island of its power."

Ragnar looked at me, surprised. "That could happen?"

I nodded, but Ulrika was the one to elaborate "Magic is not infinite. If we take too much, the island could die."

"When was the last time you asked the island for something?" I asked.

She rubbed her chin. "Several months now. So, it will be safe. Just don't let Ivar steal from you again. You won't be able to get any more supplies after this. Not for at least a few more months."

"And Yule will be long over by then."

Ulrika nodded and knelt on the sandy platform, her bare knee against the wood. Carefully, she collected four grains of sand, one for each of the elements. One by one, she dropped them in the milky lake. The three of us watched them vanish, the distant dripping the only noise in the heavy silence.

"As the keeper of your heart, I come to you with a request," Ulrika began with a solemn voice that echoed through the cavern. "We are in great need of grains, vegetables, and eggs. Meats and fruits would also be enthusiastically accepted. But we will gladly take whatever you can provide us, small or large. And in return, I will continue to protect the heart of this island until the day I die."

24

LILIA

"Well, that bag of oats was the last of it." Ulrika pounded the side of the wagon with a fist that was twice the size of mine. "Seems you're all loaded up now. You sure you don't want to stay the night?"

While we'd been inside the cavern, the inky blue of dusk had pushed the sun below the horizon. Scudding clouds dampened the moonlight, and a harsh breeze blew in from the distant sea. I'd thrown on the cloak I'd packed in Ragnar's wagon, but the chill still seeped through the wool.

"It's only an hour or so back to Riverwold, and I'd really like to get back. Besides, Ragnar is well-equipped to see at dusk," I said.

Ulrika dealt him a piercing stare. "Of course he is. Makes sense."

"Makes sense for what?" I couldn't help but ask. She clearly had suspicions about Ragnar, and I wished she'd stop dancing around it. Why hadn't she thrown it all out in the open, like she normally did?

She gave Ragnar a long-considering look, then shrugged. "I'll let him tell you when he's ready. In the meantime, you two best get going if you don't want to stay. The evening is young, but it won't be for long."

Shoving down my curiosity, I threw my arms around her solid torso and hugged her tight. She lifted me from the ground, like I weighed less than a sack of potatoes, and clung to me. When she put me down, I could have sworn her eyes were glazed with tears.

"I'll be back soon," I promised her. "With an invitation to join us for Yule."

"I suppose if anyone can convince them, it's you." Smiling, she turned to Ragnar, flashing her teeth. "Take good care of her, or I'll show you why us mountain trolls have the reputation that we do."

I sighed. "Ulrika."

"You have my word," Ragnar said solemnly. "I would rather stand in the flames than have her get burned."

"Well, I would certainly hope so," Ulrika said with a crisp nod.

"The two of you are impossible." I grabbed Ragnar's arm and tugged him toward the wagon. "Come on, let's get going before you start breaking out into battle stances."

"Safe travels," Ulrika called after us.

I offered her one final wave goodbye and led Ragnar to the front of his wagon. Together, we heaved up the yokes and pulled it back onto the path that led into town. The rumbling wheels swallowed up the silence, the heavier yoke digging into my hands. We'd weighed down the wagon with sacks of potatoes, flour, oats, honey, and dried meats. It was enough food for Yule and more.

Halfway back to Riverwold, the bulging clouds cracked open and heaved out a torrential downpour of rain. The wind churned up leaves and grass, throwing it into us. Ragnar dropped the yoke, grabbed my hand, and threw aside the burlap. He lifted me up with his hands around my waist, tossing me inside just as lightning crackled nearby.

He thundered in behind me and tied the burlap shut as tight as he could get it. The wagon shook from the force of the wind.

It had only been seconds, but the rain had seeped into my cloak. It dripped onto my boots, soaking the leather. But it was so dark inside the wagon, I could see nothing but the vague outline of the crates and sacks of food piled around us.

"The Elding strikes again," I said, my warm breath frosting the air. "Hopefully, this storm doesn't endure as long as the last one did."

It had taken all day and night for the Elding to take its rain-logged clouds and wind and edge back over the sea. At least we'd been in town that time.

Now we were stuck out in the hills, cramped inside a fully packed wagon.

"At least we have enough food," Ragnar said with a quiet chuckle.

Despite the circumstances, I grinned. "Ulrika might very well track you down and make good on her threats if you eat all her food before it gets to Riverwold."

His laughter grew deeper, warmer. The sound was like a soothing heat against the chill. "I don't doubt it for a moment."

The wind gusted against the side of the wagon, rocking the wheels. I stumbled forward. Ragnar caught me in his arms. In the dark, the fiery glint of his eyes was the only thing I could see.

"You're shivering," he murmured.

My teeth were chattering, but I'd been so distracted by everything else I hadn't noticed. Gently, Ragnar unclasped the front of my cloak and tugged the wet material away from my body. It did little good. My tunic had gotten wet, and the chill had well and truly seeped into my skin.

"It's a shame we can't build a fire," I said, half-joking.

Ragnar held up his palm, and flames came alive on his skin. Sudden warmth blasted toward me, its lambent glow spilling across the cramped space. It was only now I could properly see him. His wet hair sent droplets down his cheeks, and his curls kissed his sharply pointed ears. I had the sudden urge to reach up and brush the strands out of his eyes. And for the first time, I finally did it.

My fingers tiptoed across his warm skin. Steam hissed between us. He tensed beneath my touch; his breath caught. The flames on his palm dulled to a pale flicker, but the heat remained. Even so, my damp tunic clung to my skin, and I could not shake the cold.

Ragnar frowned. "You're still trembling."

"I'll be all right."

"This could go on for hours." Jaw tightening, he glanced around the wagon. He pointed at the corner behind me. "I have some dry blankets back there. You should get out of those wet clothes and bundle up. Try to sleep if you can."

He started to move toward the back flap.

I reached for him. "Wait, where are you going?"

"I told you before, I don't mind the cold. I meant storms, too." He gestured at the small scrap of floor where I stood. "There's hardly any room in here, and you should have your privacy."

"Ragnar, don't be a fool. You can't just stand outside during the Elding." I shook my head at him, scarcely believing his words. Surely he didn't expect me to kick him out of his own bloody wagon during a storm.

The tension in his face tightened the muscles around his eyes. "There's something about me you need to know, although I'm sure you've guessed that by now."

"Yes, Ulrika's sneaky comments gave that away," I

said slowly. "But what does that have to do with any of this?"

He came closer, his flames dancing up his arms. "Because of what I am, and the magic I carry within me. Storms can be brutal to the others, but they don't hurt me. Not anymore."

I furrowed my brow, trying to make sense of his words. "Storms hurt the others? The only person I've ever met that had trouble with storms is Daella, and that's only because she's half-orc, and..." Realization thundered into me. The fire. The scent. The suggestion in Ulrika's words. "Wait, are you part orc? Why didn't you just say so?"

But even as I voiced the question, I knew that it couldn't be true. It made little sense. If he had orc in his blood, he'd have a sensitivity to fresh water, just as Daella did. It wouldn't explain his ability to conjure fire from thin air, either. Orcs could not do that.

So then what was he saying?

"I am not orc," he said quietly. "I was once something else that, like orcs, have a sensitivity to rainfall. But not anymore."

I searched his gaze and whispered, "What are you?"

He took my hand in his and pressed my palm against his chest. The mad beat of his heart pounded through me like a drumbeat, an old familiar rhythm. *Thump, thump-thump-thump, thump, thump-thump-*

thump. It was not the steady heartbeat of the folk. But I had heard it before.

Sleeping near Reykur on those cold nights.

My lungs ceased to breathe. Shaking my head, I did not dare say it aloud. It was impossible.

"You can't be," I said, my voice as soft as a feather in the air.

"I was once a dragon, Lilia. My brother and I both were. A group of orcs found us after Isveig killed the rest of our family. They wanted to save us, so they took us to a pool of water hidden in the mountains, much like the one Ulrika guards. They begged the gods to protect us from the conquering emperor. And the gods answered. Galdur magic transformed me into…whatever I am now. I'm not an elf, but I look like one, and I no longer have scales. The rain does not harm me."

He held up his arms, the impossible fire raging across his indestructible body. Awed, I lifted my hand to feel the heat of him again, understanding now why he'd always felt so achingly familiar. But the flames suddenly died, and he stepped back.

"So now you understand," he said. "Warm yourself up in those blankets. I'll be outside."

He turned away from me. His boots thunked against the wood. Undoing the ties that held the burlap in place, he took a breath, as if bracing himself for the coming onslaught of wind and rain. He might be immune to its effects, but that didn't mean he would enjoy it.

"Stay," I said.

Heaving a sigh, he shook his head. "You don't need to worry about me. I promise you, Lilia, it's fine."

Clearing my throat, I steadied my voice. "I'm not worried. I just want you to stay."

His hand fell to his side, leaving the ties where they were. As he turned, a new flame took shape inside me, burning so hotly that I forgot about my wet clothes, my tangled hair, and what little room we could share inside this space. I just wanted him to touch me, to feel me, to take me in his impossible arms.

"You're not...disgusted by what I am?" he asked in a tight voice.

"Disgusted?" Shaking my head, I rushed toward him and slid my hands up the length of his chest, resting them on his shoulders. "How could I possibly be disgusted by you?"

"I am a dragon," he said, grinding out the words. "Most people would think I'm a monster."

"You are Ragnar," I breathed. "And that is all that matters to me."

He slid his hands around my backside and lifted me into his arms. And then he kissed me.

25

The kiss was more feverish this time, like a dam had cracked opened inside him. All the pent-up emotions he hid from the world were rushing out of him and into me. I welcomed the flood. Wrapping my legs around him, I kissed him back, matching his intensity. He groaned as he stumbled forward and slammed me against the side of the wagon. The rough interior bit into my back, but I barely felt it.

His lips skimmed my jaw, leaving a trail of sparks to my ear. With his breath hot on my skin, I shuddered. He nipped at my neck, his teeth grazing me, and everything within me fell apart against him.

Whatever nerves I'd felt last time were gone. I just wanted him. All of him.

Dropping my head against the wall, I speared his hair with my fingers, gently nudging him lower. He needed no more encouragement than that. He tugged down the front of my tunic until the low-cut neckline slid beneath the bottom curve of my breast, exposing my nipple. My peak tightened in the cold air.

His warmth consumed me as his tongue drifted across my breast. I arched against him, tightening my grip on his hair.

Gently, he cupped my exposed breast and explored every inch with his tongue, lighting up my core with an ache that throbbed through me like a thunderstorm. He shifted closer; his hard length drove into the apex of my thighs.

The building heat between us settled there.

Desperate for more, I tugged at his clothes. He lowered me to the floor and yanked off his tunic, tossing it into the far corner of the wagon. My eyes consumed the hard planes of his chest, scarred by his struggles. I reached out for him. Only a second passed before he erased the distance between us again, like he couldn't bear for our bodies to be apart.

His muscles gleamed as he lowered himself over me. I slid my hands across his shoulders and chest. Every angle was like a mountain peak, built to perfection. Trailing one finger down his stomach, I caught his heated eyes in mine as he fought the urge to shudder.

"Fuck, Lilia." He palmed the wood on either side of my head. "I want to do unspeakable things to you."

My breath caught. "You say that like it's a bad thing."

He shook his head, swallowing when my hand found his belt. "I told you before. I'd never push you to do something you don't want."

"Who says I don't want it?" I whispered, my heart pounding.

"Do you?" He searched my eyes. "You can say no. Just because we've come this far doesn't mean we can't stop right now."

I unbuckled his belt and pushed down his trousers. Then I followed it with my own and pulled my tunic over my head. The warmth of him caressed my bare skin, but still I shuddered. I was bared before him now, every inch of me on full display. No one had ever seen me this vulnerable. I'd never wanted them to.

And I'd certainly never wanted to be touched like this. For a very long time, I'd thought I might never want it. But I'd finally found someone who made me *feel*. And I wanted to make him feel, too.

"I quite like what you're doing right now," I said with a sly smile. "Can't you tell?"

"Oh, turning my words back on me, are you?" His eyes slid down me to rest on my hips. He dropped to a knee before me, his powerful hands capturing my waist. My heart kicked my ribs as I watched him slowly and gently lift one of my legs and rest it on his shoulder.

"More beautiful than I even imagined." He kissed the inside of my thigh. Shivers stormed through me. Holding me in place, he drifted his mouth closer and closer to my core. With every hot breath, another tormenting blast of need clenched the ache between my thighs.

My hands found the floor behind me; my fingers curved, desperate to cling to something. His lips inched closer. He was only a breath away from the apex of my thighs now.

And then, so softly it was scarcely a touch, those lips brushed across me. I bucked against the floor, my entire body lighting up with pleasure. Ragnar's hands tightened around my hips to hold me in place, and he drove his tongue inside me.

"Oh, gods," I moaned. I felt like I was diving from the highest mountain and into the deepest chasm of the world. At least he would be there to catch me.

He lapped his tongue across me again. Stars danced in my eyes.

"You taste," he said, licking me, "so fucking sweet. I want you to sit on my face."

"What?" I breathed, my heart pounding.

"You heard me." His mouth vanished from my skin, leaving me aching for more. Lowering himself onto the floor beside me, he curled his finger and beckoned me toward me. "Sit on my face, and ride me until you come."

My nipples tightened. Breath caught in my throat, I rose from the floor and slowly lowered myself to his face, straddling him. His hands captured my backside, and he tugged me squarely onto his mouth. His tongue pushed back inside me.

Oh my gods.

My every inhibition vanished as a wild boldness came over me. I rocked against his face. His lips caressed me, sucking and tasting and licking every inch of me. I grabbed the nearest crate and held on while my pace quickened.

The pleasure within me roared. Dropping back my head, I moaned as I rubbed myself against Ragnar's mouth. His hands tightened on my backside. I could sense his own need mounting with mine, and I gripped the crate harder. The wood cracked, but I barely noticed, not even when a few apples tumbled out onto the floor.

"Ragnar," I panted. I could barely think from the ache between my thighs. I rocked against him once more, faster, harder, and so rough I was sure it would be too much for him. But he growled in response, like my unconstrained pleasure excited him.

And that was all it took.

I shattered. My body shook; a pulsing heat of fire rocked my core. Powerful convulsions throbbed through me. All I could do was cling to the crate and bounce against Ragnar's mouth. Every time I thought I was done, he flicked me with his tongue, and another wave went through me.

Eventually, I collapsed against his chest. His heart pounded against me in that unique, melodious beat. For a good long while, a cocoon of silence captured us both, the rain still drumming on the roof of the wagon.

"That was…enjoyable," I said after a long while.

"You liked that? Hard to tell," he said, his voice rumbling against me. "Hopefully you're nice and relaxed now. Ready for sleep?"

I lifted my head and met his gaze. "Oh, it's not time to sleep just yet."

His lips curled up in the corners. "Is that so?"

I slid myself lower and rested my thighs on either side of his waist, my knees against the floor of the wagon. His cock throbbed between us, as if anticipating my next move. Slowly, I reached down and wrapped my fingers around the length of him.

He shuddered. "You…are a lot bolder in the bedroom than I anticipated. And I like it."

Smiling, I dragged my hand down his shaft. "Do you like this, too?"

"Fuck yes," he groaned.

"What about this?" I whispered, shifting my body so that the tip of him grazed my core. And then slowly I slid down. His length drove into me. I sucked in a gasp. There was a flicker of pain, yes, but it was nothing compared to how good he felt inside me. How *right* it felt.

"Lilia," he murmured.

"Say my name again," I whispered back, slowly shifting up and down him.

"You are perfect, Lilia. Everything about you…is so fucking perfect."

He held on to my thighs as I gently rocked against him, the pleasure slowly overtaking the pain until it was nothing more than a distant memory. Every stroke heightened my need. My moans filled the space; the rhythm of our bodies shook the wagon.

As my pace against him quickened, Ragnar's hands consumed every inch of me. He felt my thighs, my hips, my breasts. He swept his fingers along the curve of my back, across my belly, and down the length of my arms, like he wanted to memorize every inch of me.

The heat in his eyes and the appreciative bend of his lips filled me with an intoxicating burst of desire. I leaned forward and kissed him. His hands tangled in my hair. Our bodies collided together. The soft touches grew heady, and he thrust into me as I bounced faster and faster onto him.

A hunger I'd never known gripped me by the throat, and an all-consuming climax rushed through me once again. Tossing back my head, I cried out. His hips slammed into me. Stars painted my vision. Roaring, he shook against me, his powerful quakes matching mine.

Trembling, I lowered myself onto his chest again. He was still inside me, but I didn't want to move. Neither did he. I drifted to sleep almost instantly. His touch was like a balm that I'd never known I needed. And I finally felt peace.

26

RAGNAR

"Perhaps we can stay here for the rest of the festival." I brushed my lips across Lilia's forehead, relishing the steady beat of her heart against my chest. We'd spent the entire night like this, with her warm body on top of mine. She'd dozed off from time to time, unlike me. I couldn't stop thinking about how little time we had left. As soon as Yule was over, we would have to say goodbye, even if I didn't earn enough coin to pay back my brother's debt to the Mercenaries Guild. I had to return either way, or they'd come for me.

It was impossible to sleep knowing that.

Lilia pushed up onto her palms, beaming down at me. "I'm not sure the townspeople would forgive me for choosing *this* over brewing their precious ale for them."

Smiling, I slid a strand of hair behind the sharp curve of her ear, enjoying the shiver my touch conjured. "Then we'll just have to continue this once we're back in town."

"And maybe somewhere a tad less...cramped." She looked around at the crates, wincing when she spotted the one she'd broken when she'd been riding my face the night before. Apples dotted the floor around it. Thankfully, it hadn't been the crates with the grains.

I palmed her backside, tugging her back to me. The wind and rain had quietened sometime in the night, but that didn't mean we had to invite the sun inside just yet. There were a lot of ways I could make Lilia moan and sigh and tremble and...gods, she was beautiful.

"Mmm," she said with a sly smile when she spotted how hard I was. "You don't seem to be ready to go just yet."

"I could spend days in here with you, and I would never get satiated."

I sat up, revelling in her wide hips and luminous silver eyes. I'd never met anyone more beautiful. But more than that, I'd never met anyone who looked at the world the way she did. Someone who marvelled at the beauty of it with eyes and heart wide open.

Someone who loved a dragon as if he were her family.

Gently, I lifted her from the floor. I perched her on a crate and dipped my head, kissing the sweep of her breasts. She shuddered, her luscious thighs tightening around my waist.

I slid my tongue across her nipple, teasing her. Already, I could scent her need like the headiest, sweetest perfume. I basked in that scent—craved it. My cock hardened even more.

With my mouth on her breast, I slid my finger inside her. Her wetness coated me. Fates be damned, she was already soaked. I shuddered as my need clenched my balls. But this was about her, not me. I wanted to make her moan. I wanted to make her tremble. I wanted to make her see a million bloody stars.

She let out a little gasp that did something to me. Groaning, I slid another finger into her pussy and fucked her with my hand. Rocking against me, she dragged her nails down my back. *Fuck*, that felt good.

I licked her breasts, savoring the salty taste of her skin. Fingers pulsing into her, I sucked hard.

"Ragnar," she moaned, her nails carving into my skin. "Please. I want you inside me."

"You have me," I murmured against her.

"No, I want all of you."

Need ripped through me at her words. Whatever she wanted, I would happily give her. I pulled out my fingers and spread her legs wider, careful not to let the wood scrape her skin. In the dim light of the wagon, her pussy gleamed. So wet and full of need for me.

I pushed inside her. The heat of her enveloped me, her walls squeezing tight around my length. My eyes nearly rolled into the back of my head for how good she felt. Her breasts heaved as she gasped. Gazing at me with those beautiful silver eyes—so open, so honest, so true—she inched her legs even wider.

You are going to be the end of me.

And I would gladly face oblivion to have her look at me just like this.

Shuddering, I thrust into her. Her leg hooked around my waist, and she tugged me even closer. My cock found the very back of her. That sweet little gasp popped from her throat again.

Oh, yes. That's it.

Rocking back, I thrust into her, harder this time. Again with the gasp. Her lips parted; her cheeks were growing red.

"You're taking me so good, Lilia," I told her, clutching the crate as I thrust again.

She squirmed. The heat of her pussy blazed around me, more wetness coating my cock. And the last remaining dregs of my self-control snapped.

I felt the uncontrollable rush of my power coming over me.

Gritting my teeth, I pulled out and flipped her around. Fire erupted along my back, scorching my skin. I slammed into her to the hilt, her backside bouncing against me. The crate tumbled to the floor and splintered everywhere.

"Ragnar," she gasped. Her legs hit a sack, and potatoes scattered across the floor.

Fire still blazing across my back, I took ahold of her hips to keep her steady. And then I inhaled slowly. I forced my fire to still. Carefully, I started to pull out of her, but she reached back, grabbed my hand, and held me there.

"Don't stop," she whispered. "I want you to go feral for me."

"I don't want to hurt you," I ground out.

"You won't. You never would. I trust you completely."

My flames roared back to life again. "Are you sure?"

"Yes," she breathed.

"Then hold on tight."

Lilia lifted her hips and clutched the wall. I slammed into her again. The entire wagon shuddered. That untamed need tore through me once more, and my pace quickened. She cried out, her walls tightening around my cock.

I pounded harder, faster, so driven by my want that nothing else mattered. The wheels groaned; another crate smashed to the floor.

Lilia's body tensed, and then a pulsing storm went through her. She clenched around me, again and again, coming harder than she had the night before. The intoxicating feel of her pleasure only quickened my own release. My cock throbbed once, twice. And then I came so hard I roared.

When I finally quietened, Lilia sagged forward, panting. The flames on my skin died. Sweat coated her back.

"Fuck." I pulled out and twisted her to face me.

"Are you all right? Did I take it too far with—"

"Shh." She pressed a finger to my lips, gazing at me with softened eyes. "You didn't hurt me. Just like I knew you wouldn't."

I shook my head. "I lost control."

"You had enough control to keep me safe." She palmed my cheek. "That felt good for me, Ragnar. Did it not feel good for you?"

"Fuck yes," I said without a beat of hesitation.

She smiled. "I like your fire."

"I like everything about you." The words spilled out of me. Too late, I realized what they were. It was true, of course, but I didn't want to scare her away with my intensity. Fates, I'd already set fire to myself from wanting her so much.

But she didn't pull away. If anything, she leaned closer.

Somehow, the truth of me hadn't scared her away. It seemed almost impossible, like she was a lass I'd plucked from my dreams.

And one I could never keep.

27

LILIA

Halfway down the final hill, the wagon got stuck. Muddy sludge from the previous night's storm grabbed the wheels and refused to let them go. The entire thing shuddered to a stop, even with both me and Ragnar trying to pull it forward. I slumped against the left yoke, wiping the sweat off my brow with the back of my hand.

The bottom of my cloak was caked in mud. Spatters of dirt peppered my trousers, and even with Ragnar's presence, I was chilled to the bone.

I gestured at the mud-caked wheel. "Why do I feel like we've been here before?"

"Only this time, *my* wagon is the stuck one." Ragnar grinned at me, and my belly did a little flip. Even with all the mud and the cold and the persistent wind, there was a giddiness in my chest that made the adversity feel…unimportant. It was only a bit of mud.

A scrub would wash it all out. And soon, I could have a warm bath and a bowl of hot stew beside the hearth.

A shout echoed from down below. Moments later, a few of the younger boys from Riverwold came rushing up the hill. When they reached us, they were breathless, but their eyes were gleaming with hope.

"Nilsa said you'd gone to get some food for Yule. Did you find any?" a ginger-haired human boy asked, his cheeks pink from the wind.

"Steffon is threatening to call the whole thing off!" a tall, silver-haired elven boy added.

"Don't worry." Ragnar pounded his fist against the side of his wagon. "We've come bearing gifts. Want to help us get this thing out of the mud?"

Eagerly, the boys jumped in to help, and a couple more ran up the hill to join us. With five of them pushing from behind and the two of us at the front, the mud eventually released the wheels. As we carted the wagon down the path, the boys walked alongside us. And when we finally reached town, they shouted at the windows we passed by. Soon, we had an entourage. People spilled from their homes and followed us to the courtyard square. Someone grabbed a flute, and a merry tune joined the cheers.

I looked up at Ragnar, smiling. He grinned back. We'd actually saved Yule. And we'd done it together.

A fter making the grand procession to the square, we had to backtrack to the festival grounds when Steffon scolded us for delivering the food to the wrong place. But even his anxious temperament couldn't douse my good mood. Ragnar even offered to swap the wagons while we were there, putting his cart where mine had been on St. Olaf's Row and mine in its old spot beside the indigo-leaved willow tree.

I stepped back and surveyed my old familiar friend, the Traveling Tavern. Now that we had enough grains, I could get started on brewing some ale. And soon, I'd get to open up those doors to patrons again.

"You know, you didn't have to do this," I told Ragnar when he returned from distributing some bags of flours to the food merchants.

"After everything you've done, it only seems right for you to have this spot." He motioned at the tree. "Besides, your wagon looks better there than mine."

"Don't you mean after everything *we've* done? You've been with me every step of the way, Ragnar."

"Getting the food from Ulrika was all your idea."

Frowning, I searched his face, noting his eyes had grown distant. "Is something wrong?"

"No." He sighed, then cast me a smile, but it didn't reach his eyes the way the others had. "I'm only thinking my brother would have loved to see the festival come together when it seemed like it wouldn't. He always did love a good underdog tale.

When I visit his barrow, I'll have to tell him all about it."

And that was when I understood what he didn't want to say out loud. He had resigned himself to returning to the mainland even if he could not pay off that debt.

To the mainland.

The thought squeezed my heart like an iron clamp. All this time, I'd known it was an inevitability. Ragnar did not live in the Isles. He'd only come here for Yule so he could earn enough coin to settle his brother's debt. That wouldn't change just because he'd met me. It couldn't. He'd made a vow, and he was not the kind of man who could easily break one, especially not for the brother he'd loved.

It made my chest burn. My stomach didn't feel right, either. Even my eyes felt like they were being stuck with pine needles. I'd only just met this man, who was unlike anyone I'd ever known. And I would have to watch him walk away far too soon. Suddenly, I understood what it was like to be my friend.

But the last thing I wanted to do was make him feel guilty for it.

"Listen, how about we make a deal? If you help me brew the ale for Yule, you can have half the coin I get for selling it," I said.

He cast me a sharp glance. "Lilia, that coin is yours. Like I said, you've done so much for this festival. You've earned it."

"No." I shook my head. "You helped me track

down Ivar. And then you helped me haul all the food back from Ulrika's place. And now I need to brew, and I could use an extra hand. If you help me, you get half the coin. If you don't, then it's all mine. Take it or leave it. You know where to find me when you decide."

Shrugging, I sauntered away with my hands deep in my cloak pockets. If I let him see just how badly I wanted to help him, he might say no. Truth was, I wanted him to spend the rest of his time here by my side, but I didn't really need the extra pair of hands. Brewing was practically in my blood by now. I'd find it easier to just do it all myself.

The thud of his footsteps behind me brought on a smile, but I didn't pause. I let him catch up to me, then fall into step by my side.

"You did swear you'd teach me how to brew proper ale," he said gruffly. "I suppose I ought to take you up on that."

"Good. It's a deal, then," I said with a nod. "We brew the ale together. You take half the earnings. And we'll both leave here better off than we were when we arrived."

Except that wasn't entirely true. Even if we had a successful Yule now, I'd barely break even splitting the earnings with Ragnar, especially after everything I'd already lost. But no matter. It would be enough to last me a few months, and I could always return to Wyndale for a while.

"After you," Ragnar said, motioning at the path.

But instead of taking the lead, I hooked my arm around his waist. Side by side, we began.

After collecting the barrels and grains from Tomas the carpenter, we returned to the Traveling Tavern to get started on the brew. Ragnar dumped the bag of grains on the ground while I built a fire behind my wagon. We fell into an easy, companionable silence as we worked. Together, we crushed the grains and then boiled them for a few hours.

Curious merchants wandered by now and again to watch, and a small crowd began to form. Eventually, Steffon came around to give the boiling mash a very thorough inspection. He sniffed at it, then gave his nod of approval.

"Looks like everything is coming along nicely," he said, the tightness around his eyes not quite as noticeable as it had been before.

"We're only just getting started," I told him. "It'll be a few days yet before it's ready to drink, and it won't stay good for long. I'll be brewing most days up until Yule to keep a fresh supply coming."

"You're making fresh ale, then? Instead of your normal brew?" he asked, seeming surprised.

I shrugged. "I don't have the special ingredient for that. Don't worry. This will be just as deliciously sweet, I promise."

He nodded and then suddenly started when he

noticed Ragnar come round the side of the wagon. "What are you doing here? I assumed you'd be making your own brew."

"Best not. It tasted like feet."

A ripple of laughter went through the gathered crowd. Steffon even cracked a grin, shaking his head at the self-deprecating confession. From somewhere nearby came the sound of a flute, followed by the clapping of several dozen hands. At the laughter, the bubbling of my brew, and the music, my entire body seemed to sigh. *This* was so much more like it.

Steffon looked around, his own shoulders relaxing. He indicated toward the brew. "Is this stage going to take a few hours?"

"It will," I said.

"Then why don't you get washed up and put on some dancing clothes? Some of the bakers have gotten started on their breads, and others are mixing up some stews. The performers have even been chattering about taking to the stage. I think tonight we should have a mini-party to celebrate the saving of Yule."

I cracked a grin. "So, you want to celebrate the fact we get to have a celebration?"

"The festival grounds have been miserable the past few days. Some of the visitors have been talking about heading off. Let's give them a reason to stay, yes?"

"And what will I serve them?" I asked. "My brew won't be ready for a few days."

"Just enjoy yourself for once. Have some cake or some stew and relax." He took my hands in his and squeezed them gently. "You earned it, Lilia. This is all thanks to you."

"Not just me," I said. "My friend I told you about, the one I called in a favor from? She's the one who gave me all this food. And if anyone should be thanked for this, it's her."

He nodded. "Well then, you tell her she's welcome in Riverwold anytime, and I'll be sure she gets her proper thanks."

"Even if she's a mountain troll?" I arched a brow.

Surprise flickered across Steffon's face, but then he smiled. "Like I said, she's welcome here anytime. Now go get dressed. It's time for us to have some fun."

28

LILIA

My wagon was scrubbed and polished and open for business. Well, it would be if I had any ale. Ragnar had helped me set up the tables and chairs beneath the willow tree. Silver banners etched with clinking tankards hung just over the serving window, and my awning swept from the top of the wagon to wooden poles we'd shoved into the muddy ground. To make up for the sludge, we'd even carried some fallen sticks over from the forest to create a makeshift wooden floor.

I stepped back to observe the wagon in all its glory. Ragnar slung an arm around my shoulders, shoving the sharp end of a shovel into the ground.

"I see what you mean now," he said with an appreciative smile. "You've built yourself a proper tavern. This is far better than what I would have set up with my wagon."

"Thank you. It took several years to get it to this

point. 'Course, it needs a fresh coat of paint now, but it'll do."

"It will more than do, Lilia." He turned to me, brushing a strand of hair behind my ear. Everything within me tightened. "So. Yule is less than a week away."

Oh. Swallowing, I cast my gaze at the ground. "It's the sixth night from now, yes."

"How long do you normally stay in Riverwold after the festival?"

"I...usually leave at first light the next morning before most people wake. If I waited any longer, I could get stuck in the long line of carts going up the hill on the way out."

"Choosing the empty road over the crowds. That does sound like you," he murmured.

"It's easier. And it means I can be on my way to the next destination," I said, trying to explain myself.

"And where do you normally go after Riverwold?"

Sighing, I forced myself to look up from the mud and meet his gaze. But as soon as I did, my resolution began to waver. Those eyes of his always seared me, always saw through the defenses I erected around my heart. I left by first light because I didn't want to stay anywhere long enough to get attached to any one place. I was here for Yule and nothing more. There was no reason for me to stay longer.

Except for the man standing before me now. But he was leaving, too.

"Honestly, I don't know," I said softly. "I don't always have a specific location in mind. The next place I want to visit after this is the dwarven city for their annual competition, but that's not for a few more months yet. I might head to Oakwater first. I like it there a lot. It has some of the prettiest forests I've seen in my life. And…" I stopped, swallowing. I'd been rambling too much. "What about you, Ragnar? Where will you go next?"

His jaw tightened. "I suppose I'll return to the mainland. My brother's debt to Lars won't pay for itself."

"How much is it?" I asked.

"The debt?"

I nodded. "How much do you have to pay back?"

"Two hundred gold coins."

My eyes widened. "Damn."

He would not earn enough from Yule. It was impossible. Unless I gave him mine…and then it might be close. Still not enough, but close.

But then I'd *have* to remain in Riverwold, at least for a time. Long enough to earn more coin to continue on my ceaseless path. But that could take weeks. Well over a month, maybe more. The residents of Riverwold would happily buy my ale, but they were a few dozen compared to the hundreds of patrons here for Yule.

But before I could consider it further, music piped through the festival grounds from the direction of the stage.

"Let's do what Steffon said," Ragnar said, sliding an arm around my waist. "Tonight, we celebrate. We can worry about what the future brings tomorrow."

My mind wanted to latch onto the threat of what might come. What would it feel like to say goodbye to Ragnar? How would he pay his brother's debt? And where would I go next? *Could* I go somewhere next?

But the sounds of the celebration called for me. For now, I could put all that aside. It was a crisp, clear night. We had food and music and dancing. And right now, Ragnar and I had this moment in time. Nothing lasted forever. I should enjoy what I had while I could.

And so, with a beaming smile, I wound my arm around his back and followed the crowd.

After Birta the Bard played a few upbeat tunes on the festival stage, the crowd made its way through the town streets to the courtyard. Word had quickly spread that Nilsa had cooked up a big vat of stew. She'd also brought out some spirits that she'd saved for a special occasion. Apparently, there wasn't anything more special than saving Yule.

The courtyard was packed. Shoulders jostled mine, and the crush of the bodies imbued me with warmth. A few shouts peppered the crowd as Nilsa edged through the inn's front doors and leapt up onto a table. Bells jingled wildly. Her hair was even more frazzled now, but there was a luminous glint in her eye. She was enjoying this.

She called out, "I've got stew and spirits! First come first served!"

I stumbled forward as the hungry festival goers shoved toward the door. Ragnar's hand was ripped from mine. The crush of bodies knocked me sideways, and when I finally caught my balance, I couldn't spot his crimson hair through the crowd.

"Ragnar!" I called out.

Still no sign of him.

The crowd was packed so tightly now, I could barely breathe. Heart pounding, I squeezed through a gap in the bodies, breaking free of the stampede. A couple of pixies spotted what I'd done and followed just behind me, squealing when they almost got knocked to the ground. I grabbed both of their arms and hauled them out. And then we edged around the packed throng until we were on the street beyond the courtyard.

"This is madness!" one of them trilled. She swiped her dark hair out of her luminous purple eyes, blinking at the bodies still crushing each other, all in hope of some stew and some spirits.

The second pixie's wings twitched behind her. Frowning, she reached over her shoulder and patted the spot where her skin met bone. "My wings nearly got snapped in half. Someone needs to do something or people are going to get hurt."

"How?" the other asked. "No one will listen.

We're all hungry and tired. And a shot of spirits sounds lovely right about now. In fact...maybe we should try for it again."

"Ragnar could do it," I murmured, casting my gaze around for him. As tall as he was, his crimson hair would be unmistakable, and yet there was no flash of red anywhere. I frowned. He'd been beside me only moments ago. And it wasn't as though he would wander off after the crowd had crushed us like that. Wouldn't he be looking for me? It didn't make sense that he was gone.

The back of my neck prickled with the sensation that someone was watching me. Heart lifting, I turned. Had Ragnar found me? But my eyes found nothing but shadowy corners along the empty street. Everyone was in the courtyard, fighting to get inside the inn.

"Is Ragnar that handsome elf who tried to steal your tavern spot from you?" the twitching wing pixie suddenly asked.

The other edged in closer. "Do you know if he's spoken for?"

I snapped my attention away from the street. "What?"

"You know, is he spoken for? Does he have a partner?" the first pixie asked.

My chest tightened. "No. He doesn't have a partner."

The pixies exchanged a knowing look, but I'd heard enough. I started to move past them toward the alley. I had to get into the inn to make sure Nilsa was all right. She'd been outside when the crush had started. If she hadn't gotten to safety, she could be hurt.

My cheeks burned as I shouldered through the crowd, but it had nothing to do with the pixies' questions. The situation outside the inn was frightening, that was all. And it was far too warm with all the tightly packed bodies. I'd told them the truth. Ragnar *wasn't* spoken for. He did not have a partner. Yes, we'd shared a night together, but that was all it was.

That was all it could be.

If they wanted to approach him, why should that bother me? He wasn't mine. And I wasn't his.

Squaring my shoulders, I nodded to myself and forged ahead. Eventually, I reached the alley. Thankfully, no one had thought to come this way, so the path to the side door was clear. I threw it open and ran inside to a tornado of pots and pans and bean splatters on the wall. Nilsa screamed and threw up her arms to shield her face.

"Shhh, it's only Lilia," Herold said, pulling Nilsa to their chest. The two dwarves were huddling together with their backs against the kitchen door, clearly hiding from the chaotic crowd.

"Lilia?" Sniffing, Nilsa peered around Herold's protective arm. Tears streaked her face, dribbling onto the front of her apron.

"Oh, Nilsa." I crossed the kitchen in two quick

strides and fell to my knees before her. "Are you hurt?"

"No, no. Just a little rattled is all. Did you see what happened?" She scrubbed her cheeks with the bottom of her stained apron.

"Yes, it seems everyone has gone a bit feral." At the pounding of more fists on the kitchen door, I jumped to my feet and glared at the wood rattling on its hinges. I reached over Nilsa and slammed my fist right back. "Stop that! You won't get any food if you keep it up!"

The hammering ceased. The three of us waited with bated breath. When the pounding didn't resume, Nilsa sagged against the door. The bells in her hair jingled sadly.

"The past few days have been so...*dreary*. I just wanted to do something nice for everyone," she muttered.

"And you did. It's not your fault things got a little out of hand," Herold said, lovingly brushing the wispy strands of Nilsa's hair out of her eyes. Then they looked up at me. "Is there anything you can do?"

"I can tell them all to bugger off, if you'd like," I said with more bravado than was warranted. How would I make the crowd listen to me, of all people?

Nilsa threw up her hands, moaning. "But all this food. I don't want it to go to waste."

I looked around the kitchen. Empty burlap sacks were piled in one corner, and several crates of vegetables were empty, too. Steffon had given a lot of the cavern's food to Nilsa's inn. It was likely needed, too, with how much the two of them had been feeding everyone.

"Where's your elf friend?" Herold asked, scratching their beard. "He's big and burly. Maybe they'll listen to him."

I sighed. "Ragnar? I lost him in the crowd."

Nilsa's face brightened at Ragnar's name. "Herold's right. If you can find him, I bet he can help calm everyone down."

Suddenly, a loud banging erupted from the taproom. Nilsa winced, clearly imagining the damage she would find when she opened up that door. When another boom quickly followed the first, she stared at me with pleading eyes.

I held up my hands and backed toward the outer door. "All right, I'll try to find him, but I can't make any promises."

But as I pushed outside, a nagging thought prodded the back of my mind. Why hadn't Ragnar come looking for *me*? He knew Nilsa and I were close friends, and when he couldn't spot me in the crowd, he'd know I'd go straight to her side to check on her. He would look for me in the kitchen. Wouldn't he?

He'd want to know I was all right.

Except…he hadn't.

My heart throbbed painfully in my chest. Perhaps I'd gotten this whole thing wrong.

I shook my head and walked the length of the alley. No matter. We had less than a week left together, and none of this would be more than a memory years down the line.

When I reached the edge of the courtyard, the crowd had already begun to disperse. Those who remained looked tired and disappointed, casting rueful glances at the inn, where Steffon and a few other shadow demons blocked the door.

It was all under control it seemed, even if a dark cloud had settled over the celebration.

But then the screams began.

29

LILIA

The acrid scent of smoke tore through the courtyard. Terrified shouts echoed from down the road. Heart leaping into my throat, I raced toward the festival, letting my ears lead the way. The closer I drew to the meadow, the more people rushed past me, running in the opposite direction. Fear etched every face.

I spotted an elven woman fleeing with a basket of bread in her hands. Quickly, I darted in front of her.

"What's happening?" I asked, catching my balance when a fleeing dwarf nearly bowled me over.

Tears welled in her eyes. She clasped my arm, and her fingernails dug through my tunic and into my skin. "There's a fire. It's taking everything."

"A fire," I repeated numbly.

"Don't go that way. You should run." She released her grip and started off again, leaving me to stare after her, dumbfounded.

Her words repeated in my mind. *A fire. It's taking everything.*

Everything.

"My wagon," I whispered, taking off down the path again.

The roar of flames grew. Smoke curled through the buildings. In the distance, a blazing heat bathed the entire town in an eerie orange glow. When I finally reached the edge of town, I stumbled to a stop. I gazed upon the conflagration with disbelieving eyes, my lips parting.

I had hoped the woman's warnings were nothing more than an exaggeration. The fire would be small and contained. Easy to vanquish. Little damage would be left behind.

But no.

I shook my head. My face twisted in pain. Vibrant, wicked flames consumed the entire festival. They enveloped every wagon and every cart. Performer tents were nothing but ash, and the stage burned brighter than the moon overhead. It had spread to *everything.* Only the mud had prevented it from creeping into the actual town.

Stumbling forward, I caught sight of my wagon through the blaze. It was already burnt to a crisp, the awning and banners long gone. Even the willow tree had not survived the fire's vicious attack.

An arrow of pain pierced my heart. I sank to my knees, watching it all burn away. That wagon had been my life for so long, I couldn't imagine a time without it. And now only ash would remain.

"Lilia, love, you need to come away from the fire." Steffon knelt beside me and gently tugged me to my feet. Concern gleamed in his midnight eyes, his protective shadows twisting and curling around me—soothing my skin. Their touch brushed away the pain.

I blinked, and the flaming world rushed back in around me. My face felt hot, and so much smoke surrounded me that my throat burned. I coughed, my eyes watering.

I let Steffon lead me away, but I cast a final glance over my shoulder at the ruins of the festival. The fire still raged, though there was hardly anything left for it to consume now. Only blackened bits of my wagon remained. Unbidden tears streamed down my face. It felt as if someone had opened up my chest and scooped out a piece of my heart.

I coughed again, my lungs squeezing. Steffon handed me a wet cloth. Whispering my thanks, I pressed it to my nose and mouth. It did ease some of the burn.

He led me through the maze of streets to Nilsa's inn, taking me in through the back. The front door had been bolted shut. Only a few patrons were at the tables, nursing their stews with downcast looks on their faces. Nilsa was with Herold in the back corner. Her head was in her hands.

Startled, she looked up when she heard us approach. When she saw it was me and Steffon, she leapt to her feet and rushed toward me, her braided hair slapping her back and jingling madly.

"Oh, Lilia." She clasped my hands. "I heard what happened. Your wagon…is it…did the fire…?"

A lump in my throat caught my words. Clenching my teeth, I looked away.

"I'm so sorry," she whispered.

"Have you seen Ragnar?" I'd searched the town for him on our way here, but there had yet to be any sign of him. I tried not to imagine the worst—that he'd gone to my wagon, thinking he'd find me there. That the flames had consumed him before he'd gotten away.

But even then, he had to be fine. He would survive that. His body seemed immune to flames. So where was he?

Nilsa shook her head, her brow furrowing. "No, Lilia. I've seen no sign of him. It's a strange coincidence, is it not?"

"What's a strange coincidence?" Steffon asked from behind her.

I shot Nilsa a look. Earlier, I'd told her about Ragnar's past because I'd needed to talk to someone about how I was feeling. Finding him only to lose him felt overwhelming, and unburdening it all had lessened the ache. But the information about what he was couldn't go further than that. It wouldn't be fair to him unless he wanted everyone to know.

"It's just that Ragnar has some fire demon in his blood. Right, love?" Herold spoke up from their spot at the table.

Nilsa stiffened, as if realizing what she'd been about to say. "Yes, yes. The fire demon blood."

"So Ragnar could have easily started that fire," Steffon said, catching on to Nilsa's suspicions.

"No," I said, just as Nilsa said, "Yes."

"Come on." I frowned. "He wouldn't do that."

"I would certainly hope not, but…" Nilsa sighed. "Well, we don't actually know him very well, do we? He's a stranger from the mainland, and he vanished right before that fire started. I really like him, Lilia, but tell me I'm wrong in thinking he could have done it."

"You *are* wrong. Because it doesn't make any sense. There's no reason for him to burn down the entire festival," I argued.

"Are you certain?" Steffon folded his arms. "Like Nilsa said, none of us know him. What if he's involved with something that made him do this?"

I opened my mouth but no words came out. Surely that couldn't be true. If it was, everything he'd told me had been a lie. All the moments we'd shared —fake.

And perhaps they were right. He'd never told me exactly why his brother owed someone such a big debt and why it was so important for him to go back. Perhaps the fire had something to do with that.

But I couldn't bring myself to believe it.

A pounding ripped through the silence. We all turned toward the door. I almost expected Ragnar to burst through that very moment, as if our conversation had summoned him here.

Nilsa eyed the door warily. "I suppose I better open it. People are going to need some food and shelter tonight."

"I've got Tomas coming round soon to help keep things orderly," Steffon said, frowning. "We'll get everyone to line up and come inside one by one. If anyone tries to shove anyone else, they'll get kicked out of Riverwold for good."

Nilsa nodded. "I'll see how many of them are out there."

She minced over to the window and peeked through the curtain. A moment later, she bustled over to the door, shrugging. "It's only Emil."

Everyone visibly relaxed. Emil was the kind baker, who I'd originally camped my wagon beside. I trailed over to the table and slumped onto the bench while Nilsa cracked open the door and motioned him inside. As soon as the door slammed shut behind him, he pointed a crooked finger at me.

"It's her. She's the problem," he said, slowly

stalking across the taproom. The few patrons scattered around the tables fell into a tense hush.

"What are you talking about?" Nilsa demanded.

"The fire," he said, his voice wavering. "It was her dragon that did it. I saw him skulking around the woods right before it happened."

"What?" I shoved up from the bench.

"That's right," he said, nodding. "I gave him a chance, Lilia. I said I was fine with him as long as he didn't bother me and mine, but now he has. Killing things, burning everyone alive, that's what the dragons once did. And apparently, it's what they still do."

All the blood fled from my face. I hadn't seen Reykur since the incident with Ivar's wagon. I thought he'd been hiding from all the rain or hunting for food like he often did.

"Hmm, I did forget about your dragon," Steffon said, rubbing his chin.

"Reykur would never burn anyone alive," I said hotly.

"I would just like to point out that *no one* has burned anyone alive," Herold said calmly.

"Yes, well, no thanks to that dragon," Emil said, narrowing his eyes. "I doubt he knew that most everyone was *here* banging down Nilsa's door for food and drink."

"I'm telling you, he wouldn't do it," I insisted.

Steffon frowned. "You also said Ragnar wouldn't

do it. So which is it? Ragnar or your dragon? One of them must have started the fire."

I looked from Nilsa to Herold and then back to Steffon again. No one said a thing. I supposed they truly believed one of them had started the fire.

My hands clenched. "Fine. What is it you'd have me do?"

Steffon shook his head sadly. "When word gets out about your dragon, everyone will assume the worst. They'll go after him, Lilia. They'll want to run him far, far away from here. How do you think he would handle that? Would he protect himself?"

"You're asking me if he would retaliate with his fire," I said flatly.

"That's exactly what I'm asking," he said. "Would he?"

I ground my teeth. Reykur would never attack anyone unprovoked. I knew the truth of that as well as I knew my own soul. But if an angry mob went after him? I couldn't be certain he'd hold back.

"You want me to make him leave," I said.

"For the sake of peace, yes."

"I'm afraid Steffon's right, Lilia," Nilsa said with a heavy sigh. "I don't believe he'd ever hurt anyone, but it's just better for everyone if he goes now. After the fire…people are going to be on edge. They'll react badly when they find out he was near the meadow."

I lifted my chin. "If he goes, I go."

Steffon heaved a sigh, scratching the base of his horns. "Very well. It isn't as if Yule will proceed at this point. Everything's gone. There's no reason for you to remain here."

Herold rose from the table. "Now wait a minute. You can't force Lilia to leave in the middle of winter, not when her wagon got burned up with all the rest of it. She has no home."

"It's all right, Herold." I smiled sadly. "I can manage on my own. I always do. I'll just get my pack from the room upstairs, and I'll be on my way."

As I moved toward the staircase, Nilsa bustled after me. "No, I'm not having it. With the Elding the way it is, you can't go wandering the roads without shelter."

But I'd already heard enough. I reached the stairs and jogged up to the top floor. Inside my rented room, I shoved all my belongings back into my pack and hauled it onto my shoulder. I looked out the window one last time, memorizing the shape the buildings cast onto a mottled blue-gray sky. This might be the last time I ever saw them. I likely wouldn't be welcomed back here after this.

Because Steffon was right. Gossip would quickly spread. The townspeople would blame me and my dragon for all the calamity that had befallen their beloved festival. They'd likely assume I had some-thing to do with all the theft, too. If I ever stepped foot in this place again, it would not be to the sound of cheers.

Brushing the unwelcome tears from my cheeks, I strode out the door and took the route to the rear of the building rather than taking a chance with the stairs. I couldn't stand the thought of saying goodbye to Nilsa. When I reached the window, I hoisted myself over the ledge and scaled down the stone, landing in the alley. And then I took a winding path through the streets, careful to stay out of sight.

I didn't look behind me even once.

30

LILIA

My hands were empty, and the silence was louder than my wagon's rattling wheels ever had been. I lumbered up the side of the hill, aiming my steps toward the mountains looming ahead. I figured I'd pay Ulrika another visit and tell her what had happened. I dreaded seeing the look of disappointment on her face when I told her I'd failed her. Steffon had offered her an invite, but her association with me could get her driven out of town.

I didn't have much of a plan after that.

I could always return to Wyndale. My brother would welcome me into his home with open arms, and he'd expect nothing in return for it. But that was a good three weeks' journey from here, if not more. I had no food. I had very little coin. And I had no shelter.

My boots faltered on the path. Despair dogged my every step, but I couldn't let it win. I would just have to go back to the basics. Years ago, I'd learned to forage for berries during the winter months. I could collect sticks fore fire when I stopped for the night. It would do little good if the Elding hit, but hopefully those storms had moved on for good now.

I could survive long enough in the wilds to reach Wyndale.

Looking up at the sky, I brought my fingers to my lips and whistled hard. The sound echoed across the foothills. A moment later, the sound of rushing wings answered my call. Reykur swept over the distant ridge-line, his majestic form a welcome sight. He soared toward me, and his wings skimmed the tall grass. Not a single blade caught flame, like they would have only weeks ago.

There was a wildness, a freedom to his movements now, like he'd been trapped inside a cage before. His essence filled his entire frame, expanding outward. He was letting himself take up space in a world where he'd once had to hide. And I would not make him do that any longer.

He thundered to the ground only a few feet away from me. The heat of him throbbed toward me, like hearth fire. But the burn didn't come. He could control his fire now, just like Ragnar could. And that was when I realized, he must have learned it by watching him, the man who'd once been a dragon himself. The timing was too coincidental to ignore.

I ran my hand along Reykur's scales. He leaned

his head into my touch, loosing a purr of contentment.

"I'm so sorry," I murmured to him. "We have to leave Riverwold now. We'll find somewhere else where you can be you."

His luminous eyes gazed back at me.

"The fire. They think you did it."

Rearing back, he swept his head from side to side, communicating with me in a way he never had before. His nostrils flared, and sparks of his inner fire danced down his spine. And I understood his wordless voice.

"I know you didn't," I told him, speaking around the lump in my throat. "It's not fair for them to blame you. But they're frightened, and they needed someone to take the fall."

I fell silent, suddenly troubled. Steffon had been certain the fire wasn't an accident, and so he'd been searching for someone—anyone—to blame. My dragon hadn't done it, though. And I knew Ragnar wouldn't, either, despite Nilsa's warnings that I didn't truly know him.

So if neither of them had anything to do with it, who *had* started the fire?

Frowning, I turned to gaze down the hill at the distant town. Smoke curled from chimneys, lights shone in windows, and the blackened meadow stretched out to the north, where it backed up against the woods that had managed to survive the worst of the fire. From here, Riverwold looked calm and peaceful. Just another evening in the quaint little town.

"Maybe someone was just trying to stop the festival, for whatever reason," I eventually said. "That's why they set the fire."

Reykur snorted. Clearly, he wasn't convinced. Neither was I.

But what was I to do? Steffon had told me to leave. If I tried to return now, what would happen? What would I even say? They already believed my dragon was behind it. Why would they listen if I tried to warn them it was someone else?

A sudden gust of wind slammed into me, forcing me to bend my knees to stay on my feet. Thunderclaps tore through the sky. Clenching my teeth, I turned toward the mountains behind me, only to find bulbous clouds heaving with rain.

Reykur screeched and took off. He had to get away from the path of the storm or the rain would burn his scales. I broke out into a run, following him across the foothills. Pumping my arms by my sides, I dodged rocks and dips in the grass, my cloak whipping around my legs.

"Reykur!" I called after him, my voice hoarse and ragged.

Rain fell in heavy sheets, drenching me instantly. I could hardly see, but I kept my eyes on the winged figure dashing through the storm. Worry fuelled my every pounding step. Even if he managed to outrun the clouds, he'd be in pain for hours after this. I wouldn't let him face that alone.

An outcropping of rocks rose just ahead. Reykur soared toward it, the wind buffeting his wings. His talons scraped the ground as he thundered inside the cave, leaving tracks of churned earth behind him. I stumbled after him, but my foot got caught in my cloak. I fell forward and my face hit the muddy ground.

Everything went black.

I awoke to a crackling fire and a warm body pressed against mine. My head pounded in time with the beat of my heart, and my eyes felt swollen and dry. When I forced them open, I found myself in a small cave with a membranous wing covering my body like a blanket. Reykur curled beside me, his soft breaths tickling my cheeks. And just beside us, a campfire blazed.

Slowly, I eased myself out from beneath him to take stock of the situation. Rain sprayed into the mouth of the cave, painting the stones. The harsh wind was doing it damndest to reach us, but we were far back enough to stay dry. I looked down at my muddy legs. Reykur must have dragged me inside after I fell.

I moved closer to him and gently ran my fingers along his scales. He was covered in big, angry red welts. Sighing, I sat back down beside him and pulled my knees to my chest. Thankfully, my clothes were mostly dry now, but I'd lost my pack when I'd been chasing Reykur in the rain. What a pair we made.

Something glimmered in the corner of my eye, dragging my attention away from my sleeping dragon. The firelight glinted across the steel hoops of a dozen barrels stacked in the corner of the cave. Frowning, I stood, trailing across the stone ground. Those barrels looked mighty familiar.

When I reached the stack, I hoisted one of the barrels into my arms. Liquid sloshed inside and heaved against the wood. A sweet, earthy scent washed over me.

Slowly, I turned back toward Reykur. He'd cocked one eye open and was squinting at me.

I shook the barrel. The liquid sloshed some more. "Curious thing. We happened to stumble upon a cave fully stocked with what looks, feels, and smells like ale."

Reykur shut his eye.

"Ah ha." Carefully, I set the barrel back down and strode over to the dragon. "You knew these were here. For how long?"

His only answer was to wiggle his wing a bit, like he was considering flying right out of here and back into the brutal storm.

"Since they went missing?" I asked, my voice rising an octave.

He reopened his eyes—both this time. With a huff,

he pushed onto his feet, trundled over to the barrels, and—much to my shock and dismay—collected one of them by gently lifting it with his teeth.

My mouth dropped open. "Are you telling me that *you* stole my kegs?"

Reykur blinked once before releasing the keg. I took that to mean he had, in fact, taken all the ale.

I needed to sit down. All this time, Reykur had been behind it. My *dragon*. But how? And why? Unlike the pies, it didn't look like he'd actually consumed any of it. He'd just taken it and stored it here, along with…wait a minute. I looked behind the barrels. There were a few sacks of flour, grains, and vegetables hidden here, too.

I pointed at them. "Where did you get those?"

He swung his head toward the east, in the direction of the sea.

I blinked at him. "You stole back the food Ivar took? The bits he sold to the sailors? You shouldn't have done that. They—"

Reykur suddenly lowered his head and nuzzled my arm, and the rush of love pushed away any lingering exasperation. Sighing, I leaned into him and stroked his snout.

"Why'd you take my ale, eh? I'm not mad. I just want to understand," I said quietly.

He nudged me again, this time at my heart. Then his lifted his eyes to mine and blinked. Even though we didn't speak the same language, our bond allowed me to understand. He'd seen me lonely on the road all these years. And then he'd seen me with Ragnar. Stealing the ale meant nudging us closer together. It was a ridiculous plot, but it *had* worked.

If those kegs hadn't gone missing, I might never have opened myself up to Ragnar the way I had.

Sighing, I perched on a stone beside the fire and gazed out at the raging storm beyond the cave. "You wanted to see me find happiness. Even if you went about it in a very strange way, I appreciate you trying. It might have worked, too, if Ragnar hadn't left to return to the mainland."

It was the only explanation that made sense. I refused to believe he'd caused the fire. So for whatever reason, he must have left after we'd gotten separated in the courtyard. Perhaps I'd pushed too hard about sharing the coin from the brew. Perhaps he thought it'd be too difficult to say goodbye. I understood that at least. I'd vanished, too.

Reykur gave a sage nod, agreeing with me. He wore sadness in his eyes. I supposed he wished Ragnar would have stuck around, too, and not just for me. Even if he was no longer a dragon himself, he understood what it was like. And Reykur didn't have many others in his life who did.

For a long while, Reykur and I sat beside each other, watching the storm. Eventually, my eyelids grew heavy and sleep took me back in its embrace. I dreamt of dragon-shaped clouds, elven men with crimson hair and piercing orange eyes, and a painted blue wagon tugged down the road by a gaggle of happy children.

But that wasn't my life, and it never would be. And when I woke again, I was cold.

The fire had died, and my dragon had fled the cave. Once again, I was all alone. Not even the thought of seeing Wyndale again could cut through the gloom. With a heavy sigh, I pulled my cloak around my shoulders, and I headed for the road.

31

RAGNAR

I crept through the woods. Ivar was quick on his feet, but I was faster. A heavy drizzle thickened the air, but my keen eyesight cut through the gloam. I'd been following him for at least five hours after spotting him creeping around the courtyard. He'd started off at a run, clearly hoping to evade anyone's notice. As the day progressed, he'd begun to slow, but he hadn't stopped once.

What had caught my attention more than his presence was the lute tucked under his arm. I'd recognized the sleek, gleaming wood painted with decorative dragons the second I'd laid eyes on it. He'd stolen it from the bard who played at Nilsa's inn. I had a feeling there was more where that came from, too. Lilia and I never had found the missing ale.

As the day darkened to night, the chase continued through the thinning trees. Eventually, the woods gave way for the foothills that rolled westward toward the mountain peaks. Ivar slowed, casting a nervous glance over his shoulder, but I was too hidden in the brush for him to spot me.

A rumbling shook through the skies. Ivar tensed and looked up. The clouds parted, pushed aside by the powerful beat of dragon wings. Reykur tore through the sky and bellowed fire. It streaked through the night like a trail of vicious red, leaving behind plumes of billowing smoke.

My heart pounded, hearing the pain and sadness in that call. Hands tensing, I glanced behind me at the woods that led back to town. Had something happened to Lilia?

I should have said something before rushing off, but my long-buried dragon senses had taken over the moment I'd set eyes on Ivar. He was my prey. When my instincts came alive like that, it was nigh impossible to tamp them down.

Up ahead, the dragon swooped low, hurtling toward Ivar. The human screamed and flattened himself against the ground.

I shoved through the brush and approach him from behind.

"Ivar," I called out to him. "Looks like the dragon wants you to give back the lute and whatever else you stole from Riverwold."

He rolled onto his back and tossed the lute across the field, where it fell into the mud with a squelch. "I don't want it, and I didn't steal anything else. I swear! Just take it and leave me alone!"

"I saw you running away with it."

He wet his lips as I strode closer. "You're right. I did steal the lute. But I don't want it, not really. Just take it back. All I wanted was to cause a little kerfluffle and nothing more. Please don't burn me!"

I slowed to a stop, only inches away from where he cowered in the mud. "Calm down. No one is going to hurt you."

He pointed a shaky finger at the dragon in the sky. "He'll eat me. Like he ate all those pies."

"The pies you made from the food you stole," I said, arching a brow.

"I'll stop stealing things, I swear." His lower lip trembled like a leaf caught in the wind.

Sighing, I extended my hand. His eyes widened as he looked from the dragon to my face to my hand and back again, like he thought this was some kind of trick or a test. But after several long moments passed, he firmly grasped my hand.

I hauled him to his feet, ignoring the mud he splattered onto my trousers. "Good. Now here's what I want you to do. You're going to take that lute, carry it back to Riverwold, and apologize to everyone for trying to ruin their fates-damned festival. And if you do it without crying about it, I'll ask Steffon to undo your ban. And as long as you swear not to cause any more trouble. That means no fighting and no stealing."

Ivar stiffened. "You don't know what's happened, then."

"What do you mean?" I took a step closer to him, my muscles tensing. "What's happened? Did you do something else?"

"Ah." He danced a step back. "Now listen, I didn't do it, so don't you blame this on me." Swallowing, he made more space between us. "The whole festival burned down earlier. I thought that was why you were chasing me until you started shouting about the lute."

"The entire festival burned down," I repeated, trying to make sense of his words. I'd chased Ivar in the opposite direction of the festival, but I'd assumed he was merely heading back the way he'd come. I'd smelled no smoke nor heard the crackle of fire while we'd dashed through the town streets.

I narrowed my eyes, grabbed the front of his shirt, and hauled him from the ground. "Are you lying to me?"

"No," he said, his voice barely a whisper. "Why would I lie about this? That would be extremely foolish of me. You're just going to think I did it."

"And for good reason. It seems exactly like the kind of thing you'd do."

His face paled. "I'll admit I've thieved, but I would never want to hurt someone. You have to believe me."

Slowly, I lowered him back to the ground, loosing my grip on his shirt. He stumbled back, then collected the mud-drenched lute.

"I'll go with you and return it," he said, lifting his chin. "I'll prove to you I had nothing to do with this."

"Hmm." I eyed him. I didn't trust the greedy little pie man further than I could throw him, but he was right. It made little sense for him to tell me about the fire if he'd done it himself. And I couldn't waste any more time haggling with him over it. Lilia had been in the courtyard, so she would have been safe...unless the flames had spread from the festival and into town. The thought clenched my gut.

I had to go to her. I had to make sure she was safe.

And then I had to find a way to keep her by my side, even if it seemed impossible.

32

LILIA

O nly a few steps down the path, my body seemed to stop listening to me. My feet refused to budge, and the sound of my heartbeat grew loud in my ears. Now that the drizzle had stopped, the moonlight bathed the distant town in pools of silver. Laughter drifted toward me on the wind. I could picture it all so clearly. Everyone would be down and out about the fire, but they'd have picked themselves up by now.

Nilsa would have found a miracle of food and drink, and she'd be passing it around to the packed taproom, where the visitors were taking shelter for the night. The townspeople would be there, too. They'd jump in to help, passing out plates or washing up in the kitchen.

The bard would leap up onto the stage with her lute to sing about quests and adventures.

Things had gotten out of hand earlier, that was all.

Everyone had been hungry and tired and more than a little cranky. But they'd pull through. The heart of this place was good, and everyone would look around and see that Yule was still worth fighting for in the end. Even if the festival took place in the crammed town streets, it would go ahead.

It always did.

Nothing could dampen the spirits of the people of the Isles. Not the Elding. Not a fire. Not even gods-damned fear of dragons.

I squared my shoulders. There was food in that cavern. My ale was there, too. It might not be enough to create a luscious feast, but it would be enough to fill some bellies and convince them my dragon was not to be feared—so long as I could find him first…

Lifting my fingers to my lips, I whistled the call. I shielded my eyes against the bright moonlight and searched the skies for his return. Long moments passed with nothing more than the rustle of the wind in the long grass, brushing against my thighs. I frowned. It wasn't like him to stay away when I called for him.

At long last, a bellow echoed through the night sky. His brilliant wings speared the night, illuminating the dark clouds above. He dove toward me, body tumbling this way and that, like a dance of scales and wings. I couldn't help but smile. I'd only seen him dance like this once before with his siblings. It was like he'd found the song in his heart.

I lifted my hand toward him, a part of me wishing

I could join him there in the clouds. He looked so breathtakingly free.

"Lilia," a deep, achingly familiar voice called, breaking me free of my reverie.

Everything within me stilled. Lips parting, I dragged my gaze from the sky. Ragnar stood just down the path, the wind battering his face with the curling strands of his crimson hair. His hands hung heavily by his sides. But when he spread his arms wide, I ran to him.

My feet pounded the ground faster than I thought possible. He started toward me and scooped me up when I launched toward him. My arms clung to his neck; his hands palmed my thighs. I wrapped my legs around his waist and buried my face into his neck.

"You're all right," he murmured, pressing his face into my hair. "You're all right."

I pulled back and searched his face, but I didn't dare let go for fear he might vanish into thin air again. "Where were you?"

He shook his head. "Chasing after bloody Ivar. He stole the bard's lute. I'm sorry I didn't say anything before I rushed after him, but I thought he might get away if I took my eyes off him."

A laugh of shock popped from my throat. "Chasing after Ivar? That's certainly not what I expected you to say." But then my lips softened into a frown. "So you didn't see what happened to Riverwold."

He brushed his thumb across my cheek, sighing.

"Not until an hour or so ago. I was worried you got caught in the fire. I thought you might have been hurt, Lilia."

"I'm fine," I whispered, though that wasn't entirely true. Physically, I was no worse off than I'd ever been, but my heart had taken a beating. Unwinding myself from his arms, I hopped back onto the ground, trying to find the words to explain what had happened. Quickly, I filled him in. And as I spoke, the furrow of his brow deepened into a tight, angry crease.

"I can't believe they would run you out of town after everything you've done for them," he said. "They don't deserve your help anymore. You know that, right? You could just take the food and ale in that cavern and move on with your life."

"No, I can't." I gave him a sad smile. "I'm not angry at Steffon or Nilsa. All they want is to protect the town, just like I do. And truly, they want to protect me, too. They knew what would happen if the townspeople got wind of a dragon near the meadow."

"Still, it's hardly fair. He's an innocent dragon."

"Well." My smile stretched into a full-on grin. "I don't know that I'd go so far as to call him *innocent.* He stole all our ale and ate all those pies. The mischievous little thing has been scheming against us to make us work together. Some of this chaos is purely his fault. That said, I think everyone down there would welcome him with open arms if he delivered them this ale."

His lips tilted up in the corners. "And Lilia's Traveling Tavern will be back in business again."

My heart dropped. "Minus the wagon."

"Oh, hi there!" another voice called out, higher-pitched and much less self-assured than Ragnar's. A blond human hobbled up over the hill, wincing when he caught sight of me. "I ah…well, I'm sorry for all the trouble I caused. But I might have a way to make it up to you. We've got a couple spare wagons near my house. You're welcome to have one to fix up and turn into your tavern."

"The wagons at the top of that path?" I asked.

"That's right." He gave me an eager nod. "What do you say? You interested?"

"You're actually serious. Ivar, the pie man who stole all our food, is offering a free wagon to me?"

He winced. "Yeah, I am. I know it won't erase what I've done, but it's the best I can do for now. I'll even give you paint for it, if you'd like."

I grinned up at Ragnar. "Did you hear that? We've got ourselves a wagon."

The four of us camped out in the cavern for the night when the wind blew in a fresh burst of rain. Ivar did not seem at all pleased to share a living space with a dragon, but he didn't speak a word in protest. With his nervous darting looks, I had a feeling he worried Reykur would take a bite out of him for the smallest offense. I decided not to correct him.

Once the sun rose, we trundled down the hill and through the woods to the ridge near Ivar's house. Then we trundled back up again and loaded all the cavern supplies into the wagon. It was midday by the time we carted the thing into the busy courtyard outside Nilsa's inn.

The crowd hushed when they spotted us. Heart thumping, I looked around, suddenly unsure if this was a good idea. The fear in the air was palpable. A few fire demons slowly climbed to their feet, flames sparking along their skin.

Ragnar pressed a comforting hand to my back.

Ivar cleared his throat uneasily. "They look very happy to see us."

The door to the inn flung wide, and Steffon stumbled out. Shaking his head, he rushed across the courtyard, latched his hand onto my arm, and dragged me behind the wagon.

"What are you doing here?" he whispered with a feverish glint in his eyes. "It's not safe, Lilia, as much as I wish Riverwold could be a perfect place free from danger. There are a lot of people who are angry with you right now. They think you ordered your dragon to set fire to the festival."

"Tell them I didn't do it," I said.

"What? They won't listen to me."

"You're the Defender of this town. They chose you

to lead them. Tell them I didn't do it, and they'll have no choice but to listen."

Indeed, everyone gathered in the courtyard looked to Steffon with expectant expressions, as if waiting for his decision. If he condemned us, they'd force us out of town. But perhaps if he welcomed me back with open arms, they'd be less inclined to chase after us with pitchforks. I could only hope, at least.

Sighing, Steffon ran a hand down his drawn face. I felt a twinge of guilt. He'd been through it the last week, just as much as I had.

"If it helps," I told him quietly, "we brought a wagon full of food and ale."

He brightened significantly at that, casting a hopeful glance at the wagon. "You brought us food? But how?" He paused. "And also *why*? I wasn't very kind to you yesterday."

I palmed his shoulder, smiling. "Because while Riverwold is not my permanent home, it is one of many to me. And I wanted to help, regardless of what you believe about my dragon."

"And to answer your other question," said Ragnar, "the dragon is the reason for the food. He found it."

Steffon scratched the base of his horns. "Well, if your gifts can't convince them, then I don't know what will. I'm not sure I can get them on board with the dragon, however."

I sighed. "Come on, Steffon. He had nothing to do with the fire. Can't you vouch for him?"

"Bring me the true culprit, and I can." He

suddenly noticed Ivar peeking around the corner and listening in on our conversation. His gaze narrowed as he stalked toward him. "What is *he* doing here?"

I followed. "Ivar has given me this wagon so I can rebuild my Traveling Tavern for Yule. He also helped us load up all the food and ale so that we could bring it here."

"I see," said Steffon, folding his arms.

Ivar held up his hands and bowed to the Defender. "I've come to make amends. It was wrong of me to take all that food. And to start a fight all those years ago. And to take the lute. But I'm asking you to give me a second chance. Please." He cast a nervous glance up at Steffon's tense face. "I'll do whatever you ask, if you let me stay."

"This is turning out to be a supremely interesting day," Steffon said tiredly. But then he waved his hand, shrugging. "All right, fine. You help us rebuild the festival in time for Yule, and I'll wipe the past away. You can even move back into town, if you'd like."

Ivar's mouth dropped. Beaming at Steffon, he grabbed the shadow demon's hands and shook them ferociously. "Thank you, thank you, thank you. You won't regret this, I promise."

Grimacing, Steffon carefully extracted himself from Ivar's eager hands. "Yes, well. I hope not."

Steffon turned to the crowd. A feverish energy rippled through the courtyard, like every single person was a flint ready to spark. When combined, they would transform the town into an inferno of anger. I stepped closer to Ragnar, and he wound his arm around my waist in solidarity. Whatever they decided to do, we would at least face it together.

"Ah, listen everyone," Steffon called out. His voice rang through the pregnant silence. "The rumors you've heard about Lilia, Ragnar, and her dragon are nothing more than tall tales. None of them had anything to do with the fire. And to prove this, they've brought us food and drink for Yule, despite these false allegations." Steffon frowned when Ivar cleared his throat. Sighed, he added, very tiredly, "Ivar didn't do it, either."

A dwarf with a long, bouncy gray beard hopped up onto a table. "Then who did? The fire didn't just set itself. Not with all that mud!"

The crowd murmured, making sounds of agreement.

"I'm afraid we have no idea who set the fire," said Steffon.

The murmuring grew into a tittering of unease. Several tables emptied as the patrons climbed to their feet, their faces lined with frustration. I thought that might be Steffon's undoing. He'd cow to their rumblings and be forced to take back his words. But he pounded his fist against the side of the wagon to get their attention back on him. The mutterings instantly ceased, and everyone standing sat back down.

"That's the best I can give you," he said in a firm voice that brokered no argument. "I wish we knew who did it, but we don't. As it is, we will not let an innocent person—*or dragon*—take the blame for someone else's actions, even as tempting as it might be." Clearing his throat, he turned to me. "Lilia has once again gone above and beyond to help us. I think we should thank her for finding us some food and ale. *Again.* Don't you agree?"

Silence was the only answer. After a few moments, the door of the inn opened to reveal Nilsa just inside the doorway. She held up her hands and clapped, edging out into the courtyard. Herold came out behind her and joined their clapping with hers. Steffon nodded and started clapping, too. Ragnar released my waist, turned toward me, and pounded his palms together, louder than all the rest.

Soon, everyone was on their feet, hooting and clapping and shaking their fists at the sky.

"To Lilia!" someone in the crowd shouted, raising an empty tankard into the air.

"To Lilia!" everyone roared.

With a laugh, I leapt up onto the roof of my new Traveling Tavern and threw my arms wide.

33

LILIA

wo days later, a bucket of paint sat by my feet. The entire town and all the visitors had chipped in to clear the meadow of all the burnt wood and blackened remains of the festival. My muscles still ached from all that hard work, and soot stained nearly every piece of clothing I owned. It had been worth it, though.

Now that all the ashes had been carted away, the meadow looked less like an abandoned fire pit and more like a churned field, ready for the yearly crops. Ivar had donated the rest of the carts to the merchants who'd lost theirs. Like us, they were deep in preparation for Yule, which was only a few days from now.

It would be a small celebration in the end, especially compared to the ones that had come before it. But it was better than nothing. A buzz of excitement rippled through the meadow, coalescing with the sounds of hammers against wood, crackling fires, and good-natured conversation.

A small boy with fire-red horns ran up to me and held out a blue winter flower. "This is for you."

I beamed down at him, taking the flower. "Thank you very much!"

With a giggle, he ran off, his boots slapping the drying mud. I slid the stem behind my ear, smiling after him. Ragnar came up beside me and wound his arm around my waist. My colliding emotions battled for dominance. We'd spent every night together at the inn. And each one had been better than the last.

Every morning, I awoke with a smile on my face, and my soul had never felt calmer. And yet, I couldn't shake the knowledge that this soon would end. He'd leave, and I'd never see him again. Permanence had never been a thing I'd sought, but I couldn't help but wish for it now, to dream of a life where we never had to say goodbye.

"They adore you," Ragnar said, rubbing the side of my hip. "As do I."

My heart fluttered. Swallowing, I tried to find my voice but found it had abandoned me. So instead, I leaned into him, trying to memorize the shape of his arms and the beat of his heart. In the days ahead, these memories would be all I had left.

"Is something troubling you?" he asked after I took too long to answer.

Shaking my head, I pulled away. I didn't want to bring gloom upon the few days we had left together. I wanted to make the most of it, to laugh and sing and dance and wrap my arms around his neck. And so I shoved my sadness down and painted on a smile.

"I'm just thinking about all that's happened," I replied. "Against all odds, the festival will go on, and we're finally going to sell that bloody ale of mine."

His chuckle washed over me, warming me from head to toe. "It's like your ale is as stubborn as you are."

"Hey now." Grinning, I swatted at his arm. "I think you need to look at your own reflection before calling someone else stubborn."

"Oh, you think I'm stubborn, do you?" Without warning, he scooped me up into his arms and tossed me over his shoulder. Then he gave my backside a little spank. A heady warmth spread through me, and my breath hitched.

"What are you doing?" I whispered.

"I'm feeling pretty damn stubborn about making you moan."

"Oh." Flushing, I held on to his muscular back as he hauled open the wagon doors. He leapt inside with the kind of strength and dexterity I'd known few others to possess, and then he lowered me to the floor. He'd covered the wood with a soft rug, and several candles suddenly sparked to life. My heart pounded. He must have been planning for this.

With his body over mine, he gently took both of my wrists in his hand and trapped them above my head. My chest arched toward him, my body responding to his touch. The laughter in his eyes died. He leaned down and kissed me.

Everything within me sighed against him. His hand slid down the length of me and slowed near the top of my thigh. My core clenched, aching with need.

When he pulled back, I could scarcely breathe.

"Wait. There's something I need to tell you," he murmured. His hand suddenly vanished from my thigh. He loosened his grip around my wrists and sat back.

"What is it? Is something wrong?"

"Yes. And we've been avoiding talking about it." Sighing, he ran a hand through his hair.

Suddenly, I wanted out of this wagon. I didn't want to talk about the looming end to...whatever this was between us. Crying was not on my plan for the day, and I could already feel the tears threatening to make an appearance. I shimmied out from beneath his legs and launched to my feet.

"There are a lot of people out there. Someone might walk by at any moment," I said, rushing my words. "We don't even have a lock on this wagon. I'd rather not have someone like Steffon catch us rolling around naked together."

I started to move past him to get out of here. My entire face and neck felt hot. Some cold wintry air was sorely needed. But as I darted around him, Ragnar gently took my arm.

"We really need to talk about this, Lilia."

I shook my head. "I don't want to. Not right now."

"I don't want to say goodbye, either. That's what I'm trying to tell you. But I have to—"

The rising sound of angry voices cut off whatever he'd been about to say. Even from inside the wagon, I could clearly hear the words.

"Who do you think you are? Get away from there!" came Steffon's familiar voice.

And then a voice I didn't recognize replied, "Let go of me or you will sorely regret it."

Ragnar tensed, then flung open the wagon door. He leapt outside, and I followed quickly behind him. A tall, handsome fire demon with dark hair that hung to his waist stood with a knife pointed right into Steffon's frightened face. He wore a long coat and leather trousers and boots caked in mud. The way Ragnar was looking at him sent a spear of dread down my spine.

I pulled the tiny dagger out from my waistband.

"Lars," he said, his voice hard. "What are you doing here?"

Lars. That name was familiar. I scanned my memories, searching for the source. And that was when I realized who this man was. The owner of Ragnar's debt. The reason for all his turmoil and the hunt for good coin. But if he was here, then that meant...he'd followed Ragnar.

My blood went cold.

The island was meant to protect those of us who lived in the Isles. It prevented anyone from arriving here if they meant us harm. But Ragnar did not call this place home. He was just a visitor.

And it had not protected him. Was that why?

Lars folded his arms and looked Ragnar up and down. "I didn't trust you not to run when you got the chance, and it looked like I was right. Instead of earning me my coin, you're shacking up with this tavern wench."

Ragnar let out a low growl, fisting his hands. "Say what you want about me, but keep Lilia's name out of your mouth."

Lars did not look impressed. "At least your ridiculous reaction tells me my accusations are right."

"No, Lars. I did come here to earn you your coin." Ragnar stalked toward him, the tension in his body practicing rolling off his body in waves. "And I don't appreciate being spied on, least of all by you."

Lars didn't so much as blink. He motioned at the meadow and the small stalls being erected along the newly-made path. "As determined as these island folk are to make this festival a success, it's clearly doomed. You're wasting your time here."

"I am not wasting my time," Ragnar said in a low voice.

The fire demon sighed. "I tried giving you a chance to earn your coin the honest way, like you asked, but it's time to join the guild, Ragnar. You can earn it the old-fashioned way, like your brother was meant to before he got himself killed with his own damn dagger. Then and only then will you be free to go."

The old-fashioned way. My heart squeezed. Ragnar hadn't gone into detail about his brother's debt, but Lars had said enough for me to read between the lines. Ragnar's brother must have been in the Mercenaries Guild. The coin they earned came in only one way, and it was not by selling ale or painting old wagons. It wasn't even by stealing coins out of rich nobles' pockets. At times, they'd even taken jobs from Isveig himself.

As a former warrior and then a member of the rebels, Ragnar would make an incredible addition to their guild. And this man knew it.

I released a slow, shuddering breath and tightened the grip on my dagger. Lars wore a mask of indifference, but tension tightened every muscle in his body, particularly around his jaw. He'd let Ragnar come here to try to earn some coin, but he'd never wanted him to be successful at it.

He'd wanted Ragnar to fail.

"You," I whispered.

Ragnar glanced over his shoulder, his brow furrowing. "Do you know this man?"

I shook my head. "I don't know him, but I feel as if I should. Because he's the one who set fire to our festival. He tried to sabotage you, so that you'd be forced to return to the mainland and work for him."

The fire demon tensed, then drew himself up tall. Ragnar swung back around to face him.

301

"Is this true?" Ragnar asked in a voice that was barely restrained.

"The tavern wench is upset you're leaving her in this mud-hole of a festival. She'd say anything to get you to stay."

"I told you." Ragnar grabbed the front of the demon's coat and hauled him closer. "You will not say a damn word about her."

"Or what?" Lars asked in a sneer. "You'll want to kill me? Go on then. Channel that rage and join our ranks." His lips twisted into a cruel smile. "And if you don't, I'll burn this festival down again and add Lilia to our list of targets."

I rushed toward him, wielding my weapon, even though I had no idea how to fight.

A bellow sounded from the sky. Plumes of smoke billowed toward us. Reykur twisted through the air, leaving streaks of fire behind him. A square, silver contraption hung from his talons.

"Is that a cage?" asked Ragnar.

Lars saw the opportunity for what it was and twisted out of Ragnar's grip. He shot me a furious look, then took off across the meadow, his long cloak billowing behind him.

"Fuck." Ragnar grabbed the bucket of paint. "I can't let him get away. If he returns to the mainland without me, he'll add your name to the bloody list."

"What are you going to do with a bucket of paint? Don't you want this dagger instead?" I shouted helplessly, watching him dash after the fire demon, who was already halfway across the meadow by now.

A heavy sigh sounded from behind me. I turned to spy Steffon sagging against the side of the wagon and puffing from a sweetly-scented pipe. He blew the smoke at me, then waved it in the air. "Want some? It's very relaxing."

I pointed at the two men darting around the cluster of carts. "There's a fire demon mercenary running from an elf and threatening to burn the whole place down again. Also, I have a dagger, which you should probably be mad about."

He tipped his head back, gazing at the cloudy sky above. "Don't forget the dragon flying around with a cage."

I couldn't help the laugh that popped from my mouth. "It certainly can't get any stranger than that."

"Oh no." He wagged his finger at me. "Don't tempt fate like that. I'm sure it can come up with countless ways to make this year's Yule one that will long be remembered."

Shaking my head, I joined him at the wagon. I rested my shoulders against the wood and watched my dragon swoop ever closer to Ragnar and Lars. They'd slowed now that they'd reached the northern side of the meadow, where the mud had yet to fully dry. Every now and then, one of them would stumble. The sound of their squelching boots joined the chorus of Reykur's growls. It was too amusing for the concern to take root inside me.

Steffon held out his pipe. I took a puff. Almost instantly, a lightness filled my head.

"Want to make a bet on what happens next?" he asked, his eyes half-lidded.

"My dragon is going to trap Lars in that cage," I answered.

He nodded. "I won't bet against that."

Indeed, as Reykur drew close enough that his wings cast a shadow across Ragnar and Lars, he released the cage. It slammed into the ground only inches away from them both. Lars tried to run, but Ragnar caught his arm and tossed him through the open door. Then Ragnar slammed the bars right into Lars's shocked face.

"Told you." I smiled. "My dragon saves the day."

34

LILIA

O nce a lock had been procured, Reykur carted Lars out of Riverwold. I had a feeling he was taking him to the mines, where other captured criminals had been put to work by the dwarves. The world would be a better place with one less mercenary out there, running around stabbing people or setting fire to people's homes.

Ragnar was quiet as we walked back to the inn. He was covered in mud from head to toe, but he scarcely seemed to notice. I supposed it had all come as a bit of a shock. He wouldn't have expected that world to follow him here.

Nilsa fussed over him once we trudged inside, and she shooed him up the stairs for a hot bath. I found a spot at one of the tables and nursed a tankard of water. The hearth was roaring and the crowd was abuzz with conversation. But the easy calm from Steffon's cigar smoke had abandoned me.

I gripped the tankard like it was keeping me tethered to the world. If I loosened my hand, I'd tumble into the jagged ravine below.

Everything had turned out fine. Ivar had turned over a new leaf, and the true culprit of the fire had been caught. Ragnar wouldn't have to worry about repaying that debt any longer.

He had no reason now to return to the mainland.

I swallowed the aching lump in my throat, but it refused to budge. Ragnar could stay, if he wanted. He never had to go back.

But he hadn't looked relieved after my dragon flew off, taking a caged Lars with him. If anything, his eyes had grown far more distant.

There was a chance he still wanted to leave. A goodbye now would hurt far worse than it would have before. Because it would be his choice.

I heaved a sigh, wishing my water was a big old barrel of ale. Maybe Nilsa could scrounge up some spirits for me.

Heavy footsteps tapped the floor. Ragnar rounded the table and dropped onto the bench across from me. Damp curls spilled across his shoulders. Nilsa must have found some clothes for him, as the pale gray tunic was just a tad too tight, highlighting the impressive strength of his biceps. He braced his arms on the table, noted my tankard of water, and motioned for Nilsa to bring him one over.

After a moment, he tapped a finger against the table. "Well."

"Well," I repeated.

"I had no idea Lars was involved in any of this."

"I can imagine it came as a bit of a shock."

"More than a bit." He ran his fingers through his hair, spraying water onto his shoulders. "I saw Ivar upstairs just now. Turns out he met Lars at the docks when that ship came through last week. Guess what kind of conversation they had."

I leaned forward, my curiosity greater than my lingering melancholy. "Don't tell me Lars put him up to the food theft."

"Encouraged more like, but still. It sounds like he's had his hands in all of it. I wouldn't be surprised if he got the crowd worked up the other day in the courtyard."

I nodded. I'd felt someone watching me a few times. Bet that was him, too.

"So he was behind everything. Except for the ale, of course."

He chuckled. "At least we can say your mischievous dragon has more than made up for that now."

"Right." My smile dropped, and I fiddled with the handle of my tankard. "He captured the man your brother owed."

"Yes, the leader of the Mercenaries Guild." He frowned at the table, avoiding my eyes. "Lilia, it's time for me to go. I can't stay another night on this island."

My heart pounded. I'd been afraid he'd say these very words, but not quite so soon. I'd assumed he'd stay for Yule, at least. Hands tensing around the tankard, I shoved the disappointment and hurt as far behind my crumbling walls as I could, though they seeped through the cracks like a flood after the storm.

The words spilled out of me before I could stop them. "You don't need to worry about him any longer. Reykur will take him to the mines, where he'll be a prisoner for a very long time."

"And the mercenaries back home will search for him. He would never come here without telling the others his plans. When he doesn't return in good time, more of them will come." His voice sounded pained. "They'll find me, which means they'll find you. And like Lars, they'll try to use you against me. I would never put you in harm's way like that, Lilia."

"No, you don't understand." I leaned forward and grabbed his strong, rough hand. "The magic of this place won't let the mercenaries come here. No one can step foot on these islands who mean its people harm."

"Hmm. The island let Lars come here just fine."

"I know. I think it's because you are not its people," I said. "Not yet anyway."

He drew in a sharp breath, as if he finally understood the implication of my words. The island would stop the mercenaries from stepping foot on its shores, just so long as Ragnar decided he wanted to remain here and call these lands his home. But he would have to turn his back on everything he'd once known, and perhaps that was too much to ask of him.

At least, I hoped it would work. I couldn't be certain.

"We would have to stay here on Hearthaven?" he eventually asked.

"No," I said, noting the use of the word 'we.' "You can *travel* anywhere you'd like. You could even return to the mainland for a time, but these islands would be your home."

Suddenly, he rose, moved around the table, and took the seat beside mine. "It would only be my home if you were with me."

I searched his gaze. "Do you mean that? If you want to go back, I won't blame you for that. We've only known each other for a couple of weeks. And if you stay with me, you won't have a house and a plot of land and a picket fence. All I do is wander."

"I'd spend forever wandering the world with you," he murmured.

A hopeful smile crested my lips. "Does that mean you're going to stay?"

"Of course I'm going to stay. It's all I wanted since you scolded me for having bitter beer." Standing, he hoisted me into his arms and kissed me fiercely. I slid my hands into his silken hair, sighing against him. All the tension in my body fled, the clouds of my mind clearing for the sun again.

I hadn't realized how badly I'd wanted him to stay until he said he would. Those long nights on the road would never again be so lonely. I could not wait to travel the world with him.

I pulled back and smiled. "Here's to adventure and endless horizons."

"And every night spent with you."

35

LILIA

The morning of Yule, we awoke to a flurry of snow. Ragnar and I walked outside hand-in-hand, tipping back our heads to bask in the cascade of silver specks. They landed on my cheeks and nose with the gentle touch of winter. Children raced by, their arms spread wide and giggles spilling behind them.

"I can't believe it snowed for Yule. It's never done that before," I said.

Nilsa waddled up beside me with a beaming smile on her face. "*I* can believe it. Did you hear what happened in the meadow?"

For a moment, dread was the only emotion I could conjure. After the past few weeks we'd endured, *something else* happening the meadow was the last thing I wanted to hear.

"You seem happy," I said slowly, squinting at her. "But I'm almost afraid to ask."

She chuckled. "Everything's fine, Lil. Your friend showed up a few hours ago with a tall tale about the island. Turns out, it decided to gift us with some more food for the festival. Not only that, but the meadow grew back overnight. It's a field of green now. Funny, huh?"

"Wait. Ulrika's here? And she brought more food with her?"

"That's right. She's in the meadow, helping everyone get things set up. Quite strong, that one."

"I have to go," I said quickly, starting off down the path. It seemed against all odds that Ulrika was here and that the townspeople had accepted her so easily. I hoped to Freya it was really her and not some impersonator trying to weasel their way into the good graces of the Riverwold people. Ragnar had decided to stay in the Isles. I'd truly hoped that had fixed the mercenary problem.

But what if I'd been wrong? What if the island still refused to protect him?

As I broke out into a run, Ragnar called out, "Lilia, wait!"

"Oh, she'll be fine," answered Nilsa. "Let her go see her friend. I need you in the kitchen. We have some hot breakfast to prepare for at least a hundred people. Come along, stop gaping at her like that."

Despite my worry pounding through me, I couldn't help but smile at the thought of Nilsa wrangling Ragnar into helping out in her kitchen. Something told me his flour measuring skills weren't much better than his ale brewing.

But I didn't stick around to find out. I ran through the streets until I reached the festival grounds at the edge of town. Big fat snowflakes dusted the wagons, transforming the verdant field into a sea of white. Spikes of grass poked through it, and a scattering of flowers curled up toward the sun in patches of pink and yellow. My feet slowed, my breath hitching. Nilsa had told me the magic of the island had turned this muddy, fire-raged meadow into the living, breathing thing it had been before, but it hadn't felt real until now.

"Lilia, there you are!" a husky voice called out from deep within the tents. A moment later, Ulrika emerged. Her gleaming horns were coated with snow, and a wreath of flowers curled around them. Even in the brisk, wintry morning, she wore her leather brassiere lined with fur and a matching skirt that barely covered her backside. She waved me over, grinning from ear to ear. Her tusks flashed beneath the sunlight poking through the falling snow.

I followed her into a tent where crates nearly filled every inch of available space. Her head brushed the burlap top, and her horns almost snagged the rough material.

"Can you believe it?" she asked proudly. "The island gave me some more food!"

I shook my head at her, smiling. "I didn't even

believe it was you when Nilsa told me. How did this happen? Did you ask for more?"

"Nope." She shrugged. "It just gave me more. After I heard about the fire, I assumed the festival would get shut down. Next thing I knew, the island gave me crate after crate after crate of food. I figured it wanted me to bring it here."

"It's a Yule miracle," I said.

"That it is. And thank you for suggesting I come." Ulrika lowered to one knee and wrapped her beefy arms around me. For a moment, I didn't move, still surprised by the new revelations. But then I leaned in, wrapped my arms around her neck, and hugged one of my oldest friends for a very long time.

That night, Yule came alive beneath the stars. Tomas the carpenter had used every ounce of the Vindur sand I'd traded with him to keep the Elding at bay for the night. A cloudless sky was the reward, and the brutal wind we'd endured the past weeks had finally stilled. A wintry cold had settled onto the meadow, but while cheeks were flushed, I had yet to spot a single person shiver.

I bustled around the tables we'd set up around the wagon, depositing tankards of beer along with bowls of Nilsa's finest stew. Every seat was taken; clusters of patrons hovered nearby, chatting and laughing the night away.

Ragnar tugged another keg from the back of my new Traveling Tavern and hoisted it onto one shoulder. He wore his signature sleeveless tunic. It was deep blue edged in silver to match the new banners hanging along the outer wall of the wagon. We'd even managed to pull together a new awning—crimson, this time.

I smiled his way as upbeat music piped toward us from the nearby stage. Dancers whirled past, twirling ribbons through the air. And in the center of it, Reykur perched on a bed of blankets, sending out waves of soothing heat to everyone. He'd been getting a lot of snacks for his efforts. A lot of pats on the snout, too.

My heart had never felt more full. We'd had to fight so hard for this, but that made it taste all that much sweeter. There was enough food to go around and more, my ale was selling quickly, and I had a new brew ready to go if my kegs emptied.

And Ragnar was here.

Once this night was over, we'd stay a few extra days before putting on our walking boots and making our way across the Isles. I couldn't wait to show Ragnar my world.

With a hop in my step, I weaved through the tables and back to where he was preparing the keg for the line of patrons waiting for ale. He hefted it up onto the table, and I edged in front of him, tankard in hand.

His arms slid around my waist, and he nuzzled my ear. "You look beautiful tonight, Lil."

Dropping my head back against his chest, I smiled up at him. "Wait until you see what I plan to wear to bed."

"Oh, I like the sound of that already." His lips trailed across my neck. Sparks of luscious heat followed. As he held me close, I relished the feel of him. This was the first night in what I hoped would be a long line of them, with Ragnar serving ale by my side, a freshly painted wagon to call my own, and an open road full of possibility.

EPILOGUE
LILIA

ONE YEAR LATER

"Look at you!" Nilsa proclaimed, rushing up the hill. Her beaming smile felt like home, one of the few I'd ever known. She waved several pies in the air, then tossed them up to Reykur and his siblings as they swooped low overhead.

"Don't tell me you've forsaken the bean stew for some pie now," I said with a laugh. "I might start to think you like my dragon more than me."

"Oh hush." She wrapped her arms around my waist and hugged me tight. "You know I have a vat of the stuff ready and waiting for you at the inn." Pulling back, she gave Ragnar a once-over. "Well, looks like you've kept your promise. She's alive and well. And judging by her smile, she's happy enough."

Rivelin and Daella came around from the rear of the wagon, their fenrir, Skoll, bounding along beside them. They were hand-in-hand, like always, steam hissing into the air where they touched. I'd convinced them both to come along this time. They'd jumped at the chance and brought Skoll and the rest of the dragons with them.

Nilsa cocked her head at them. "Who's this now?"

"Nilsa, meet my brother, Rivelin, and his partner, Daella."

"Oh, I've heard of you. The half-orc." Nilsa loosed an appreciative whistle and eagerly took Daella's offered hand. "I must say, it's an honor to meet you. Surviving the conqueror like you did. That was mighty brave of you."

"You would have done the same, I'm sure," Daella said, smiling.

"Bah!" Nilsa swatted at her. "You're too kind. What's your favorite food, dear? Let me guess..." She cocked her head, looking Daella up and down, taking in her cropped shirt and the way she leaned against my brother's shoulder. Not for support, but because they didn't much like having more than the smallest gap of air between them, if that. "A pasty. I bet you love a good mushroom and cheese pasty."

Daella's cocked her head, brow raised. "How in fate's name did you figure that out?"

"I have a gift." Nilsa winked and motioned for our party to follow her back down the hill to where the town was already bursting with visitors. We hadn't come so early this year. I didn't feel the need to be so territorial about my spot anymore. No matter how packed the meadow was, I'd find somewhere to park my wagon. We'd have a lovely Yule, enjoying our time together. That was all that truly mattered.

We followed Nilsa down the hill. When we reached the path that cut through the stone buildings and into town, she swerved toward the meadow instead. I left the others to jog ahead and fall into step beside the dwarf.

"No need to go to the grounds just yet," I told her. "I'm sure Rivelin and Daella would love to get off their feet and enjoy some food beside the hearth."

"Oh, they're fine. They look as sprightly as you do." A small smile tickled her lips. "Besides, I can't wait to show you what we've done."

I squinted at her. "Nilsa, don't tell me you're making a big deal out of the Traveling Tavern."

She held up her hands and laughed. "It wasn't my idea. You can blame Steffon and Ivar when you see them."

"Steffon did something?"

"That's right," she said smugly. "Seems you made an impression on him."

We rounded the corner. Verdant grass rolled across the meadow, peppered with a multitude of flowers. They were vibrant and alive, despite the chill in the air. Carts and wagons and tents packed the winding paths, and a gleaming new stage hunkered near the entrance, where a pixie bard sang with a band of dwarves. Folk wandered through it all, talking and laughing and shopping at the stalls. Yule wasn't for a few more days, but the celebration had already begun.

Nilsa pointed through the festival. There, by my old spot, a vacant patch of land remained. A new willow tree had sprung from the ground, so tall and rich with indigo leaves that it looked like it had been there for decades, at least.

"But how?" I whispered, too awed to say more than that.

"The magic of the island stuck around after last year's Yule." She gestured at the grass, the flowers, and the tree. "Ulrika thinks it wanted us to have this, even without us asking. I suppose we have your kind deeds to thank for that."

"Nilsa, all I did was bring back the ale that my own dragon stole from me."

"And you could have just kept it for yourself after you found it." She shrugged. "So there you go. Steffon saved that spot for your Traveling Tavern. It's yours if you want it."

Ragnar came up behind me. "I've got a better idea. I'll take it for myself and brew my own ale. I know how to make the good stuff now."

I elbowed him in the side, grinning up at him. "Do that, and you'll have me climbing into your wagon in the middle of the night to steal it."

"Oh, you can climb into my wagon anytime you like, darling."

"Oh boy." Nilsa fanned herself. "I might have to make myself scarce." She whirled on her feet, waving her hand toward my brother, who'd stopped a few feet behind us. "Rivelin, Daella, shall I show you to your room while these two get the wagon all set up?"

"That would be wonderful, as long as Skoll can come, too."

"Of course he can!"

Thanks, Nilsa," Daella answered, patting Skoll's furry head.

The dwarf beamed up at the orc. The four of them wandered off into town, leaving me to stare at the new willow tree. If I hadn't known better, I would have said it was the same one as before, all drooping branches and vibrant leaves.

"Happy?" Ragnar asked as he wound an arm around my back.

"The happiest."

"You truly love Riverwold."

"Of course." I looked up at him, my cheek brushing his shoulder. "Don't you?"

He chuckled. "It's lively, that's for sure."

"It's a shame you've never experienced this place in a normal year. All you know is last Yule's utter chaos. It couldn't have left a good impression on you."

Gently, he pulled away and took my hands in his. Searching my eyes, he said, "Riverwold is where I fell in love with you, so it's one of my favorite places in the world." He rubbed his thumb along my jaw. "You know I've loved traveling with you this past year, especially to the dwarven competition, but I don't want you to stay on the move just for me. If you want to make a home here, I'll make it with you."

My breath caught. "You'd do that? You'd stay here for me?"

"I would stay anywhere for you."

Smiling, I palmed his cheek. "I do love Riverwold, it's true. But I love the road more, especially when you wander it with me."

"Then we'll wander as long as you want." He brushed his lips against mine. "The only home I'll ever need is you."

GLOSSARY

DRAUGR - those who bond with dragons and channel their power

FENRIR - wolf-like creatures who can form powerful bonds with folk

FILDUR - the elemental magic of fire

FOLK - beings in tune with the Galdur; includes elves, orcs, pixies, trolls, fenrir, demons, giants, kraken, and dwarves

FREYA - the ancient goddess of the elements

GALDUR - the elemental magic that runs through the bones of the earth; can be controlled by rare sand

JORDUR - the elemental magic of earth

MIDSUMMER GAMES - a annual celebration that takes place in Wyndale, complete with a tournament; the winner may ask for one gift from the island

THE OLD GODS - ancient beings who crafted the world and gifted the folk with Galdur

VATNOR - the elemental magic of water

VINDUR - the elemental magic of air

YULE - the annual winter festival to celebrate harmony, bounty, and happiness, and to bless the coming year

Acknowledgments

First and always, thank you to my husband for letting me bounce ideas off you, even when they were a bit ridiculous (like the mischievous dragon).

Thank you to everyone who helped me bring this book together: Noah for the skillful editing, Deandra for the beautiful illustration, Sylvia at The Book Brander for the gorgeous typography, and Rachael for both the map and hardcover design.

And the biggest thank you to all the readers who have shared, reviewed, and shown so much love to the first stand-alone in this series, *Forged by Magic*. This one is for you.

Also by Jenna Wolfhart

Falling for Fables

Forged by Magic

Brewed in Magic

The Mist King

Of Mist and Shadow

Of Ash and Embers

Of Night and Chaos

Of Dust and Stars

The Fallen Fae

Court of Ruins

Kingdom in Exile

Keeper of Storms

Tower of Thorns

Realm of Ashes

Prince of Shadows (A Novella)

About the Author

Jenna Wolfhart spends her days dreaming up stories about swoony fae kings and stabby heroines. When she's not writing, she loves to deadlift, rewatch Game of Thrones, and drink far too much coffee.

Born and raised in America, Jenna now lives in England with her husband and her two dogs.

www.jennawolfhart.com
jenna@jennawolfhart.com
tiktok.com/@jennawolfhart

Printed in Great Britain
by Amazon

42857991R00192